ONCE UPON NEVERMORE

The Jinx Hamilton Series - Book 13

JULIETTE HARPER

Prologue

My pen hovered over the grimoire page. I almost imagined the wings of the phoenix on the barrel planting themselves on the hips of the writing instrument in consternation.

"What?" I asked, trying not to sound defensive.

The nib descended to the paper and scratched out, *"How many times will you attempt to write of things about which you have no knowledge?"*

"That is not fair. I was there for this story."

"You were there for part of the story. Ask for help."

The pen was right. To give this story the dimension it deserves, I reached out to those who shared the adventure with me.

Part of this story belongs to Festus McGregor, part to a dragonrider named Blair McBride, and part to a figure lifted from the pages of literary history—Edgar Allan Poe.

I come into the tale late and out of a desire to prove a point to my husband. That's difficult to admit.

A woman should have a better reason for traipsing off to an

alternate timestream when she's only just escaped being trapped in another.

What happened to me in the Land of Virgo added unknown elements to our lives on many fronts. To understand those changes, you must enter the mind of a madman and delve into the politics of a citadel high in the Spica Mountains.

The people and creatures you will meet there are part of our world now. Their presence will affect Festus's work recovering the Temporal Arcana and will influence the family Lucas and I have started.

You know that a vision came to me when I reopened the temporal rivers. What I saw that day comes true within these pages. The consequences of my actions reawakened an old conflict, one fought in a dimension none of us could have imagined.

There's no right way—no single way—to tell a story. This one takes a different path than the adventures we've shared in the past, but it inaugurates a new phase of our lives.

We re-discover a forgotten magic, a way of life thought to be extinct, and awaken hope in the heart of a man long lost to himself. If you think you know Edgar from the pages of history, give him a second chance. He's not who his detractors made him out to be.

He committed many crimes in the name of forbidden love. Under a similar influence, any of us might do the same.

Grant him the favor of a second impression. Grant us all the favor of your patience. And with that, let the story begin.

Jinx

Chapter One

Baltimore, Maryland, 1849

Seneca ignored the discomfort of cold rainwater soaking his feathers. If he didn't deliver the terms of the devil's deal Reynold Isherwood had offered, Edgar would die.

But to save his friend, Seneca faced burying the poor man alive.

The raven banked over the city and turned toward the hospital, passing a church steeple where, in mere hours, the bells would ring.

Iron bells!
What a world of solemn thought their monody compels!
In the silence of the night,
How we shiver with affright
At the melancholy menace of their tone!

Tolling bells fascinated Edgar, among the many preoccupations he developed in London during his boyhood.

One such fascination had set him down the path to this very night—his love of the antiquities housed in the British Museum. As often as possible, Edgar stole away from his steparents' home in Russell Square to wander the galleries.

If only Seneca and not Isherwood had found the lad there that afternoon in 1817. The curious child of 8 or 9 years wanted only to see the newly installed Elgin Marbles.

Critics claimed Lord Elgin stole the priceless treasures from the Greek government. A theft of a different sort, however, was about to take place in their shadow—the theft of a soul.

By happenstance, Reynold Isherwood, the Ruling Elder of Fae Londinium, had business in the museum that same afternoon. He was, himself, interested in the Parthenon statues.

Isherwood strolled into the temporary gallery and saw a boy with an unruly shock of black hair falling across his high forehead. The child's dark, brooding eyes passed hungrily over the carved friezes and metope panels hanging above his head.

Something in the boy's expression inexplicably moved Isherwood. He recognized loneliness and sensed the child's desperation to be held in the esteem of a mentor.

Seneca didn't believe Isherwood meant any harm when he joined Edgar on the bench and spoke to him of the Pantheon and the Greek thinkers, but ambition calls to ambition.

Even at so young an age, Edgar yearned to prove his cruel stepfather wrong. The child wanted to discover within himself the artistry that made his dead mother a renowned stage talent. He hoped to exhibit genius, but he *burned* to know fame.

The two agreed to meet again before Edgar's school term resumed. Then when the boy returned to his classes in Sloane Street, Isherwood arranged to meet with him periodically.

Facilitating the ruse in the human realm was child's play for the powerful wizard. A bit of persuasion magic established his identity as an "uncle" to the school officials; a spell of forgetting erased their memory of his presence afterwards.

When the family returned to the former colonies in America, Isherwood simply traveled there by portal, explaining his comings and goings to Edgar as "business."

He did not reveal even a hint of his true nature until Edgar was a man with a man's failings. Then the mirror calls began.

For thirty years, Isherwood nurtured a mentoring, almost paternal relationship with the troubled young man. Ostensibly cultivating Edgar's writing talent, Isherwood used the aspiring author's compositions as a weapon without his knowledge.

Edgar became an unwitting pawn in the War of Bibliophile Aggression between the Kingdom of Nevermore and the Confederation of Magical States.

Could he really be blamed then for breaking the truce that ended the war by committing the common human mistake of falling in love?

The sheer irony of fate made the object of Edgar's passion a high-born Fae woman named Lenore—the sister of the Master Publishers of Nevermore.

"I cannot spare his life, Seneca," Isherwood said, steepling his fingers and eyeing the raven perched on the edge of his desk in the Office of the Ruling Elder. "Edgar has angered Nevermore. Why can he not accept the story that the wretched woman is dead? Would you have me risk a resumption of the war for the sake of a human's romantic failings?"

Cocking his head to the side, Seneca said, "Reynold, this *human* thinks of you as a surrogate father. Be reasonable. He was drinking."

"This situation does not afford me the luxury of sentiment. When he drinks, Edgar becomes dangerous and reckless. You yourself inspired one of his lamenting compositions."

"I went to him at your behest to tell him that he would find Lenore *never more* to allay his curiosity about the terminology. I said nothing of the land itself!"

"Need I remind you that he set your visit to verse and published the work to considerable notoriety?"

"I can handle him."

With painful effort, Seneca pressed and won his case. For four years Edgar abided by Isherwood's rules, but in 1849, haunted to the depths of his soul by grief for the loss of Lenore, Edgar again set his pain to verse.

This time when Seneca appealed to the Ruling Elder for mercy on behalf of his friend, Isherwood threw the papers on his desk and yelled. "I care not what he calls her, Seneca. He has gone *too far*. Read the ending of the fourth stanza. *Aloud.*"

Reluctantly the raven complied, "*. . . the wind came out of the cloud by night, Chilling and killing my Annabel Lee.*"

"What," Isherwood demanded, "do you have to say to *that*? He wrote of the Wind from the Cloud. Lenore's kinsmen have demanded his death."

"Would you kill a man of weak will for loving a woman as vibrant as Lenore?" Seneca asked. "Does she not share a measure of guilt for her preoccupation with the human world?"

"Lenore has been dealt with. Now Edgar must face the consequences of his actions."

"We can make him disappear in other ways," Seneca insisted. "Do not take his life. You are better than that, Reynold. Think of the lad you met in the museum. Think of the child who wanted a father and looked to you to fulfill that role."

Isherwood rose from his chair and walked to the window, staring out at the foggy Londinium streets. "Fine," he said at last. "Send him into the temporal streams, to the Land of Virgo where time knows no constancy."

When Seneca asked for leniency, he had not expected an offer of cruel exile instead. "Reynold, a human will go mad in such a place."

Turning away from the window, the wizard said coldly, "Edgar may choose death or madness. I offer no other terms."

The finality of the ultimatum sat heavily on Seneca's heart. He landed on the window ledge and peered into the hospital room. Edgar lay on the bed, agitated and feverish, the light of a single oil lamp illuminating the scene.

The raven waited for the nurse to mop her patient's brow and leave before using his beak to tap an intricate, rhythmic pattern on the glass. At the final blow, the pane shimmered and liquified. Seneca stepped through, shaking out his feathers, and glided to the end of the bed.

"Edgar," he said softly. "*Edgar*, wake up. It is I, Seneca, with news from Londinium."

The man's eyelids fluttered as he struggled to focus on the raven sitting at his feet.

"Are you the angel of death?" he asked weakly.

"Of the many names I have been called," the bird replied, "'angel' was never among them. Look closer."

With difficulty Edgar focused. "Seneca," he said at last.

"Correct. If you do not wish to die this night, you must listen to me."

The delirious patient shook his head. "I listened once before when you sat upon the pallid bust of Pallas above my chamber door. You gave me no hope that night. Why should I believe you now?"

"You must believe me because I bring a message from Reynold."

"Reynold!" Edgar cried out. "*Reynold* is the architect of my misery."

Footsteps sounded in the hallway. Seneca hastily retreated into a corner muttering an incantation that blended his inky form into the shadows as the nurse re-entered the room.

Bending over the bed, she said, "Did you call for someone? Who is Reynolds?"

"A fiend," Edgar replied, clutching at her arm. "A devil from hell."

"You've been dreaming," the woman murmured comfortingly. "The fever makes you say these things. Rest now."

When they were alone, Seneca returned to the foot of the bed. "Do not call out like that again," he warned. "We don't have much time. Surely you must have known ultimately Reynold would exact a price for your success, for the ideas he gave you, for the knowledge of the possibilities that lie beyond the human sphere?"

Struggling to remain lucid, Edgar said, "He does not punish me for those things. He punishes me for her."

"He does," Seneca admitted. "But I have brokered a compromise. If you accept the terms, you will live, Edgar."

The bird swiftly laid out the details of the proposed banishment. "You will awaken in a land that will challenge your sanity. Do not give in to the madness. Your life's journey will not end in that place. You must accede to this solution. I cannot tell you how or when, but you will escape to live once again as a free man."

Quieter now, Edgar studied Seneca. "Will I be able to find Lenore?" he asked hoarsely.

"*Nevermore*," Seneca said. "No matter what happens to you, do not forget *Nevermore*."

Edgar's head thrashed against the sweat dampened pillow. "You speak in riddles, bird! First you open a door to salvation, then you dash that hope to pieces!"

Hopping onto the mattress, Seneca sat squarely on Edgar's chest. "*Look at me,*" he commanded sharply.

When he held the man's complete attention, Seneca said, "*Nevermore* is not a pronouncement, Edgar. It is a place—a concept—a reason for your continued being. I cannot send you there, but I can save your life if you agree. Beyond that, you must find your own way."

"Do as you will," Edgar muttered, his eyes closing from exhaustion. "I still know not if you are bird or devil, but do as you will."

"I am your friend," Seneca said. "Sleep, Edgar. Sleep so that you might awaken in a new land. We will meet again. On that, you have my word."

At the window Seneca looked back at the figure lying in the bed. The raven couldn't change what he had to do, but he could take steps to ensure the condemned wretch enjoyed some material advantages.

Exiting the same way he'd entered, Seneca flew to a low-hanging branch on a nearby tree. He spread his wings and focused his mind on the hospital, speaking the words of the incantation he'd written in his shop in Londinium in preparation for this task.

Form from function, function from form.
Split thy substance to shelter this man.
Remnants of reality carry him beyond the coil.
Seek the mountains in the Land of the Maiden.
There, supply his needs, shelter his body.
Anchor his mind until the day of his return.

A ghostly double of the hospital flickered against the building, hanging suspended in the night air. Inside, Edgar opened his eyes and whispered, "Lord, help my poor soul."

As a cold wind rippled through his feathers, Seneca invoked the trigger, "*Vi inmortalium fiat.*"

By the power of the Immortals, let it be done.

The architectural doppelgänger shimmered and melted into the darkness. Somewhere a clock struck three.

The witching hour.

Chapter Two

Mountain Range off the River of Virgo, Spica Citadel

Black shadows swept over the jungle and sent small creatures scurrying for cover. Overhead, the dragon riders of the Spica Citadel cut through the slanting rays of the setting sun.

One after another, the beasts peeled out of formation to make for the ten rows of arched alcoves ascending the cliff face. The warrens offered room for a hundred dragons, but now sheltered only twenty-five.

Tangled vines crept across the outer limits of the fortress, pulling the hewn stone into piles of collapsed rubble. In time, the jungle would take back what the First Flight had carved from its heart.

Blair McBride angled her yellow drake, Giallo, toward a well-tended landing pad on the highest level. The dragon's talons reached for the deep furrows gouged in the flagstones. He came to a halt inches from a clump of scraggly wildflowers.

Sliding from her mount's back, Blair encircled Giallo's neck with her arms. Standing more than six feet at the shoulder, the dragon towered over his slender partner.

"Thank you for missing them again," she whispered, burying her face in the soft, heated skin behind Giallo's ear.

The drake's voice rose in her mind, learned but primitive, the words tinged with the alien accent of his kind.

"Weeds, a sheòid."

Blair's heart clutched at the endearment.

My hero. My valiant warrior.

The pet name used only by Giallo and Blair's dead father.

Giallo felt her emotions surge along their telepathic bond. He raised a muscular foreleg and drew her close.

"Adair. Absent but beloved. Companion to my sire."

Blair closed her eyes. "I miss them all. Father. Mother. Your dame and sire."

Dragon and rider stood together in silent remembrance. Blair's parents. Gruff, good-natured Adair. The gentle Esme, her ebony tresses shot through with silver. Giallo's dame, the sleek black drakaina, Lintonth. His sire, the crimson, Eovro.

Blair tended the wildflowers in remembrance of her mother, a woman whose soft whispers coaxed living things to bloom.

In her imagination Blair heard the voices of her family gathered round the fire pit in the evening. Against the background of jungle sounds, Adair regaled his daughter with stories of the Otherworld.

Like all the First Flight riders, he and Esme had left their home and came to the Spica Mountains at the order of the Ruling Elders. The dragon wings dispersed the Temporal Arcana and accepted exile to guard the scattered artifacts.

Now Adair and Esme and their mounts were gone, but Blair and Giallo remained.

"No sadness, a sheòid," the dragon purred. *"We are the last, but we survive."*

The last.

But were they? What lay beyond the jungle and down the River of Virgo?

Blair yearned to discover the answer, but the Dragon Master Kian treated her curiosity as dangerous sedition.

"Imagination fails Kian," Giallo said. *"He is not Jaxon Frazier. We control our piece of the skies,* a sheòid. *You and me. Tomorrow let us fly farther. See the Great River for ourselves."*

Straightening, Blair said, "And Kian thinks *I'm* the rebel. Are you going to Eingana this evening?"

Giallo shifted uncomfortably, his claws scraping the stone. *"She shows her temper since the egg."*

"Eingana is waiting for her offspring to hatch, you big oaf. It's been only a single rainy season since Miriam fell to her death. Eingana has a right to be erratic."

Few dragons survived the loss of their rider. For what seemed an eternity after Miriam failed to secure her saddle cinch and plunged into the jungle, Eingana refused to eat or leave her stall. The drakaina blamed herself for being unable to reach her careless partner before Miriam struck the ground.

The fact that Miriam used a saddle at all spoke to her lack of skill. The best flyers rode the bare backs of their beasts. The physical connection deepened the telepathic link. Only those who never fully shed their fear of the skies relied on tack as a crutch.

Giallo's tireless companionship saved Eingana, and now he shrank from a display of maternal hormones?

Blair freely shared her train of thought with the drake, who looked properly shamed.

"Later," he said. *"We flew long today. Warm straw beckons. Let me nap before I must face Eingana's temper."*

"Coward," Blair said sternly, but she was teasing. "Have your nap, but don't snore and set the bedding on fire and *don't* sleep the night away. When I return from the dining hall, I expect a report on Eingana and the egg."

Twin columns of steam issued from Giallo's nostrils in a dismissive snort. *"Females. Leave my duties as sire and mate to me."*

As he lumbered toward the archway, Blair called after him, "I meant what I said about the snoring."

"One time I flamed the straw," the dragon grumbled as he disappeared into the stalls. *"For this never am I to know peace."*

Chuckling, Blair moved through the entrance and continued into her quarters. Passing into her bedroom, she stripped off her leathers and threw the garments on the bed, still thinking about Giallo's suggestion that they fly beyond their patrol route.

What Master Kian didn't know wouldn't hurt him, but if he discovered the transgression, Blair would find herself flying over the swamps to the north until the rains came again.

Her gaze tracked to the portrait of her parents hanging on the wall. In the days when Jaxon Frazier led the Flight, Adair and Esme served an heroic purpose. As second in command, Adair flew at Jaxon's side, administered the affairs of the Citadel, and died protecting his friend and master.

Esme died trying to save them both.

The loss of the flight's three principal riders opened the door for men of lesser nerve like Kian to step forward. What had once been a proud drakonic order now ran on routine and mediocrity, guarding an empty jungle out of habit more than purpose.

Other than one crazy hermit living near the waterfall, the riders hadn't seen another living soul in decades.

"What would you tell me to do?" Blair asked the image of her father. "You and Uncle Jaxon taught me about the far places. The Middle Realm, Cibolita, the great Fae cities like Londinium. Am I so wrong to want to see the world where once we owned the skies?"

Giallo's sleepy voice pushed at the edge of her reverie. Blair opened her mind and let him in.

"You awaken me and miss your meal, a sheòid. Go!"

"What have I told you about eavesdropping?" Blair grumbled.

"You think too loud."

Sighing, Blair changed clothes and started down the interior staircase to the dining hall ten levels below. As she descended past the mostly empty floors, she found herself grappling with what had become an ever-present worry.

At the current rate of decline, drakonculture would die in the Spica Mountains. Eingana and Giallo's egg was the first to be laid in at least twenty-five rainy seasons. Already plans were being made to rear the whelp in the traditional way—confined to small quarters to contain its growth.

But what if that very program of husbandry had played a role in the dragons' failure to successfully conceive and hatch their young?

Nothing could diminish the visual and physical impact of a dragon the size of a stout draft horse. Left to develop on their own, however, the creatures might attain triple their cultivated proportions. Wouldn't allowing them to exist in their natural state also make the dragons healthier and happier?

Below her, a door opened and laughing voices filled the stairwell.

"You can't hit a dragon's backside," a male voice taunted.

"Bold talk," a woman answered. "Come with me to the archery range after supper, and I'll make you eat those words."

Blair smiled. The rivalry between Davin and Maeve was an old one, tinged with a fair amount of flirting. Everyone expected them to announce their betrothal when the rains came, and the riders could enjoy a long vacation from daily patrols.

Quickening her pace, Blair caught up with her friends. "She always wins, Davin. Why do you keep setting yourself up for defeat?"

"Ah," he said, sweeping his wild mane of black hair away from his face. "Hello, Blair. It's all an elaborate trap, you know. One day I'll strike and show her the skills of a real marksman."

"Will you now?" Maeve said, her blue eyes sparkling against her dark skin. "The day that happens, our dragons will tumble from the sky in shock."

The three fell into step, descending the last two turns of the stairs together. "How did you and Giallo make out today?" Maeve asked Blair. "You flew the waterfall route, didn't you?"

"We did," Blair said, as they came into the dining room. "The Hermit watched us from his window like always."

They weaved through the loose collection of trestle tables to reach the sideboard where the three or four surviving servants laid out the platters each night. The ritual was nothing but a remnant of the formality that once marked meals in the Citadel. Riders and servants ate side by side now with no thought of station or status.

"I feel sorry for the Hermit," Davin said, piling his plate with meat and vegetables. "Who wouldn't slip into madness alone out there in the jungle?"

An old woman caught Blair's eye and motioned the trio to her table with an upraised hand. The riders accepted, as they did each night.

When Blair slid in beside her on the bench, Marta patted her on the knee. "Did your patrol go well?" she asked, including the others in the question with a fond, maternal look.

After they each assured her that they'd enjoyed an uneventful day, Blair fixed Marta with an appraising look. "Are you feeling better?"

Sighing, the old woman said, "Today yes, tomorrow perhaps no. Aged bones do as they will."

"Are you using the ointment the healers compounded?" Blair pressed.

"Do I smell of camphor and rosemary?"

Davin let out a burst of laughter. "Leave her alone, Blair. You know Marta does as she pleases."

Before Blair could voice her concerns about Marta's casual attitude toward self-care, Master Kian dragged a chair to the head of the table and joined their group.

The short, thick-set man administered the Citadel's affairs with an egalitarian hand for the most part, but he insisted on regimentation and repetition. That, coupled with his demeanor of absolute authority, made Blair regard him with alternating surges of amusement and annoyance.

Dispensing with greetings, the Dragon Master focused his attention on her. "How fares the Hermit?"

Everyone at the table knew Kian meant the question as a test to see if Blair had maintained her assigned flight plan.

Maeve shot Blair a warning look that telegraphed the message, *"Be nice,"* while Davin focused his attention on his plate.

Marta, however, looked the Master square in the eye and said in a scolding voice, "Kian! Is that any way to greet your riders after a hard day's work?"

No one else in the Citadel would have rebuked Kian so directly, but Marta had known the man all his life.

"Sorry," he said gruffly, "good evening. Now, Blair, what of the Hermit?"

"Unchanged," she said. "The path to the waterfall shows consistent wear. Broken branches in the jungle suggest he approached the river yesterday."

Chewing contemplatively Kian nodded, "I'm not surprised.

He goes frequently to the waters. The sight of the river soothes him."

When Blair stiffened, Maeve shielded her face from Kian's view with her napkin and mouthed, *"Don't!"*

In recent days the flow of the River of Virgo had reversed itself without warning. The change touched off furious speculation among the riders, but Kian allowed only a few—those he regarded as the most obedient—to fly the waterway to inspect the alteration for themselves.

Blair was not among their number, though she asked repeatedly to be given the assignment. Kian was baiting her—and enjoying it.

Recognizing the tactic, Blair said, "A man who lives in such isolation deserves a source of comfort. I could do with a view of the river myself."

Completely ignoring the second half of her statement, Kian waved a dismissive hand. "The Hermit lives as he chooses. We've offered him the shelter of these walls many times."

Marta put down her soup spoon. "His mind is broken. You shouldn't use the Hermit's disadvantage as an excuse to withdraw the offer of friendship."

Blair wanted to laugh at the red flush that climbed up from the Master's collar, but she knew better.

"Marta," Kian said, "you remember when the Hermit and his strange dwelling appeared in the jungle. The leaders of the First Flight went to him that very day."

"And when," Marta countered, "was the last time kindness was extended to the wretched man?"

The Dragon Master blinked. "It has been many rainy seasons."

"Then," the old woman said, rising from the bench, "were *I* the master of this Citadel, I might afford some thought to *that*."

Pausing to give Blair's shoulder an encouraging squeeze, Marta shuffled away to supervise the clearing of the dishes.

No one at the table spoke. Exerting a visible effort, Kian regained his composure and gestured toward a rider named Llewellyn who sat at a nearby table.

When the man came over, the Master said, "You flew the river today?"

"Yes, sir."

"Well, out with it. How did you find the stream?"

"Flowing steadily in the opposite direction."

Waving Llewellyn back to his place, Kian tore off a fresh piece of bread and gave Blair a smug smile. He'd rubbed the issue of the river in her face twice in the space of five minutes and seemed quite pleased with himself.

Blair felt her temper spark. Maeve saw her friend's jaw clench and tried to intervene.

"Come on, Blair," she said, moving to leave the table. "Davin and I are going to the archery range."

Ignoring the invitation, Blair said, "Master Kian, don't you think it's time we pursued an *explanation* for the change in the river's flow?"

Suppressing a groan, Maeve sank back into her chair. Kian didn't bother to hide his triumphant look.

"*We?* You have nothing to say in the matter, Blair McBride."

"Every rider in this wing has something to say in the matter," she retorted hotly. "Especially if the alteration in the river points to a change in the Citadel's mission."

All eyes in the dining hall were now on Kian and Blair.

"The Citadel's mission remains steady," Kian said tightly. "Just as it has been since the days of the First Flight."

"How do you know?" Blair asked stubbornly.

"I know," Kian replied levelly, "because I command this Citadel and you do not."

Struggling to control her anger, Blair said, "How can you possibly believe that a river suddenly changing its direction not be a matter of concern for everyone in this room?"

"When there is something about which you should be concerned," Kian said flatly, "I will tell you."

Springing to her feet, Blair said, "Which will be *never*, because you can't imagine anything ever changing. You're perfectly content to let us wither at our posts until the last dragon and rider die on this mountain. How do you know we aren't being shown the way to return to the Otherworld? How do you know that the mission we were sent here to fulfill no longer matters? If Master Frazier were alive, he would explore all the possibilities."

Kian took a deep breath, his face hot with barely controlled fury.

"You presume to speak for a dead man," he said. "We are not *destined* to return to the Otherworld. We were given a charge to settle in these lands and in these lands we will remain. That is our mission."

"It is the *mission* of every being of free will to lead their lives according to the call of the Natural Order."

Now almost purple with rage, Kian said, "You have much to learn about duty. Leave the hall and think well before you speak to me in this manner again."

"Good evening, Dragon Master."

"Good evening, Blair McBride."

Blair stormed toward the exit with Maeve and Davin at her heels. At the door to the stairwell, Davin said with bemusement, "That went well."

"Come with us to the range," Maeve said to Blair again. "Work off your anger."

"No," Blair said, "I'll see you at morning roll call. Really, I'm fine."

They watched as she strode toward the exit to the walled courtyard at the base of the cliff.

"She's going to the jungle," Maeve said. "Maybe that's for the best."

"Best for her," Davin agreed, "but not for anything unlucky enough to get in her way."

Chapter Three

The Fairy Mound in Briar Hollow, North Carolina, Rodney, A Rat

Halfway between the space the humans called their "lair" and the store upstairs, Rodney stretched luxuriously in his recliner. He wiggled his toes and repositioned his long black tail with happy satisfaction.

On the opposite wall, *Lord of the Rings* played on the iPod Touch that served as the rat's big screen TV. The fairy mound created the private space for Rodney and helped him decorate the interior with all the amenities dear to a rodent's heart.

His rat-sized laptop claimed the center of the desk beside overflowing bookshelves packed with biographies, detective stories, philosophy, fantasy, and history. During his studies with Lucien St. Leger, the seneschal of the Knights of the Rodere, Rodney learned to love books of all kinds.

With plenty of witches in his life to work the miniaturization spells, Rodney now had a library that fit his size instead of books that threatened to topple over and squash him. He also had a pantry filled with snacks, an exercise wheel, and a proper bathroom because wood shavings had never been his thing.

A furry bean bag functioned as his mattress, giving the rat a warm nest away from any chaos or interruption. Rodney loved his people. He considered himself the most fortunate of rodents, but privacy mattered too—as did security.

None of Rodney's friends knew he guarded a great treasure—the Eighth Wand of the Chosen, given to him by the ghost of the Cherokee witch Knasgowa, Mother of the Briar Hollow Coven, known as the Daughters of Knasgowa.

Hewn from the golden ash of the World Tree for the wizard Merlin, the wand now rested on brackets near Rodney's chair waiting for *"one who . . . has yet to be born."*

In the beginning, Rodney checked the wand daily for any sign of change, but over time, he noticed its presence less and less. At the moment, his full attention was on the screen of the makeshift television where Gandalf was making his stand against the Balrog.

Rodney giggled at himself as he mouthed the famous line, *"You shall not pass!"* He didn't even realize the vibrant red stone on the wand's tip had begun to pulsate until he reached for the bowl of popcorn on the end table.

Startled, Rodney pushed himself upright and cautiously approached the wall display. He leaned closer and watched the outline of a dragon etch itself into the wand's shaft only to gasp and jump back when a small burst of flame shot out of the creature's mouth.

The phrase used by Medieval cartographers to describe the unknown flitted across the rat's thoughts.

Here be dragons.

Dragons meant unexplored territory . . . and danger.

∼

Londinium, Archives of the Bureau of Enchanted Artifacts and Relics (BEAR)

Wereparrot Jilly Pepperdine extended a wing and delicately turned the page of the journal lying on the table. When she and her wereraven partner, Lucy George, arrived at BEAR headquarters in Londinium that morning, they agreed to a plan of divide and conquer.

Jilly plowed into the official journals of the individual Ruling Elders. Lucy sorted through reports written by the Bureau's Recovery of Magical Objects (ROMO) Agents six months before and after the imposition of The Agreement.

Passed under the ruse of protecting the *nonconformi* species from human bigotry, the now defunct decree once segregated the Middle Realm (also known as the In Between) from the Fae Otherworld and the Human World.

Recent events, however, exposed a secret clause that outlawed travel within the Fourth Realm—time itself.

Like all Fae, Jilly grew to adulthood understanding the three levels of reality held in coherence by the global grid of Mother Trees. Now she had to shift her worldview to accommodate the thirteen Temporal Rivers pouring into the Middle Realm.

Jilly hadn't been present when Jinx Hamilton, the Witch of the Oak, re-opened the great rivers. Now, however, the wereparrot functioned as part of a team charged with recovering the Temporal Arcana, the navigational instruments that allowed for accurate travel along those waterways.

The head BEAR librarian, a barn owl named Hortense Tyton, regarded Jilly and Lucy suspiciously when they presented their credentials. Her onyx eyes glinted behind severe gold spectacles when she asked, "Have you been trained in the proper handling of archival documents?"

Opting to err on the side of diplomacy, Jilly said, "Yes, but please do explain any special procedures. We want to follow the facility's rules to the letter."

Mollified by the parrot's deferential manner, Hortense softened slightly. "Do not use your talons or beaks to turn pages or handle documents. Wingtips only. I'll be at my desk if you require assistance."

With that, the owl spread her wings and flew into the exposed beams. She settled into a loft office that gave her a clear view of the researchers working in the collection.

"*Wingtips only,*" Lucy mocked, ruffling her feathers.

"I'm the parrot," Jilly said. "Impersonations fall under my skill set."

"Sorry," Lucy said, "I have a thing about owls."

Tilting her head quizzically, Jilly asked, "Bad experience?"

"My parents sent me to boarding school shortly after I fledged," Lucy replied. "The headmistress was a wereowl. Dreadful beast. Constantly hovering over us and asking who did this or who did that."

The parrot started to laugh, but hesitated when she realized Lucy hadn't consciously chosen the word "who" as a joke. "She used informants?"

"She did," Lucy said, "and *I* roomed with one of them."

"That sounds dreadful. Follow the rules, and I'm sure Hortense won't bother you."

Jilly promptly forgot the whole exchange until hours later when Hortense let out with an ear-splitting screech. "*Molting* is *NOT* allowed in the collection."

"It was *one* loose tailfeather," Lucy said, her voice sharpening to an irritated caw. "You've never lost a feather?"

"Not on the job, I most certainly have not," Hortense replied tersely. "How do I know you don't have mites?"

Jilly dropped her beak onto the table and groaned. The owl just had to go *there*, didn't she?

Taking flight, the parrot glided swiftly across the reading room alighting between Hortense and Lucy.

"Ladies, please," she said. "We're all civilized avians here. Let's not resort to insults."

Lucy tried and failed to contain her temper, only stoking the argument with her next comment.

"This mouse-chasing barn pigeon started it."

Hortense clacked her short beak with steely precision. "I will not take that from a mite-infested corn thief."

"What did you call me?" Lucy asked with quivering outrage.

"I called you . . ."

Jilly silenced them both with a piercing whistle. When she had their attention, the parrot said pleasantly, "Lucy, why don't you pay a call on Seneca in Blackfriars? It's been a long day. I'll tidy up my things and meet you there so we can take the portal back to Briar Hollow together."

Lucy opened her beak to say something, but closed it when Jilly shook her head. Giving her partner a curt nod, the raven lifted off the table and flew out the main entrance.

"I'm revoking her privileges," Hortense snapped.

Marshalling all her patience, Jilly said, "Please don't make me speak to Director Rosmarus about this."

"Rosmarus is a *werewalrus*," the owl said. "He couldn't possibly comprehend the intricacies of a cross-species avian dispute."

"Odo might understand better than you imagine," Jilly said, adding with emphasis, "especially when *I* explain it to him."

Jilly's use of the director's first name wasn't lost on Hortense. "You know Director Rosmarus?"

"We belong to the same cribbage club," Jilly said innocently. "I've seen him at least once a week for the past 35 years."

The angry fire in the owl's expression faded. "There's no

need to bother the Director with a trivial squabble. Agent George may continue to work with you in the library."

"Thank you, Hortense. I knew you'd be reasonable about this."

"But I won't put up with molting."

Now it was Jilly's turn for impatience. "One feather does not a molt make."

Grudgingly conceding the point, Hortense flew back to her office, and Jilly returned to her littered work table.

The parrot had hoped to find something definitive to take to Festus McGregor, the werecat head of their team and her "gentleman friend," but once again they'd come up empty-winged.

They still didn't know the identity of the agents who dispersed the Temporal Arcana *and* they had no explanation for multiple jumbled references to something code named "Spica."

Jilly hated to return to the lair with more questions, but she had cross-referenced every database BEAR maintained to no avail. Until they could decipher the meaning of "Spica," Jilly feared the search for the missing time artifacts amounted to a wild goose chase.

And geese had a well-deserved reputation for being foul tempered.

As did Festus.

The thought of the perpetually grumpy yellow cat warmed the parrot's heart. He preferred to spend his life on four legs in his small house-cat form—an accommodation to an old injury—but he willingly shifted to human form to date Jilly.

Smiling at the prospect of seeing Festus in Briar Hollow, Jilly lifted her wings to take off, but not before she stole a covert glance at Hortense.

The owl appeared to be napping with her head tucked under her wing. Satisfied that she could make her exit unmolested, Jilly signaled to one of the assistant librarians to pick up her materials.

As she did, a single bit of down worked loose and floated toward the surface of the desk. Horrified, Jilly snatched the offending fluff out of mid-air with her beak and hastily stuffed it into her breast feathers.

Hortense didn't stir as Jilly carefully launched off the table and made straight for the door. Clearing the entrance, the parrot banked left and let out the breath she'd been holding. Festus owed her dinner for this research assignment—a *nice* dinner.

Chapter Four

Londinium, A Shop in Blackfriars

Lucy barreled toward the front door of BEAR headquarters at full speed, waiting until the last possible second to caw loudly, *"Coming through!"*

The panic-stricken brownie doorman dropped his copy of *The Londinium Times* and lunged for the red emergency button. A klaxon sounded, and the doors began to grind apart.

The raven tucked her wings and sailed through the narrow opening like a black bullet, chuckling as the outraged attendant yelled after her, "*Birds!* Do you always have to show off?"

Executing a mid-air roll, Lucy yelled back, "Yes, we do!"

She surged skyward, using powerful wing strokes to diffuse her anger and frustration.

Once clear of the rooftops, Lucy leveled out and flew toward the Thames rather than cut straight across the city to Blackfriars. She wanted to follow the river, taking in the busy barge trade and enjoying the glint of sunlight on the water.

In the Human Realm, the Thames flowed muddy brown, but here in the Otherworld it sparkled like a sapphire. Lucy merged into the heavy flow of wereavian traffic, dodging pigeon couriers and waving at birds she recognized.

Rejuvenated by the exhilaration of flight, the raven pegged a perfect landing on the window sill of a dingy shop. Two and four-legged customers went through the narrow front close; winged visitors came to the rear and tapped on thick glass that had been new when Elizabeth I sat on the throne.

Shuffling footsteps approached. The latch clicked and the window swung back to reveal a short old man in a frayed work shirt and ratty cardigan. Gold spectacles framed his rheumy blue eyes set between a magnificent pair of mutton chop sideburns.

"Aren't you supposed to be working at the BEAR archives?" he asked, stepping aside as Lucy hopped over the window frame.

The raven examined him speculatively, making a sniffing motion. "Key Man are you wearing aftershave?"

"Birds can't smell," he snapped.

"*Au contraire, mon ami,*" Lucy teased. "Ravens are known for their olfactory acuity. I would think you'd know that since your brother is a raven."

"We don't sit around smelling things," the Key Man grumbled, turning on his heel to walk away.

Lucy stopped him with a surprised squawk. "Your pants are ironed!"

The curtains at the front of the room parted as a second black bird twice Lucy's size came in from the front of the shop. "My brother has, I believe, an assignation with a member of the fairer sex."

The old man pursed his lips, "I do not have an assignation, Seneca. I'm going to my Miniaturist Society meeting, just as I have every week for the past seventy-five years."

"True," Seneca agreed, hopping onto the cluttered worktable, "but I believe this is only the second week that Miss Millicent Steingruber will be in attendance. It is also the first instance in my memory, as Lucy has observed, that you've pressed your trousers to spend an evening peering through a magnifying glass with your model-building cronies."

"That will be enough out of both of you," the Key Man declared stoutly. "I have no intention of running myself late playing word games with insolent black birds."

With that, he stormed through the curtain. Seconds later the bell on the front door jangled followed by a slam and the sound of keys in the lock.

Seneca and Lucy exchanged a look before they both burst into laughter.

"It wasn't nice of us to needle him so," Lucy said. "I'd like to see the Key Man doing something other than crafting bling for you to enchant."

The larger raven finished studying the notebook that lay open on the desk before flipping the volume closed with his beak. "Female companionship would be good for my brother," he agreed. "We have both become quite complacent in our perpetual bachelorhood."

"Does he have a name?" Lucy asked, perching on a chair arm by the fire.

"Who?" Seneca asked. "My brother? Of course he has a name."

"But you never call him anything but 'my brother' or 'Key Man.'"

"Having a name and *liking* that name are not the same thing," Seneca replied, settling on the opposite chair. "Brother would be even less amused with me if I shared his given appellation. Did you and Jilly complete your work at BEAR headquarters?"

Lucy ducked her head sullenly. "No," she said. "I more or less got myself kicked out."

"Allow me to hazard a guess," Seneca said drily. "You ran afoul of Hortense."

"Foul is a good word for that creature," Lucy said darkly. "Her pin feathers are always in a twist over something."

"What did you do?"

"I didn't *do* anything. One of my tail feathers dropped in her precious Special Collections Department."

"You haven't been taking the anti-molting potion I gave you," Seneca accused her.

"It tastes like the bottom of a chicken coop, Seneca," Lucy complained. "Would it hurt you to flavor the concoction?"

"We are discussing a finely formulated magical potion, Lucy," the raven replied in an arch tone, "not bottled soda water."

"Pop."

"Excuse me?"

"It's called soda *pop*."

Seneca dismissed the correction with a curt clack of his beak. "Did you fly all the way to Blackfriars to discuss the nomenclature of carbonation with me?"

"No," Lucy said, "Jilly suggested I wait here until she finished looking at the journals of the Ruling Elders."

The statement sparked Seneca's interest. "Any elder in particular?"

"She's been working on the Isherwood journals," Lucy replied. "Lord knows there are plenty to go through. How long did he serve, anyway?"

Seneca cocked his head to the side as if considering the question. "Isherwood's first term was sometime around 1184, as I recall. Reynold was in office on and off for roughly 832 years.

Before his untimely demise he served consecutive terms for two centuries or so. How much progress has Jilly made?"

"I think she pulled the volumes from the 1840s today, why?"

The raven offered an avian version of a shrug. "Mere curiosity. I've known all the Elders, whether they cared to acknowledge the connection or not. At one time I would have called Reynold my friend. Shall we pass the time with a game of chess?"

The offer of a match from a worthy opponent distracted Lucy from the abrupt change of topic. Positioning themselves at the game board, the two ravens began to play.

Engrossed in formulating her strategy, Lucy also failed to understand that for the next hour Seneca not only defeated her twice, he also extracted operational information from her with the skill of a master interrogator.

By the time Jilly tapped on the back window, Seneca possessed a complete understanding of all references to the mystery word "Spica" uncovered by the BlackTAT team during their investigation.

As soon as his guests departed, Seneca moved to the desk, took down a number of notebooks from the adjacent shelves and consulted pages in each volume. Preoccupied with his task, the raven didn't notice the passing hours.

Satisfied at last with the fruits of his reading, Seneca dipped his beak in a pot of ink, and made rapid calculations on a pad of paper. He circled a number and sat back.

"One hundred and sixty-seven years, Edgar," he said softly. "Have you been able to keep your wits, lost in the Spica Mountains for that long?"

The raven jumped when a voice from the curtained entrance said, "What if he has not?"

Startled, Seneca looked at the clock on the wall. "Hello, Brother. How the hours fly. Did you enjoy your meeting?"

"I did," the old man said, moving to warm his hands at the fire. "We are building a transdimensional miniature of the British Museum. This evening I concentrated on engineering a replica of the hidden entrance to the International Bureau of Indefinite Species headquarters with the assistance of Miss Steingruber. She does wonderfully steady work."

Dropping any hint of teasing, Seneca said, "Her family are renowned watchmakers."

"They are," the Key Man agreed. "Milli . . . Miss Steingruber has invited me to view the family collection."

"I envy you so rare an opportunity."

"Seneca, you didn't answer my question. What if Edgar has not kept his wits, marooned in the Lands of Virgo?"

The raven paused, wiping his beak against the blotter. "If he has not," Seneca said finally, "we stand no chance of liberating Lenore from her prison in Nevermore or retrieving the Compass of Chronos."

"Without the Compass and the missing pieces of the Copernican Astrolabe, the Temporal Arcana will never function properly. The weight of time will collapse the rivers and take the Middle Realm with it. The Otherworld will be forever severed from the Human Realm. You must share Edgar's story with Festus."

"No," Seneca said firmly, "*Edgar* must share the story. Only he possesses the details that will allow us to move against Nevermore."

The Key Man stared contemplatively into the flames. "There are no better operatives in the three realms than Festus and his team. They could enter Nevermore, retrieve the Compass, and get out quickly. Lenore brought the troubles with her kinsmen on herself."

The raven looked up sharply. "You would leave Lenore in a living grave?"

The old man shook his head. "I wouldn't want to, Seneca, but neither do I wish to see us trifle with the Neverlands. When last you went there you were a man. You came home a raven."

"I have made my life what it was intended to be," Seneca said firmly, "as have you. Surely you must have known, these many centuries, that our business with Nevermore was not complete?"

The Key Man shivered and tugged at his shapeless sweater. "I have," he admitted glumly, "but I have also been more than content to let sleeping dragons lie."

"Ah," Seneca said softly, gazing into the flames, "never forget, Brother. The dragon that sleeps is the most dangerous dragon of them all."

Chapter Five

Briar Hollow, Werecat Festus McGregor

Okay, let's drop the fourth wall and talk shop.

First, I'm Festus McGregor—up to my whiskers bailing out the bipeds—*again*.

For readers who know the story of Jinx Hamilton's journey with magic, I understand you don't need crib notes.

But, in case we have people joining us mid-adventure, we're laying a trail of background crumbs. Nobody likes getting gnawed on by the Big Bad Wolf of Confusion.

Normally, Jinx does the first-person narration solo. This time we're sharing the job. You'll understand why as the story progresses.

Broad details first.

Jinx inherited a store from her Aunt Fiona Ryan, which she now runs with her best friend, Tori Andrews. The building sits atop a fairy mound in Briar Hollow, North Carolina.

When humans look down the basement stairs in the building they see a cobweb-coated monument to hoarding and poor inventory management. A select few of us, however, walk down the stairs and into a different layer of reality occupied by the living and working space we call the "lair."

There's a lot down here. This isn't a real estate ad, so keep up.

More recent facts.

Jinx has a new husband: Lucas Grayson. Think of him as a sort of Fae secret agent/detective working for an agency called the Division for Grid Integrity. You know, if James Bond and Humphrey Bogart had a kitten—with a fedora.

Anyway, at the wedding reception, a malfunctioning portal sucked Jinx and one of the bridesmaids, Glory Green, into an alternate timescape.

A big *thing* ensued, during which nobody, and I do mean *no body*, considered the inconvenience the whole mess posed for *me*.

For starters, I had to postpone beginning my job as a Blacklist agent.

That one you can figure out by the name. We deal in sketchy, sometimes dangerous, artifacts—which would be why the items are blacklisted.

Our mission statement boils down to: keep idiots from doing stupid/nefarious things with magical doodads.

When I *did* report for duty, the higher-ups slapped me with a "special assignment" directly tied to Jinx and Glory's misadventure—find and reassemble the Temporal Arcana.

Cue esoteric background details.

Time travel used to be allowed in the Fae world. Then it wasn't. All the navigational items that made accurate timefaring possible—the Temporal Arcana—were scattered.

Now the Ruling Elders want the stuff back.

Hurdle Number One: the high and mighty Elders under the leadership of Reynold Isherwood (now conveniently dead) destroyed or magically redacted all records pertaining to where they dumped the damned artifacts in the first place.

Currently the only piece of the Arcana we have, the Copernican Astrolabe, is missing a few pieces—and it resides in the custody of a pirate captain named Miranda Winter. Payment for her help in getting Jinx and Glory back.

Her custody of the astrolabe coupled with my assignment put me in an awkward position. During the rescue mission, I called Miranda's timefaring ship the *Tempus Fugit* a "tub."

Who knew nautical types get touchy about derogatory references to their boats?

I dragged my butt to Cibolita, the Middle Realm port where Miranda currently drops anchor, and apologized with a case of rum. I need Miranda and the astrolabe to start looking for the remaining time-related junk.

Fortunately Miranda accepted both the booze and the olive branch. That's one personnel problem ticked off my list.

I'm also responsible, however, for a PAW-Ops team comprised of elite operatives named Booger, Leon, and Marty. They and my second-in-command, Rube, are Fae raccoons known collectively around BEAR as the Wrecking Crew.

Me and the boys have knocked off more ROMO jobs than I have claws to count. We're the best in the business. When the Elders wanted me to give up the team, I refused. I told the old stuffed robes point blank they could chase down their own missing junk.

Hissing and spitting ensued; I won.

When Rube and I have to be off on Blacklist gigs, the number three man on the team, Booger, will take point. I need Rube with me on the Blacklist work because even though he's a wisecracking pain in my backside, he's also a top shelf professional with talent and integrity.

Compliments I will deny uttering if so much as one word leaves this page.

Shifting gears from one-off artifact retrievals to a long-term operation presented certain . . . *challenges* . . . from Day One.

We—being me, Rube, Jilly Pepperdine, and Lucy George—showed up at the BEAR archives to consult with the agency's chief wereowl librarian, Hortense Tyton.

Within five minutes the tight-feathered old . . . broad . . . branded Rube "a refuse-diving ruffian" and pegged me for "yellow, Scotch-swilling alley scum."

I extended my claws and asked Hortense if she'd ever considered a career as a stew ingredient—which would be when Jilly sent me and Rube back to Briar Hollow.

That suited me fine.

Rube suffers from the worst case of distractible researcher syndrome I've ever seen. He also knows the publisher of *The National Dumpster Diver*. Bad combination.

Besides, like most cats, I'm happier working at home.

After I was named the head of BlackTAT (Rube came up with that, short for Blacklist Temporal Arcana Taskforce), the fairy mound got my attention late one afternoon by showering my desk with confetti.

It could have been worse; the sentient lump of dirt has been known to communicate via glitter-gram.

"Something I can do for you?" I said, shaking confetti off my whiskers and staring up at the ceiling.

The tiny paper squares shifted direction and headed out of the seating area in front of the fire. When I didn't follow, the downpour stopped, intensified, and formed a giant index finger, which promptly crooked twice in my direction.

"Can't you just draw me a picture?"

The confetti switched to a more "editorial" gesture.

"Okay, *okay*," I said, "you don't have to be rude about it. I'm coming already."

The paper trail led me past the treehouse where the Wrecking Crew hangs out.

(Yes, we have an underground treehouse. I told you there's a lot going on down here.)

Rounding a corner, I found myself looking through a doorway into a brand new war room specifically tailored to the needs of one werecat, four raccoons, and two werebirds.

To steal a phrase from Rube, *suh-wheet!*

For those of you who think the "lair" might be getting a bit out of hand, let me put your concerns at ease. The fairy mound occupies the outer layer of the In Between. The subterranean "footprint" is not limited by or equal to that of the store overhead.

With each addition, the available space becomes more expansive. Hard as it may be to imagine, we aren't piled on top of each other. Think of the fairy mound as a small town *under* the small town that is Briar Hollow and you'll be okay.

Once we moved into the war room, I called Stank Preston, the ferret scientist who heads the Blacklist Containment Division. Mr. Stinky Weasel gets all the sexy tech first, and I wanted some.

I now own the world's largest iPad—fifty-five inches of high-definition gorgeousness I call the MonsterPad, a proper all-purpose command center for a feline of my stature.

That catches you up on everything except the change in the portal system. You don't need to understand the mechanical details of the glitch that sent Jinx and Glory back in time.

You *do* need to understand the basics of the system that connects the Three—now Four—Realms.

For as long as I can remember, going from one location to

another in the Three Realms meant hopping through a series of dedicated portals. As soon as Jinx opened up the Temporal Rivers, the portal system shrank to a more streamlined version of itself.

Travelers approach a portal and tell the matrix where they want to go. Sure it's more efficient, but the damn thing actually *asks* for a destination.

Like most felines, I'm not big on change, but Bastet's litter box! Portals aren't supposed to talk, something I make a point of saying every time I'm forced to use one.

It's been scientifically proven that swearing relieves pain. Sardonic wisecracks have a similar analgesic value, or at least they do for me.

Jinx copes with changes and dilemmas by writing.

On top of all my other duties, I have an ancestral obligation to guard the Daughters of Knasgowa. That means more than showing up to fend off the latest threat; Jinx is my friend. In the weeks following her return, I worried about her.

She spent hours working on the story of what happened in that alternate version of Elizabethan England and coming to terms with what she had to do there.

Circumstances forced Jinx to leave a man named Axe Frazier to die in the Tower of Londinium. She took his daughter, Naomi, out of harm's way and promised to get her the care she needs for tuberculosis—a fatal disease then, curable now.

More than once I've ducked under the hem of the enchanted curtain covering the entrance to Jinx's alcove at some ungodly hour of the morning to check in on your favorite author. Even after committing the events to paper, however, Jinx hasn't fully recovered from the experience.

On the day this story begins, a casual observer looking into the lair would have glimpsed a "normal" day; that illusion came with a short shelf life.

I lounged in front of the MonsterPad in the war room,

checking the feeds from the GNATS micro-drones (Group Network Aerial Transmission System) we keep stationed around the courthouse square up at street level.

After about 2.5 seconds, Rube's buzzsaw snores got the better of me.

Jumping onto the conference table, I sauntered down to where the raccoon lay sprawled amidst a litter of salsa bowls and tortilla chips. A well-placed blow across his black mask brought the lazy varmint back to consciousness sputtering indignant protests.

"*Hey!* What the *heck*, McGregor? You keep beating on me like that, and I'm gonna rat you out to Jilly. She says you gotta work on your interior personnel skills."

One of Rube's more annoying habits involves murdering the English language with impunity. "*Interpersonal.*" I said. "And my skills are fine, thank you. I got your attention, didn't I?"

Rubbing at his jaw and pretending to pop the joint back in place, the raccoon replied sourly, "You ruin my nap for the fun of it or you want something?"

"I *want* your report on those files from the archives," I replied, adding with saccharin sweetness, "if it wouldn't be too much trouble."

Before he could answer, a raven glided into the office, forcing us both to duck. Lucy landed on the hanging perch over the filing cabinet.

"Hello, gents," she called out. "Rube, be a luv and lend a gal a paw, will you?"

"Sure, toots."

Seizing the excuse to get out of catching me up on work I felt sure he hadn't done, the raccoon waddled to the end of the table. He used a chair to bridge the distance to the counter. "Whatcha need?"

"A seed bar," she replied. "Honey coated please. I'm famished."

A second set of wings sounded from the door. Jilly arrived in a flash of red and gray. After sticking the landing, she leaned over and ran her beak along the line of my ear in greeting.

Yeah, yeah. I know. A cat and a parrot make an odd pairing. May I remind you we are both capable of assuming human form? Which is as far into my business as you're getting.

"Hi," Jilly cooed playfully, "fancy meeting you here."

Ignoring Rube's snicker, I said, "Hello, yourself. Good day at BEAR?"

Jilly danced back and forth, cocking her head to one side. "Lucy, would you like to answer that?"

The raven pecked visciously at the seed bar. "It wasn't my fault. That owl has an attitude."

Stifling a groan, I said, "What happened with Hortense this time?"

Lucy flexed her wings in annoyance. "For starters, it's impossible to concentrate with that white face of hers peering down from the rafters. Then, she had the *nerve* to accuse me of *molting* in the reading room."

I looked at Jilly. "I'm guessing that's some kind of bird-on-bird insult?"

The parrot nodded. "Lucy shed a tail feather, and the next thing I know, the two of them are in a squawking match about mites."

"*Which*," Lucy said, stabbing at her seeds like the bar was Hortense herself, "I do *not* have."

Jilly lowered her voice. "Lucy gets this way when she's hungry. I scanned everything we found today. Stank transferred scans of the materials I flagged to the BlackTAT server. I'm afraid you're not going to be pleased."

"Don't tell me," I said, "more cryptic 'Spica' references?"

"Dozens."

She hopped across the table to stare at an elaborate display spreading across two old-fashioned bulletin boards. Lines of red string connected photos of possible time artifacts—the Pelekinon of Apollo, the Hourglass of the Horae, the Dioptra of Janus—to snippets of text containing the word "Spica."

We had redacted copies of supply ordinances for what appeared to be building materials. Numbered personnel deployment orders completely blacked out and even inventories of books.

What the heck was this "Spica" thing, and what had to be erected to contain it?

Rube scrambled back over the chair and joined us. "Before you got here, doll, I was about to tell Grumpy Whiskers I got us a lead on something when I was doing my homework last night."

The raccoon looked at me smugly. "One of the benefits of being nocturnal, not creep-us-curler."

I started to belt him again but dropped my paw when Jilly shot me an admonishing look.

"The word," I said, through clenched teeth, "is *crepuscular*. You speak English as well as any of us. Admit it. You decimate the language purely to annoy me."

Unfazed, Rube plowed on. "The point being, I actually stay up all night doing stuff, unlike Mr. Active at Dawn and Dusk with twelve hours of napping in between."

Beaks get in the way of an actual smile, but I spotted amusement in Jilly's eye. "Don't you start in on me, too. Restorative napping contributes to my analytical process."

"Of course it does," she said, extending a wing to pat me on the shoulder. "What did you find, Rube?"

Grinning from ear to ear, the raccoon said, "Okay, so, I still got no idea what this Spica thing is, but check this out."

He went to my desk, stood on his hind legs, and started to tap icons on the MonsterPad.

"You're gonna clean those handprints off my screen when you're done," I grumbled.

Ignoring me, Rube pulled up the image of what looked like a cursive *M* with a funny hook on the right side.

"What the hell is that?" I asked.

Lucy hopped onto the table. "It's the symbol for Virgo. The Maiden."

"Bingo," Rube said, his black fingers flying over the screen. "The constellation is associated with this chick Persephone..."

"Hold it right there," I stopped him. "You can pronounce 'Persephone,' but you can't say '*crepuscular*'?"

Snickering, the raccoon went on. "This chick Persephone was Demeter's daughter. She was a real looker. Hades, the god of the Underworld had like zero game with dames, so he goddess-napped her."

"Does anyone know what he's talking about?" I asked with frustration.

"I do," Jilly said. "The Persephone myth explains the seasonal change from summer to winter. Zeus brokered a compromise so that the girl spent half the year with her mother, the Goddess of the Harvest, and half with Hades. How is Virgo related to Spica?"

Rube nodded over his shoulder toward the display. "All that stuff Festus asked me to look at had the sign for Virgo up at the top. Kinda like a stamp or something. Look."

Images filled the screen, each an enlargement of a document. A faint Virgo symbol no larger than a pinhead adorned their upper right-hand corner.

"How in the name of Bastet's whiskers did you manage to see that?" I asked, impressed in spite of myself.

"I figured," Rube replied, "that if nobody was coming right

out and saying what this Spica thing is, maybe they was saying something between the lines, so I looked extra close."

And that level of intuition would be why I tolerate the raccoon's constantly running mouth.

"You ever heard of cutting to the chase?" I asked. "Did any Fae agency in operation when the Agreement was forged use the Virgo symbol?"

"Hold on," Rube said, "I ain't done yet. We gotta talk about Spica."

It's a good thing I have naturally low blood pressure. "You are on my last nerve cell, Rube. Get to the point."

The raccoon shook his head. "You late for your worming again?"

"*Rube...*"

"Okay, okay. Spica is the brightest star in the constellation Virgo."

He switched the screen to display the map of the Rivers of Time, which Miranda'd donated to our team from her cartographic pirate stash. Rube pointed to a thin line running off the River of Virgo—a tributary called Spica.

Then, using two fingers to enlarge a section of the map, the raccoon highlighted a mountain range with a tiny Virgo symbol sitting on one of the peaks.

"I'm thinking," he said, "we oughta go check *that* out."

As much as it pains me to admit it, I agreed with him.

Chapter Six

Abandoned Building, The Jungle Below the Spica Mountains

Light fascinated him. Shadows under the jungle canopy fell thick as night one minute, only to be bathed by brilliant sunbeams the next.

Often, in the moments before nightfall, a single golden shaft pierced the tree cover at the precise angle to strike the mirror's surface.

Then, the reflected illumination filled the cluttered room Edgar called home and transported him to far away parlors lit by oil lamps.

In that life, strangers gathered to hear him speak. Sometimes, in fanciful moments, he spoke still, addressing the emptiness, reciting from memory lines of his poetry, verses from *before*.

Edgar could have chosen any place in the five-story building to call home. During the long duration of his exile, he examined every floor inch by inch.

When he first awakened, uncertain if he'd dreamed the

conversation with Seneca or if the bird had come to him that rainy night, Edgar sprang from his deathbed.

Weak, but animated by desperation, he stumbled through the corridors, calling out for a doctor, a nurse... a friend.

Then, with only silence for a response, he collected himself, located proper clothing, and went in search of food and supplies. He found everything he needed except answers—nothing but the fractured memory of a black bird perched at the foot of his bed.

What had Seneca said?

"Nevermore is not a pronouncement, Edgar. It is a place—a concept—a reason for your continued being. I cannot send you there, but I can save your life if you agree. Beyond that, you must find your own way."

How could living entombment in a jungle filled with demons be a path to anything but madness?

The raven cautioned him to keep his sanity if he hoped to find Lenore again. That gossamer dream sent Edgar down a dogged path of self-preservation.

Initially, he thought to establish his base on the ground floor, but the proximity to the jungle made him feel exposed and vulnerable. Instead Edgar chose an open area on the second floor to craft a comfortable cave.

The adjacent rooms of the central sanctuary became his storehouse, home to every useful or interesting item the building offered up.

Edgar barricaded the stairwells against intruders and developed a routine of watching the surrounding clearing from multiple vantage points.

He scoured the premises and drew to himself the society of familiar things. Ransacking drawers and cabinets, Edgar gathered every scrap of paper along with an odd collection of quills and pencil stubs.

Next he dragged a desk down from the administrator's office and nailed a shelf above its scarred surface. There, he arranged a regimented line of scavenged ink bottles.

Edgar reasoned that, so long as he could write, he could maintain a degree of stability, but the fear of scarcity tormented him.

Holding a vessel of ink to the candle flame, he measured the contents. How many days before the bottle ran dry, forcing him to open the next? How long until the day when none of the precious fluid remained?

Edgar broke down and wept the day he realized the ink level never changed. Then he received the miracle of the papers. If he filled twenty pages in a day, twenty fresh sheets awaited him on the morrow.

Determined to move forward with gratitude, Edgar sought the solace of routine, a challenging task in a place where time refused to be kept.

The hands of his pocket watch might spin wildly only then to freeze and refuse to budge. Some "days" passed quickly. Some "nights" lasted an eternity.

The coming of the rains offered the only event on which to peg a count, but Edgar stopped when the marks he notched in the doorframe reached one hundred.

What difference did it make really?

Starved for the company he'd once scorned, Edgar engaged in heated conversations with himself, an exercise that taught him to expect and ignore the rudeness of inanimate objects.

Regardless of the brilliance or intricacy of his arguments, no chair ever spoke up to laud Edgar's intellect. No table chimed in with a counterpoint. The silent mantle kept its counsel.

Oddly, Edgar never engaged in debate with the man whose visage regarded him from the shining silver of the mirror.

Some inner wisdom insisted that were he to dialogue with

his own reflection, Edgar would surely tumble over the mental precipice on which he teetered with precarious precision.

He never deluded himself. He accepted that a degree of native imbalance followed him into exile—a series of struggles that historically weighted the course of his life.

Never quite given to drinking in excess, but still vulnerable to the bottle.

Loose with money and weakened by the desire to wager. A gambler with no talent for winning.

At times, Edgar's memory called up the faces of the jealous rivals who envied his facility with words.

How merrily they gave testimony to his pre-existing lunacy!

They labeled him a drunkard when he was not.

They linked his name to drugs that he did not take and debauchery in which he did not engage.

Had any one of those critics offered so much as a crumb of human understanding, they would have seen the true source of Edgar's torment: lost love.

Deprived of his sweet Virginia, the innocent child he took as his wife, and then denied the enchanting woman whose brilliant intellect pierced his soul, Edgar looked toward the future and saw oblivion.

Then on a cold, wet night a black bird offered him the chance of consolation.

"*Nevermore is ... a place ....*"

A place where, if Edgar could believe Seneca's word, he might find Lenore.

> *Tell this soul with sorrow laden if, within the distant Aidenn,*
> *It shall clasp a sainted maiden whom the angels name*
>   *Lenore—*
> *Clasp a rare and radiant maiden whom the angels name*
>   *Lenore.*"

Quoth the Raven "Nevermore."

If only he had not misunderstood the bird's message that first night!

Sweet Virginia lay locked in a mortal struggle with consumption that would last two more agonizing years. Lenore seemed lost.

Reconciling with and obeying Reynold Isherwood offered Edgar the chance to regain his footing. Reynold insisted on a single proviso: do not write of Lenore or her beliefs again.

But how could Edgar honor that promise? How could he not share Lenore's perception of the universe as God's manuscript? Or attempt to describe the cold breath of the metaphorical creature she called the Wind from the Cloud?

Reynold overlooked the prose poem Edgar called *Eureka* because the work garnered public ridicule and generated only piddling sales, but the poem *Annabel Lee* enraged his mentor. It was for the crime of that composition that Edgar accepted banishment over death.

A beam of light interrupted Edgar's reverie. It reached the scratched and spotted surface of the mirror. Edgar walked toward the glass and studied his reflection.

He found himself remarkably unchanged. Thick dark hair combed high over his forehead descended into curls at the temples. Neither his hair nor his mustache had grown with time.

In conditions that would have left other men disheveled and unkempt, Edgar continued to look like what he was—a 19th century gentleman enduring a form of solitary confinement.

The same heavy pouches drooped beneath his melancholy eyes, betraying a life of sleepless nights, but Edgar could not blame the insomnia on his current environs. The solace of sleep habitually eluded him.

Glancing to the left and right as if expecting to be overheard, Edgar faced his reflection and spoke to it for the first time.

"Have I succeeded in safeguarding the treasure that is my sanity or did it slink away some dark night leaving me bereft?"

To his relief, the reflection held its tongue.

Suddenly suspicious, Edgar leaned forward and peered deeper into the glass. His writings explored realms of existence both macabre and compelling.

Edgar knew well the superstition with which many beings regarded mirrors. Reynold came to him often in the surface of a mirror. Proof that strange creatures and foreign lands resided beyond the looking glass.

With some trepidation, Edgar laid his hand against the cool surface. Had the means of his escape been hanging there on the wall all along?

He recoiled from the thought. Surely the winged demons that came at dawn and dusk each day implanted such notions in his already troubled brain.

The demons worried Edgar. If he could not exorcise their presence from his vision, he would never be completely certain of his lucidity.

From his position crouched low against the window, Edgar watched the devils daily. They first arrived only hours after he awakened, offering aid and asking him to live with them in their black mountain fortress—pretty temptations offered by fallen angels astride hell beasts.

Edgar refused, drawing on half-remembered religious phrases to drive the evil ones away.

In time, Satan's minions left him in peace, but they never left him alone. He felt the demons in the skies overhead, waiting and watching for the day when his mind shattered.

But Edgar had made a single deal with a single devil—Reynold Isherwood. He would sign no other black contract.

In the hours between the demon flights, Edgar, like a fellow writer whose works he admired, sought to heal himself by walking.

Born in a city by the sea, Edgar felt drawn to the mighty river lying to the north. The sound of flowing water settled his jangled nerves. The river became one of the few constants in his life until that constancy altered.

The river had always flowed toward the setting sun. Now, overnight, the water's motion pivoted eastward.

Scaling a massive tree and using the field glasses he had discovered in the building, Edgar thought he could make out a new waterfall in the distance, one whose waters seemed to tumble off the face of the earth.

By what force could a river reverse its flow?

By what power could cascading waters form overnight?

What did these signs portend for him?

Could they offer a means of escape?

But an escape to *where*? To Nevermore?

That nagging thought gave Edgar pause. Finally accustomed to the jungle, he was both tempted by and fearful of potential differences—even if those differences might return him to the company of humankind—to the company of Lenore.

With bitter irony he recalled the words of his walking friend. *"The question* [Edgar] *is whether you can* bear *freedom."*

Whether you can bear to begin the search for Nevermore.

Chapter Seven

Briar Hollow, Festus

After Rube showed us the map, I placed a mirror call to Miranda Winter in Cibolita. We arranged to meet that evening in the bar at the Crow's Nest, the inn where she rented rooms.

Since Rube had a prior commitment—the weekly poker game with the other members of the Wrecking Crew—and Lucy was looking forward to movie night in the lair, I seized on the opportunity to spend some quality alone time with Jilly.

I suggested the two of us have dinner before our meeting with Miranda. Jilly accepted the invitation and ducked into one of the changing booths off the war room.

There are logistics shifters have to consider. Going from two to four legs—or two wings as the case may be—presents nothing more complicated than a cast off pile of clothes on the floor.

Going the other way, however, leaves you with nothing but your birthday suit.

The fairy mound thought about that, providing changing

rooms complete with wardrobe cabinets. When Jilly emerged, she'd put on a lovely blue silk dress and pulled her silvery hair up in an elegant twist.

I suddenly found myself as tongue-tied as a kitten smoking nip for the first time.

Thankfully, I had shifted as well, opting for khakis, a white shirt, and a sport jacket. On my best day, I could never look as good as Jilly, but at least I was presentable.

We could have skirted the seating area around the fire and gone to the portal unobserved, but Jilly thought it would be rude not to let Darby know that we wouldn't be present for dinner.

Like all brownies, Darby has a knack for household management. He keeps us fed and watered in style and is such an outstanding housekeeper he coaches competitors for Domestic Chore Decathlons.

Appearance wise, he looks like a garden gnome and a leprechaun had a kid—that is when he chooses to pop in. Brownies have the power of invisibility and enjoy working their home and hearth magic largely unseen.

My reluctance to go through the seating area was tied directly to the epidemic of nosiness currently rampaging through the lair. Said stroll amounted to a pre-date perp walk in front of everyone who had gathered for the evening.

While it's common knowledge Jilly and I are seeing one another, I'll be glad when we get past the "couple of the moment" stage of our relationship. All those adoring, approving looks make me want to hack a hairball.

Not that it doesn't please me that everyone has readily welcomed Jilly into the extended family, but I don't see why they have to make such a big deal about me having a girlfriend. I'm just the other side of 100; I'm not dead yet.

Thankfully, we walked into the middle of a distracting

dispute between Glory and her new writing partner, Rodney the Rat. Since he came into possession of a rodent-sized laptop, the little twerp has entertained delusions of being the next Hemingway.

When Glory was absent from Briar Hollow, the rat took up the slack and wrote her advice column for *The Briar Hollow Banner*. Now, he hangs out at a roll top desk on a shelf over Glory's workspace. As a finishing touch to the hardcore author look, he's taken to sporting a miniature green visor like the old telegraph operators used to wear.

Jilly and I walked into a one-sided heated argument between the two creative partners. Glory was wailing about the correct way to respond to an inquiry from a letter writer who signed herself "Hooked on a Feeling for a Loser."

Rodney can speak, but he chooses not to for reasons that are entirely his business. We've all learned to play a mean game of charades since he showed up in Briar Hollow.

Typically, Glory has no difficulty understanding him, but that evening she had worked herself into a state, flinging about references to Elvis and the "little baby Jesus." Sure signs of agitation.

I'm not going to take the time to give you the ups and downs of Glory's backstory. She entered our lives as a spy disguised as a tiny green witch plastered on the side of a coffee cup.

Trust me. Glory wasn't clever enough to do that to herself. In her desire to emulate the singing abilities of the King, she tried to double cross a wizard and failed.

Glory's back to a normal size and complexion now, unless she gets strung out about something. Stress causes her to green up and shrink down, hence my bevy of nicknames for her, including "Pickle" and "Gherkin."

Here's the worst part. She's dating my son, Chase, and insists on calling me Dad—which I allow *only* because she had a rotten childhood.

Hearing our footsteps, Glory turned to me and said, "Oh *Dad*, you are just an answer to my prayers to the little baby Jesus. Rodney and I do *not* agree about how to respond to Hooked on a Feeling, and I'm just *so* upset I can't make heads or tails of what he's trying to say to me."

I looked around the room. There were more than enough people present who could take on the role of translator, and they all instantly got busy doing something else.

Chase sat by the fire playing chess with Colonel Beauregard T. Longworth, our resident ghost who enjoys corporeality so long as he's wearing the Amulet of the Phoenix.

He and Chase stared so hard at the chess pieces on the board between them, I expected their next moves to be executed telepathically.

Shoving my hands in my pants pockets, I leaned over the desk and put myself on eye level with the rat. "What shaking, Rodney?" I asked.

That touched off an elaborate series of mime movements which I interpreted on the fly. Turning back to the Pickle, I said, "Rodney agrees with Hooked on a Feeling. Her husband is a loser, and she should leave him. I'm not sure, but I think he said something about the guy buying a $2000 riding lawnmower?"

Glory made a scoffing sound in the back of her throat. "They live on *six* acres," she said. "Six *whole* acres! He made a good case for *needing* that lawnmower."

From the vicinity of the hearth Tori's mother Gemma Andrews chimed in, "A herd of goats would have been cheaper."

Glory actually stamped her foot in frustration. Outside a B-movie, I've never seen anyone try to pull off that move. For a good reason. It makes you look like you're trying to kill imaginary cockroaches.

"Don't any of you have any romance in your souls?" the Pickle asked. "Hooked on a Feeling and Loser were *high school sweethearts.*"

"Scrap and I were high school sweethearts, too," Gemma pointed out. "That didn't stop him from leaving me for a younger woman or taking up with a couple of skanky vampires."

I may not be the most diplomatic of souls, but I was glad Tori wasn't in the lair for that accurate, but cringe-worthy assessment of her absent father. Actually, he's absent because he's dead, but that's another story.

Judging that Glory had plenty of teammates for a game of kick the lovelorn can, I said, "As much as we hate to tear ourselves away from this scintillating conversation, we're going to Cibolita for dinner at the Crow's Nest."

Jinx, who was sitting at the table working on the monthly books for the store, looked up. "Are you going to see Miranda?" she asked.

"Yes," Jilly replied. "We need to discuss a potential BlackTAT expedition up the River of Virgo with her."

Interest immediately ignited in Jinx's expression. "Did you get a lead on Spica?"

"Maybe," I said. "Rube picked up a potential clue in some documents that points to a mountain range lying along a tributary of the River of Virgo. I want to run it by Miranda. She knows the historical pirate maps better than anyone."

"Tell her I said hi," Jinx said, reluctantly resuming her bookkeeping, "and let me know what you find out."

I told her I would and quickly ushered Jilly out as the argument between Glory and Rodney heated up again. Approaching the portal, I jumped when a pleasant voice asked, "Destination, please?"

"I am never gonna get used to this," I said. "A damned portal shouldn't talk."

"So you say every time," Jilly murmured, patting my arm consolingly, "but you do have to admit it's more convenient."

"Convenient, yes," I growled. "But does she have to sound so damned *cheerful*?"

My date shook her head. "I'm guessing you don't have a GPS unit in your car."

"Good guess," I said. "The last car I owned was a Model T. Everything's gone downhill since."

Sighing with exaggerated tolerance, Jilly spoke to the portal. "Cibolita, please. Preferably on the street in front of The Crow's Nest inn."

The portal matrix changed color. "Ready at your pleasure, madam."

Still grumbling, I offered Jilly my arm. As we stepped through the opening, I said, "Has anybody figured out where that voice comes from?"

"No," Jilly said. "People have started to refer to her as the Attendant. She's developing a reputation for being unfailingly polite. And accurate."

I couldn't argue with that assessment since the portal dropped us out mere feet from the front door of The Crow's Nest. The sign over the door read, "Travelers welcome. Brigands beware."

The caution against brigands was, in my estimation, the precise reason Miranda Winter chose to move in over the bar. The pirate captain relishes her brigand status, tempering the lawless streak with a wicked sense of humor. She enjoys rubbing the questionable legality of her business affairs in the face of management.

In this case "management" happens to be a satyr named Lou —a *nonconformi* with the body of a man and the hindquarters of a goat.

Right after the lifting of the Agreement, Lucas and Rube

hauled Lou out of the Mixologist International convention at the Mirage in Vegas. Not only was he losing his horns playing blackjack at a six-deck shuffle table, he was scaring the natives. No small feat in Vegas.

They concocted a cover story and got the guy into Gamblers Anonymous. Unfortunately, the experience left Lou with a strait-laced streak, making him a perfect target for Miranda's sharp wit.

The proprietor himself welcomed us when we walked through the door, ushering us to a lovely table by a window overlooking the port. Lou's delicate hooves clacked across the floorboards in rhythm with his detailed recitation of the evening specials. The Crow's Nest might look like a dive, but reserve your judgment until you've had the coq au vin.

When we were settled with glasses of wine, I looked out over the ocean formed by the confluence of the Rivers of Time. What had been a barren plain, now lies submerged under sparkling waters christened the Sea of Ages by the locals.

The thirteen rivers surround the ocean like hours on a clock face—plus one. Cibolita sits at six o'clock between the Rivers of Taurus and Aries with Ophiuchus and Scorpio directly opposite at the "top" of the dial. From where I sat I could see our potential destination, the River of Virgo, at roughly two o'clock.

The landscape made for a dramatic view. Each temporal river descends earthward through a jagged hole in the sky. That evening the setting sun created thousands of rainbows in the mist surrounding the suspended waterfalls. Flocks of birds flew through the splashes of color and without warning, a lone whale breached the surface of the water.

The sight brought me forward in my chair. "Did you see that?" I asked Jilly.

Lou answered from my elbow, our salads balanced in his hands. "The marine life started showing up last week. No one can explain it. The temporal rivers are freshwater, but the Sea of Ages is salty."

"There are lots of unexplained things about the Rivers," I said, picking up my fork. "For one thing, how can that much water pour into the sea without filling the whole valley?"

The satyr held up a pepper grinder and gave me a questioning look. When I nodded, he began to crank the implement over the greens on my plate.

"We all wonder about those kinds of things," he said, "but no one really cares. After centuries of dry dock, Cibolita has become a true port city again. We endured generations of being cut off from the ocean; now we're home."

The proof of his words lay in plain view—pirate ships and merchant freighters that once floated at anchor in mid-air now rocking gently along the wharves.

Yeah, you need to get used to that idea. The schooners we're talking about fly *and* float.

I spotted the *Tempus Fugit* in a prominent berth, along with several other of Miranda's vessels. As one of the leaders of a group that once styled itself as the "Temporal Resistance," Miranda dedicates the bulk of her energies to mapping the Rivers of Time and helping us reassemble the Temporal Arcana.

The mariners who made names for themselves as "pirates" under the Agreement are the descendents of great explorers. They want their heritage back; I don't blame them.

Chapter Eight

Cibolita, The Crow's Nest, Festus

Miranda knew when we entered the tavern. She knows everything that happens in Cibolita, but she was nice enough to let us have dinner before appearing beside the table.

"Mind if I join you?" she asked. "I like the view of the port, and the dining room is quieter than the bar."

There are worse fates for a werecat than being seen in public between two gorgeous blondes.

Don't take that the wrong way. I'm a look, don't touch kinda guy. Jilly has my full attention, but when Miranda Winter walks into a room, every man in the place with a pulse—and even those that don't—takes notice.

The captain's fondness for leather pants accessorized with daggers creates a certain... *presence*.

Miranda has the long, graceful lines of the Elvish people, mixed with the raw physical power born of a life at sea.

During our time on the *Tempus Fugit*, I saw those slender hands grasp the ship's wheel and turn it against a stiff breeze.

The captain can climb the rigging of her vessel with nimble ease, and I suspect when push comes to shove, she can throw a punch.

Drawing back one of the chairs, Miranda signaled Lou to bring her a drink. He didn't have to ask her pleasure. Three fingers, bourbon. Neat.

"So," Miranda said. "Rube found something."

I took a small tablet out of the breast pocket of my jacket and handed the device to Miranda. The screen displayed the documents Rube had shared with us in the war room.

After I explained the multiple Spica references and the Virgo mark, Miranda took a contemplative sip of her whiskey.

"Let's take this discussion upstairs," she suggested. "We need to look at the original of the chart Rube showed you and compare it to other maps. That will give us a better picture of the terrain around the Spica tributary."

When I reached for my wallet to pay the bill, Miranda stopped me. "Dinner's on me," she said, signaling to Lou at the bar who nodded his understanding.

We followed the captain to the second floor and down the long corridor to a heavy oak door. Miranda produced a skeleton key from her vest pocket and let us in.

If I hadn't known we were above the tavern, I would have taken the setting for the captain's cabin in the stern of the *Tempus Fugit*.

Tall, narrow latticed windows rose to the ceiling on the back wall, leaning out toward the Cibolita port. Brass rails secured the books on their shelves, but Oriental rugs softened the wood floors.

"I like what you've done with the place," Jilly said. "It suits you."

"Lou had a fit when I said I wanted to remodel," Miranda

replied, crossing to a cabinet and removing a series of charts. "He changed his tune when I told him I'd pay for the work."

She brought the charts to the rough hewn table in front of the windows that served as her desk. "The Rivers of Time are multi-layered entry points to an infinite variety of lands and time frames. All my life I've studied the exploits of the great temporal captains and wanted to sail those same waters."

"I bet your mother was thrilled that you were hanging around with a bunch of pirates," I said.

Miranda laughed. "My mother *was* a pirate," she said, "and not just any pirate. Maureen Winter was a captain of the *Temporal Coast*."

The words carried an unmistakable pride, but the title meant nothing to me. "Sorry," I said. "I'm not up on my pirate lore."

"The captains of the *Temporal Coast* are the direct descendents of the original temporal mariners," Miranda explained. "There were thirteen, one for each of the Rivers of Time. In those days, the timefaring trade was highly territorial. I'm descended from the captains who controlled the River of Capricorn."

"Will that present a problem with our traveling the River of Virgo aboard the *Tempus Fugit*?" Jilly asked.

Miranda unrolled an oversized nautical chart, weighing the corners down with the candlestick, a spy glass, a compass, and a wicked looking dagger—a spare, I guess, since she had one in her belt and another in her boot.

"During the centuries that we labored under the Agreement," she said, "territorial bickering didn't serve our greater cause. We're all free to navigate the temporal waterways. Every Captain of the Coast has access to the necessary charts."

The way she worded the statement, I realized she was including herself in that number.

"What do the other captains think about you working with BlackTAT?" I asked. "And controlling the Copernican Astrolabe."

Miranda shot me that wicked grin I was rapidly learning to appreciate. "They think it best to mind their business. The mistress of the *Tempus Fugit* answers to no authority but time itself."

With the chart firmly secured, she went back to the shelves and returned with a ship's log. I read the name embossed in gold on the front cover: *Capt. Daniel Winter.*

"Daniel was my great-great-grandfather," Miranda said. "This is the logbook he kept when he was master of the *Tempus Fugit*. He sailed the ship up the River of Virgo and partway down the tributary of Spica."

Opening the heavy cover, Miranda turned the pages, scanning the lines of elegant antique handwriting until she found the entry she wanted. Then she read aloud:

> *Today we entered the tributary of Spica off the Virgo River. We find ourselves in a tropical land. The sounds from the banks frighten the men. The superstitious fools believe they have seen strange creatures flying above the trees. We have detected nothing of potential value. If no marketable commodities are identified by noon tomorrow, I will order our return to the main river so that we might go in search of more profitable lands.*

"Did they turn around?" I asked, privately wondering what creatures would qualify as "strange" to a crew of Fae pirates from Cibolita.

"They did," Miranda said, "but so far as I know, no other temporal captain traveled farther down the tributary than Daniel."

Jilly leaned over the table and searched for the mountain range where Rube'd spotted the Virgo symbol.

"Here," Miranda said, handing her an oversized brass magnifying glass. "This might help."

Peering through the lens, Jilly located the site. "There it is," she said. "Do you have any idea why the symbol would be placed high in the mountains?"

"None," Miranda said, shooting us that grin again. "But I'm dying to find out. When do we leave?"

"Are you going to be game for pretty much any mission we throw at you?" I asked.

"Probably," the captain admitted. "You have to understand that we've been locked out of the temporal waters for hundreds of years. I've yearned to make these excursions. There's not a lot you're gonna be able to propose that will scare me, Festus. If you're looking for me to be the voice of caution in this outfit, you've got the wrong woman."

Chuckling, I said, "I'm not looking for a voice of caution. I only wanted to verify that Rube had his facts right before greenlighting the op. How soon can the *Tempus Fugit* be ready to sail?"

"This minute," Miranda said. "I've made a few modifications. The vessel can now be operated by a crew of one. Me."

Jilly arched a slender brow. "What about Drake?"

She was referring to Miranda's first mate.

"What about him?" the captain asked.

The two of them exchanged one of those female looks ending in a shared laugh that makes men distinctly uncomfortable.

"Tell me you didn't slit the guy's throat," I said. "I don't want to have to do the paperwork at BEAR to cover a homicide."

Miranda chuckled. "Trust me," she said. "If I slit Drake's throat, it would have been *justifiable* homicide. He's back in Las Vegas managing one of the vessels berthed at our Isla de

Chronos base. It gives him an opportunity to swagger around and play big bad pirate."

"He's good at that," Jilly observed drily.

The women shared a second laugh at Drake's expense, but this time I joined in with confidence. I've met Drake Lobranche. He's not lacking in the self-esteem department. Which is good, since he's a pint low on brains.

"Remind me not to cross you two," I said.

Jilly slipped her arm through mine and leaned against me. "You don't have to worry about staying in my good graces," she said with sparkling eyes. "But I can't speak for Miranda."

"You're solid with me," the captain said. "I like cats. Your kind bring good fortune to a voyage."

"I hope you're right," I said, looking down at the tiny Virgo symbol on the chart. "We have zero idea what we're going to find in those mountains."

The pirate rubbed her hands together with almost gleeful anticipation, "That's the best part," she said. "The unknown."

Famous last words if I ever heard them.

Chapter Nine

The Spica Citadel

Blair returned to the Citadel in the small hours of the morning. She slipped over the garden wall and into the darkened lower corridors of the complex unseen.

Once she was inside, the guards on duty nodded as she passed. Blair wondered for the thousandth time if the daily patrols and personnel postings accomplished any practical purpose. Security at the fortress seemed more a matter of form than function.

Since Master Jaxon's death, the riders had slowly transitioned from soldiers to scholars. Most riders filled their free time working on manuscripts, cultivating gardens, conducting experiments in compounding medicines from jungle plants—in short, anything to stave off boredom.

Were any of them really so different than the "mad" hermit in the jungle?

Earlier during the night, Blair watched him through the windows of his strange dwelling, pacing the length of his favorite room, lost in agitated thought.

Even in what Blair saw as their moribund state, the Citadel riders relied on the discipline of their training and the companionship of intellectual pursuits to avoid such a fate. Those protections, however, wouldn't hold forever.

Dragon eggs weren't the only thing lacking in the mountain fortress. No children ran through the hallways or scrambled along the ledges as they had in years past.

Blair was among the youngest, but unlike the blossoming relationship between Davin and Maeve, no fellow rider had caught her eye.

The daughter of Adair and Esme McBride would be a catch, but Blair knew too well that the McBride name alone would not guarantee a child of hers would be to the dragons born.

In the old days when the Flight resided at Drake Abbey in the Otherworld, new recruits joined their ranks on an annual basis, infusing the Flight with fresh blood and talent.

Miriam's death proved that circumstances of birth did not a Dragon Rider make. Destiny and training were the critical factors.

Dragons refused to bond with all but a select few, those in whom they sensed the calling.

Blair knew Eingana carried heavy guilt for creating an imperfect link with a girl who had not been gifted by nature with the necessary talents to fly through the skies on a dragon's back.

But Kian shared a measure of the blame even if he did not acknowledge culpability. The Master granted the dispensation for Miriam to ride with a saddle over the objection of the older, more experienced riders, something Jaxon Frazier never would have done.

Kian believed his choices protected the Flight's heritage, but he persistently ignored two glaring possibilities: the dragons were in danger of dying out and so were the people who husbanded them.

Before she began the long climb to her quarters, Blair glanced down the stairwell and saw the glow of torches from the cavern beneath the fortress.

Like all Citadel riders, she knew about the relic stored deep within the cliff. The Flight came to the Spica Mountains expressly to guard and look after the Hourglass of the Horae—the temporal artifact charged with controlling the periodicity of life.

The grains that slipped through the narrow channel between the bulbs of the glass measured the natural portions of the hours. When the grains stopped, so did the flow of time.

Though unschooled in temporal navigation, Blair understood the Hourglass to be the essential artifact required for travel along the most esoteric temporal routes.

The artifact allowed timefaring mariners to freeze the passage of the hours. In that suspended state, they could use complementary instruments, like the storied Copernican Astrolabe, to take accurate bearings of their position.

Beyond its navigational function, the Hourglass formed a crafted representation of the virtues of the Natural Order and symbolized lawful conduct, justice, and peace.

Through the years, those same values came to be inculcated in the traditions of the Flight. Kian counted on the riders' instincts to avoid chaos through obedience to the rules, thus perpetuating his policies.

As she began the long ascent to her bed, Blair inwardly cursed the Master's retrogressive attitude.

Davin and Maeve listened to her when she vented her frustrations, but if the changes in the River of Virgo presented an opportunity to alter their lives, would they seize it?

Blair found the prospect of being the sole rebel in an otherwise tight knit community more troubling than Kian's stubborn refusal to even *contemplate* change.

As she entered her quarters, she tried to soften her footfalls on the stone floor, but Giallo heard her anyway.

"Dawn approaches, a sheòid. Soon we fly. Sleep."

"I'm too tired to sleep," she replied, taking a blanket from the back of her father's old chair and heading toward the stables.

Settling in the hay with her back to Giallo's side, Blair rested her head against the dragon's shoulder.

Giallo began to purr. *"You came to me as a child. Scared by the night. Esme pretended displeasure. Remember?"*

Blair smiled. "Only the next morning. There were plenty of times when Mother came out here to talk with Lintonth after the rest of us were asleep."

"That you were not to know."

Blair began to idly weave two pieces of straw together. "Children always understand things parents don't think they know."

Giallo sighed. *"I am old. A clever rider. A clever son on the way. Too much."*

"You aren't old, and you don't know the whelp will be a boy."

"True," the dragon conceded. *"A son. A daughter. Either will bring me joy. Your heart is burdened, a sheòid. Speak."*

Blair's response surprised the dragon. "Do you feel a difference when you fly without me?"

After considering the question, Giallo said, with mock gravity, *"Solo flights are far quieter."*

Jabbing an elbow into the dragon's ribs, Blair said, "That is *not* what I meant."

Chuckling, Giallo said, *"How is it for you in the jungle, as your true self?"*

"I feel freedom in both places."

Giallo stopped purring. *"No lies. You felt free. That is no longer true."*

"You heard about what happened with Kian in the dining hall," Blair grumbled. "Dragons are worse than gossipy old fish wives."

"Fish wives shout," Giallo said. *"Dragon minds whisper. You fear you are alone. Also not true."*

Blair sat up and turned to look into one of Giallo's emerald eyes. "What does that mean?"

"I wish my whelp to grow fully as Nature commands," Giallo said. *"Kian will order otherwise."*

She took a moment to digest that information before asking quietly, "What are you suggesting, Giallo?"

"That we fly the river. Witness the change."

Dragon and rider stared at one another for the passage of a heartbeat.

"Tomorrow is too soon," Blair said at last. "Kian will be expecting us to do something like that after the scene I made in the dining hall. We have to wait a day or two."

Giallo nodded. *"Wise. We must seem to make better choices than Kian offers."*

"Kian doesn't offer *any* choices."

"Correct."

Worrying at her lip, Blair said, "Have you thought about what happens after this rogue flight of ours?"

"I cannot think what I do not know."

"If we do find something out there that makes us consider leaving the Citadel," she persisted, "Kian isn't just going to let us fly off with his blessings. He could try to stop us."

"No dragon in this Citadel will fight his kind, a sheòid. Between rebellion and permission, Kian will permit."

Blair laid her hand on Giallo's cheek. "He might let *us* leave, my old friend, but he won't let the only dragon egg to be laid in more than twenty rainy seasons go so easily."

"A greater dilemma," Giallo said, "but first let us fly the river.."

"Agreed," Blair said. "We'll go day after tomorrow."

Chapter Ten

Cibolita, Festus

Our expedition promised to supply Miranda's appetite for the unknown with a gourmet meal; I felt myself heading toward a major hairball.

That queasy "need to toss" feeling started when I asked a simple question, "How long do you think we'll be gone?"

Even though I was in human form, I felt my whiskers droop when the roguish pirate answered. "It is a *temporal* river, Festus."

"Meaning?"

"Meaning, your guess is as good as mine."

Resisting the urge to remind her she was getting paid to take the guesswork *out* of these voyages, I said, "Are you telling me we could be gone for years?

"It could *feel* like years," Miranda admitted, "but don't worry. We should resume engagement with our regular timestream as soon as we re-enter the Middle Realm. Now, if we were to stay away past the limits of the temporal reset..."

A vein in my temple started to throb. Normal math puts a

twist in my tail; time calculations have me reaching for the Scotch bottle.

Jilly read my expression accurately and stepped in. "If you had to *guess*," she said, "how long will we be gone from the perspective of the people here in the Middle Realm and in Briar Hollow?"

Miranda picked up a pen and started working equations on a pad of paper. The henscratch looked like a stage prop from an Einstein biopic.

"I'd say anywhere from four days to a week," she said finally. "Look on the bright side. Roaming around the timeverse adds to the length of our life experiences. We will age while we're out there, but the span of our life is calculated in our native timescape. According to the theories of . . . "

My hand shot up, palm out. "Stop," I said. "Traveling on the temporal rivers gives us more life experience without cutting our lives short. Right?"

The captain rewarded my synopsis with a raised eyebrow. "I bet you were fun in class discussions."

"Yeah, just call me 'Cut to the Chase' McGregor," I grumbled. "Let's move off the theories and on to making an actual plan."

While Miranda and Jilly discussed logistics, I sat down with Great-Grandpa Dan Winter's log book. Good thing the guy never tried for a career as a travel writer. He described the countryside along the Virgo River and its tributaries for profit potential only. There was no mention of native peoples—if there were natives—or any "imports" hanging around the neighborhood.

The chance that we might run into expatriate *nonconformi* bothered me more than the prospect of dealing with indigenous peoples.

We have too much to cover for me to teach a seminar in Fae History 101 or deconstruct Fae Latinate translations. It is, however, important for you to understand that the Agreement was originally forged for the express purpose of "containing" the *nonconformi* species.

The *nonconformi* are not "people" you'd expect to run into on the average street. Here's a real life example. When Jilly and I arrived in Cibolita, we immediately sidestepped a Mongolian Death Worm.

Blood red and capable of spitting acid when annoyed, MDWs can also shoot lightning bolts out their backsides. Smart people don't irritate five-foot long spiked crawly things with fiery flatulence for no good reason.

This MDW seemed placid enough. She was carrying a book bag slung over her neck spikes that read, "Declutter my bookshelves? I don't need that kind of negativity in my life."

Still, I played exceptionally nice, and said, "Excuse me, ma'am," as I moved out of her way. She gurgled something in Mongolian that sounded friendly and oozed down the thoroughfare.

The Ruling Elders weren't completely off-base when they crafted the original part of the Agreement. Humans don't react well to Mongolian Death Worm level "diversity." The Elders relegated all life forms that did not qualify as visually "normal" to the Middle Realm for their "safety."

Nothing in the historical record, however, suggested those species then confined themselves to the primary layer of the In Between. In the centuries since, the *nonconformi* could have become widely dispersed and evolved in directions unknown to Fae ethnobiologists.

The Middle Realm offers more than enough perceptual "challenges" on any normal Wednesday without the potential "extras" I kept ticking through in my head.

Fae scholars speculate Lewis Carroll modeled the upside-down nature of *Alice's Adventures in Wonderland* on the In Between. We might find bouncing around from one time stream to another disorienting, but Middle Realm inhabitants take that sort of thing in stride.

Miranda didn't seem troubled that she couldn't give me an estimate of how long we would be away. Temporal Mariners regard the forward motion of their lives as the only valid existential constant.

Wherever and whenever a timefaring sailor finds himself, is, in his estimation, precisely where destiny means him to be at that moment.

At the end of our consultation, we agreed to set sail the next afternoon. Before heading back to Briar Hollow, Jilly and I decided to walk down to the wharves for a closer look at the new waterfalls bracketing the port.

We left the Crow's Nest and made our way through the city marketplace—a vibrant bohemian mélange of sounds, smells, and colors.

As a crossroads city, Cibolita has the unmistakable air of both a frontier town and a pirate base. Thrillseeking adventurers from across the Three Realms find their way into its crowded, noisy streets.

We threaded past vendors hawking food and drink, all the while keeping a sharp eye out for pickpockets. A street hustler tried to lure me into a quick round of three-card Monte as we worked our way clear of the crowds and turned toward the waterfront.

At the top of the platform erected to provide visitors with a view of the ships at anchor and the majestic descent of the River of Taurus, we paused to mark the passage of a shooting star. Its blazing trail added extra drama to the panorama spread before us.

The mighty cascade plummeting toward the Sea of Ages only feet from where we stood should have deafened us with its roar. Instead, in a testament to the topsy-turvy nature of the

Middle Realm, Taurus reached toward the Sea of Ages on a mere whisper of sound.

An unmistakable sense of peace settled around us. Jilly looped her arm through mine as she stared up at the waterfall. "It's beautiful, isn't it?" she breathed with awe.

Out of the corner of my eye I followed the contours of her strong profile outlined in the moonlight. "It is beautiful," I said, "and so are you."

Turning toward me fully, a teasing smile played across Jilly's lips. "You are a romantic at heart, Festus McGregor."

"If you tell anyone that, I'll deny it," I said, faking a warning grumble.

Laughing at my gruff answer, she said, "Your secret is safe with me." Then getting back to business, added, "Are we taking the Wrecking Crew with us?"

"No," I replied. "BEAR sent me the specs for a ROMO job before we left Briar Hollow. It's a milk run. I'm going to let Booger lead the team. He's been doing good work. It's time he tackled a retrieval solo."

Jilly nodded. "That's a good decision. Delegating authority will be essential if you're going to continue to lead the ROMO team in addition to the BlackTAT work."

"I don't want to give up the team," I said. "We don't know where the search for the Temporal Arcana will take us. I intend to keep my paws on all of the resources at our disposal."

"Greer told me almost the same thing yesterday," Jilly said. "She's not about to leave Lucas alone at the DGI when they've been partners for so long, but she plans to stay connected to our work as well."

The red-haired Scotswoman, Greer MacVicar, adds a special flavor to our Scooby gang in Briar Hollow. Drop dead gorgeous and given to wearing black head to toe, she's technically a vampire—in particular, a baobhan sith.

If you mapped her Fae lineage, Greer would come out as a sort of fairy—one with sharp teeth and a taste for blood. She's especially fond of feeding on young traveling businessmen.

That last bit makes her dietary needs more manageable than you might imagine. Once a month she drops in on a convention somewhere, gives an attendee a false but enjoyable memory, and comes away sated and re-energized.

I consider Greer to be a good friend and most certainly a force with whom to be reckoned.

"I'm all for Greer keeping her hand in with us," I told Jilly as we started back toward the center of town. "The various Fae agencies have spent centuries carving out petty territorial niches. We need less ego and more cooperation."

The sound of nightingales singing overhead made us both look up. Unlike their Human Realm counterparts, Fae nightingales are dreamy, iridescent birds that provide spectacular light shows in the evening as they head to their roosts.

The flock circled low over the rooftops, painting a glowing trail against the deepening night sky.

Watching them with admiring eyes, Jilly murmured, "*The nightingales are sobbing in the orchards of our mothers.*"

"*And hearts that we broke long ago have long been breaking others,*" I finished.

Delight filled her features. "You didn't tell me you like poetry."

"Well," I replied with self-deprecation, "it helps that Auden began that poem talking about drinking whiskey straight at Dirty Dick's and Sloppy Joe's."

Jilly's lyrical laughter fell on my ears as a joyful counterpoint to the nightingales' songs.

"That's more like it," she said. "I would expect you to be in possession of a wide repertoire of dirty limericks."

To live up to my reputation, I regaled her with a few examples during the remainder of our walk.

I can't describe the pleasure I take in the company of a woman who appreciates the totality of my nature. Jilly doesn't require me to be on my best behavior. She takes me as I am.

In her large form, she's a Phoenix.

Think about that. A mythical bird that routinely goes through self-immolation and rebirth doesn't tend to get hung up on fake posturing or pretension.

Jilly has chosen to date an irritable, lame, werecat who opts to spend most of his time as a yellow tabby. She's good with that.

And I'm good with dating a gorgeous woman who is by turns a spectacular African Grey parrot and a flaming symbol of death and resurrection.

Ain't love grand?

That's how I felt as we stepped through the portal to return to Briar Hollow. My dreamy sentimentality lasted exactly the length of time required to pass through the matrix.

The first thing I heard on the other side was Glory's whiny voice asserting that the "little baby Jesus" would never forgive her if she advised a woman to leave her one true love. Apparently, she and Rat Boy Rodney had yet to resolve their differences about Hooked on a Feeling.

Now, however, Rube and the entire Wrecking Crew sat in a circle of chip sacks and candy bar wrappers scattered around the hearth, joining the debate.

"All I'm saying is that dames will put up with a lot of crap from a guy so long as they're getting something in return," Booger said as we walked into the lair. "When I take a chick on a dumpster dive? I always make sure to leave the primo garbage for her. You know, it's like a gentleman thing."

He spotted us as he cracked a can of Mountain Dew. "Back

me up here, McGregor. Just because Loser is a, well, like, you know, *loser*, that don't necessarily mean he's a bad guy."

Rodney ripped off his green visor, threw the head gear on top of the shelf in front of the desk, and stomped on it.

Stifling a laugh, I said, "Booger, I'm going out on a limb, but I don't think Rodney agrees with you."

Turning to Greer who sat reading in her usual chair by the fire, I asked, "How long has this been going on?"

"An eternity," the baobhan sith replied. "I venture to say none of the members of the Wrecking Crew with the possible exception of Reuben have sufficient success in the romantic department to be engaging in this debate, but that has scarcely dimmed their enthusiasm."

Booger let out with a healthy burp. "What ain't dimming our enthusiasm is the fact that the snacks is holding out."

"Rube," I said, "if you can pull yourself away from this riveting psychological discussion, Jilly and I need to speak with you. Booger, did you get the mission profile I emailed you?"

"Roger that, Big Tom," he said using my GNATS call sign. "Me and the boys is heading out first thing in the morning."

"You're sure you can handle the assignment?"

The raccoon made a stabbing motion toward his chest. "You wound me, McGregor. Like Caesar getting his salad sliced."

I didn't bother to disentangle that culinary mash of history. "Okay," I said. "Don't start any trans-dimensional episodes I have to clean up when I get back from the Middle Realm."

Shaking his head Booger said, "You're turning into a real old lady, you know that?"

Leaving the others to their debate, Rube followed us into the war room. Scaling one of the chairs he plopped himself on the table. "So," he said brightly, "was I right?"

"Miranda's maps confirm the presence of the Virgo symbol

in the mountain range lying along the Spica tributary," I said. "We're leaving tomorrow."

"*Suh-wheet!*" he responded gleefully. "I was afraid I was gonna be stuck around here answering letters from the lovelorn all week."

Jilly, who had stepped into the changing room, fluttered out and landed on the back of one of the chairs. "Where's Lucy?" she asked. "I need to fill her in on the plan."

"Everybody's over at Lucas and Jinx's watching a movie," Rube said. "Me and the boys had enough poker for one night and we wasn't into a rom com. Besides, it was more fun yanking Rodney's chain. Seriously, Hooked on a Feeling needs to blow that pop stand."

Chuckling, I said, "The part where Rat Boy stomped on his visor was priceless. I hope someone got video."

Jilly clacked her beak in disapproval. "You are both *awful*," she said. "Poor Rodney is so earnest."

"Which would be what makes him such a good mark," Rube replied complacently.

The parrot ruffled her feathers. "I suggest we let Lucy enjoy her evening until the film is over. That encounter with Hortense Tyton was terribly unpleasant for her."

Rube smacked the side of his head and began to dig in his waist pack. "Geez! I'm glad you said that, doll. I almost forgot."

He produced a pencil and notepad and began to scribble.

"What are you writing?" Jilly asked curiously.

Without looking up, Rube said, "I ain't never kept much company with birds. I'm making a list of things that ain't nice to say so I don't give you dames no offense. Should 'molting' go ahead of 'plucked chicken' or after?"

Lifting one clawed foot to scratch at her head, Jilly considered the question. "Put them on the same line."

"Gotcha," Rube said. "And mentioning mites?"

"It simply isn't done."

Concentrating, Rube sounded out the words as he wrote them. "Simply . . . ain't . . . done."

While they continued their discussion of avian etiquette, I excused myself to shift back to four legs. I'd negotiated the entire evening without one ill considered bird joke; I felt like the cat who ate the canary.

But unlike Rube, I didn't need crib notes to tell me to keep my feline self-satisfaction private.

Chapter Eleven

The Spica Mountains, Edgar

Edgar watched from his tree perch for hours. Using the field glasses, he methodically examined the landscape. The countryside appeared unchanged, but the river moved steadily east.

He remained preoccupied and lost in thought until that reliable inner alarm signaling the demons' return began to sound. Only then did Edgar reluctantly descend.

Still, he wandered aimlessly toward home, his mood temporarily lightened by the fresh air. Overhead the clamor of tiny primates reminded him that the oval green fruits with their sweet yellow meat should be ripe.

Following the monkeys, he filled his pockets with the precious treats, a welcome relief from the dull tinned food the building supplied.

Edgar lingered briefly, watching the agile creatures swinging effortlessly through the branches. Once a student of science, he knew a community of European scholars had begun to speculate about a developmental link between primates and humans.

While the monkeys' lively presence and intuitive intelligence offered him his only relief from solitude, they lived free of the worrisome concerns that plagued mankind. If such a link did exist, to Edgar's thinking, the creatures' life course took the wiser path.

Approaching the clearing around the building, Edgar studied the structure. Assured that his elaborate warning traps and snares were undisturbed, he entered via a back stairway. On the second floor, he placed the fruit on the table and went to the window. The skies were empty.

Turning toward the room, he studied the clutter with a newly critical eye. Moving to the cot, Edgar smoothed the wrinkled blanket and tucked the edges beneath the mattress.

In his former life, he'd maintained punctilious habits, declining social invitations when his depleted fortunes prevented him from dressing in the style he deemed appropriate.

Now, for the first time, Edgar recognized the creeping entropy of slovenliness. The prospect troubled him. Even at the worst moments of his life, he had not been utterly without the capacity for some discipline. Where had he found the inspiration for that minimal degree of order?

On impulse, he lifted his hands and examined the long, slender fingers stained with ink. Writing—purposeful writing had been the source of his discipline. Surely that touchstone remained within his grasp.

Crossing to the desk, Edgar picked up the story he'd been working on the evening before, forcing himself to concentrate on the words with an editorial eye. The tale started well enough, but midway the narrative thread disappeared.

Distressed, he pawed through his most recent manuscripts and extracted another. He found the prose utterly indecipherable. Feeling a rising sense of panic, Edgar frantically rifled through piles of papers.

On sheet after sheet he recognized promising ideas, but none taken to fruition. Lucid passages lay buried beneath avalanches of gibberish. How was this possible?

Consumed by his impromptu literary audit, Edgar missed the regular demon flyover. Hours later in the light of candles he did not remember lighting, he sat in the middle of the floor surrounded by drifts of documents.

Not one of the stories, poems, or essays contained a completed argument or intact plot. In despair, Edgar started to bury his face in his hands only to freeze in mid-motion.

Ink.

He could not recall a time when his skin had not been stained by ink.

A working writer's veins flowed with that alchemical elixir formulated from iron salts and tannic acid. Writing with honesty and passion made for messy work. Solid prose and poetry sprang from wellsprings of ink.

The irony of it!

The reversed current of a mighty waterway brought him to stand on the shores of a congested swamp of words.

If a river could alter its flow and bring to him a burst of clarity, he could take pen in hand and write his way to an answer. When Edgar reached for a pen, he reached for that which made his heart beat.

Pen and ink would show him what he must do next.

Lenore once said that to make writing come to life, an author must regard the act of laying ink on the page as the casting of an enchantment.

Struggling to his feet, Edgar went to his desk for fresh paper. There, on a separate shelf hanging to the right of his work surface, sat the evidence of his greatest moments of despair—his little cabinet of horrors.

The plank held an empty bottle labeled "Poison," a hangman's noose, a straight razor with a stained blade, and a folded sheet of paper bearing the inscription, "To Whom It May Concern."

Lenore's voice rose in his thoughts. "An enchantment cannot be cast without intent, Edgar."

From the age of two, when he witnessed his mother's strangled, tubercular death, Edgar's intent had been to understand death. What would happen if he applied equal focus to the business of living?

A year before Reynold Isherwood sent him to this place, Edgar attempted suicide with laudanum. Unaccustomed to the drug, he fell unconscious before he could ingest the fatal dose.

His efforts to seek the solace of death here in the jungle, Edgar attributed to the uniqueness of the circumstances. Even Robinson Crusoe did not face demon-filled skies, and fate delivered to him a companion and helpmate.

Men of far greater mental fortitude than Edgar possessed could not have endured this land. He'd tried the poison from the hospital's pharmaceutical stores first.

On the evening he meant to commit the deed, Edgar first walked through the jungle, listening to the birds in the canopy and enjoying one last time the scent of the fragrant, exotic flowers that sprang from the mossy places.

Then he returned to his rooms, penned a letter of farewell, drank the deadly liquid, and waited.

The sun edged toward the horizon, the demon riders returned to their dark Citadel, and the sounds of the night awakened in the jungle, but Edgar did not die.

He did not die two days later when he sliced his wrists with the razor and watched in chilled astonishment as the blood drew back into his veins and the flesh knitted together.

He did not die when he threw himself from the roof of the building with the noose knotted around his neck. The rope unraveled and Edgar landed on a verdant mattress of grasses that had not been there the day before.

The quest for death became a game, but no method he explored sent him to the place where he imagined he would see his dear mother, the stepmother whose kindness blunted the harshness of his childhood, his dear Virginia—and most of all, Lenore.

The very building to which he had been taken to die and from which he had been consigned to unutterable loneliness would not allow him to snuff out the spark of life.

Resigned, Edgar set himself to burn away the indefinite passage of time with the sop of physical labor. He poured his energy into the arrangement of his home, barricading the stairway, and furnishing the second floor space.

As he went about his work, Edgar commenced an animated series of self-debates. He presented arguments and counter arguments for the cosmology he elucidated in his greatest masterpiece, *Eureka*.

He recalled to his mind the conversations with Lenore that formed the genesis of his central theory: the universe was but a manuscript and each man's life the thread in the master plot.

In the lecture that presaged the writing of *Eureka*, Edgar assured his baffled listeners the Master Writer crafted only perfect plots.

Critics treated Edgar's magnum opus with scorn, a rejection that still gnawed at his heart. How could the great transcendentalist Emerson write the ephemeral *Oversoul*, a spark he insisted existed in all men, and receive acclaim when he, Edgar, had intuited the origins of the universe only to be ridiculed?

Now, with sharpened hindsight, he confronted the acid tone he brought to his work as critic and reviewer. Was it any wonder he possessed few friends among the literati?

In those days, he charged his detractors with the sin of envy. He was, after all, and notwithstanding periods of poverty, the rarest of all creatures—a writer who successfully made a living with his pen.

But now he considered, for the first time, the role he played in his own downfall. If, however, his view of the Universe was correct and what he now faced was nothing more than a plot twist, Edgar could find the true thread of his story again.

Impulsively, he put out his hand and swept the shelf clean, scattering the instruments of his unsuccessful death. The empty poison bottle struck the floor and shattered. The razor came to rest atop the glittering shards the blade, perfectly underlining the words, "To Whom It May Concern."

Life concerned Edgar. No, it consumed him. Being unable to die was not the same as living. Suddenly, and without warning, Edgar wanted desperately to live.

Drawing back the chair, he laid a fresh sheet of paper on the blotter, dipped his pen in the well, and began.

Chapter Twelve

Briar Hollow, Festus

Jilly and Lucy share an apartment in Londinium, but since we'd be leaving for Cibolita the next day, the werebirds decided to roost for the night in Briar Hollow.

After trying and failing to get some shut-eye myself, I wandered into the lair looking for Greer. I can always rely on the baobhan sith to keep me company for a late-night conversation and a drink.

I didn't expect to encounter Jinx, but I found her sitting at the table with a whole cherry pie—still warm from the smell of it—a pint of Ben & Jerry's *Pistachio Pistachio* and a spork, the perfect implement for binge eating the thick, flaky slices and soft, gooey ice cream.

"What," I said, "are you doing up at this hour eating *that*?"

"Beats me," she said, stabbing the spork into the pie. "I woke up craving cherry pie and pistachios. As always, Darby delivered. Want some?"

Making the universal open-mouthed cat face for "yuck," I said, "By Bastate's tuna breath, I most certainly do *not*."

From the vicinity of the hearth, Greer set her book aside and said, "Fancy a dram of Scotch instead?"

Finally. Someone with a particle of sense. "Does a litter box have sand?"

Laughing, Greer poured herself three fingers and put an equal amount in a quaich for me—technically a "bowl," but with more Highland ancestral elan.

The vampire carried the drinks over and touched her glass to the rim of the quaich. "*Slàinte.*"

"*Do dheagh shlàinte,*" I responded.

We enjoyed our whisky in silence for a moment before I smacked my whiskers, and said, "Did Glory and Rodney solve Hooked on a Feeling's problem?"

"A compromise was reached," Greer said, "a rather intricate proposal involving the return of the lawn mower followed by couples counseling. I predict that Loser, when presented with the terms of the deal, will choose John Deere over Hooked on a Feeling."

Helping myself to another lap of the Scotch, I said, "Do you think people actually take Glory's advice?"

"They do," Jinx said, scraping the last of the *Pistachio Pistachio*. "I know it's hard to believe, but people in the shop talk about her column all the time."

Shaking my head, I said, "Hard to believe doesn't even cover it."

Polishing off the last bite of pie, Jinx surprised me when she said, "Greer, would you mind if Festus and I went into the alcove for a private conversation?"

No pun intended, but the baobhan sith has bat ears. If Jinx wanted to step behind the sound barrier enchantment blanketing her private sanctuary, something was up.

Gracious as ever, the baobhan sith returned to the fire and

her book. I caught a glimpse of the title on the spine: *Gibbon's Decline and Fall of the Roman Empire*.

"Weren't you there for the decline and fall?" I asked as I walked by.

Without looking up, Greer said, "Yes, but it amuses me to read Gibbon's characterizations. He makes Caligula sound more like a choir boy than the depraved lunatic I knew."

I filed the comment under "ask for more details later" and followed Jinx into the alcove. The instant she drew the fabric behind us, she said, "I need you to promise me something."

Jumping into the nearest chair, I circled a couple of times before arranging myself with my front paws tucked under my chest. "Okay. What would that be?"

"Please promise me that you will be extra careful on your BlackTAT missions. I need you to come home in one piece."

That furrowed my eyewhiskers. "Staying in one piece typically tops my 'to do' list," I said. "What's up with you tonight? You're not usually the nervous Nellie in this bunch."

Jinx claimed the desk chair and passed her hand over her eyes. The weariness of the gesture conveyed a level of fatigue well beyond simply being up and hungry in the middle of the night.

"There are some details about our return from the 16th century I haven't shared with anyone—not even Lucas," she said finally.

"What details?"

She wrestled with indecision and then made her choice.

"Whatever you tell me stays between us," I said. "You ought to know that by now."

"I do," she said. "It's . . . it's not easy to explain."

"Then start with the easiest part."

"I didn't go into the portal we opened expecting to re-open the Rivers of Time."

Her words came out in a rush that filled me with sympathy. Everybody looks at Jinx as the Witch of the Oak—the *Quercus de Pythonissam*. She didn't ask for her powers . . . well, okay, she *did* ask, but accidentally.

The poor kid didn't know what she was getting into. She's learned fast and done some amazing things, but there are moments when I know Jinx would like nothing more than to be a normal shopkeeper in Briar Hollow with a regular life.

"Of course you didn't expect to open the rivers," I said reasonably. "You didn't even know they existed."

"True," she admitted, "but that's not the most complicated part. I had a vision inside the matrix."

The word "vision" made the fur on the back of my neck stand up. Nine times out of ten visions spell trouble. "What did you see?"

"My unborn daughter."

Puzzle pieces scrambled into place in my head. Up in the middle of the night. Craving cherry pie and pistachio ice cream. "Bastet's whiskers! Are you . . . ?"

"No, no," she said hastily. "I'm not pregnant, but I saw a girl I know was my daughter with Naomi and Orion. The two of them have a role in my child's destiny."

The Orion she was referring to would be the stinking mutt . . . excuse me, *wolf* . . . Glory brought home from the 16th century.

"Is that everything?" I asked.

"No," Jinx admitted. "When I finished writing about our time travels, my pen added something without any direction from me."

She reached for her grimoire, opened the book, and turned the pages toward me. Standing and stretching, I put a paw on the chair arm and leaned toward the desk.

"*The hunter. The healer. The way home.*"

"What the hell is that supposed to mean?" I asked, easing back into a sitting position.

Jinx's brow furrowed. "I don't know. Orion was the hunter in Greek mythology, and the lost Zodiac sign, Ophiuchus, is associated with the healer Asclepius."

I picked up one hind leg and scratched at my ear. "That's not a lot to go on."

"No," she said, "it isn't, which is why I haven't said anything. I don't know what's in store for my daughter when she's born, but I do know that you're the only person I trust to be her Guardian. That's why I need your word that you'll take care of yourself so you can be there for her."

The slight edge of desperation in her voice was not lost on me. Reaching forward, I put one paw on her knee. "Witch of the Oak, I promise to guard my life so that I may guard yours, that of your children, and each of the Daughters of Knasgowa."

Jinx smiled at the formality of the pledge, but some of the tension drained from her body. She laid a hand over my paw. "Thank you, Festus . . . and don't say 'children' plural. I'm scared enough about the idea of keeping *one* safe."

"As a parent, I can tell you that never goes away."

She sagged, but for comical effect. "Great. Anything else I need to know?"

"We could talk about diapers."

"No, we could not."

Chuckling, I said, "Okay. I should try to get some sleep. We're leaving from Cibolita tomorrow afternoon. Don't stay up all night, okay?"

"Okay. See you in the morning."

As I jumped down and moved toward the curtain, Jinx said suddenly, "Hey, is your hip better?"

"Yeah," I said, stretching my hind leg to show off the

improved flexibility. "Jilly has me seeing some woo woo practitioner in Londinium."

Jinx's brows rose. "Define 'woo woo.'"

Clearing my throat self-consciously, I said, "He sticks needles in my hide and has me doing . . . uh . . . Eastern-based stretching."

She didn't fall for the euphemism. "Eastern-based stretches as in yoga?"

Throwing a quick glance at the still drawn privacy curtain, I said, "Not so loud. For Bastet's sake do not tell anyone."

Jinx grinned. "You really like this woman, don't you?"

My skin started to grow warm under my fur. "Don't tell anyone that either."

"Festus, everyone knows already."

Lashing my tail in annoyance, I growled, "Getting out of here and confronting unknown dangers in uncharted lands is going to be a walk in the park compared to all this friendly *interest* in my life."

Even though she was enjoying watching me squirm, Jinx took pity on me. "Go on to bed, but don't forget your promise."

"I won't," I said, pulling the curtain aside with my paw. Then I looked back at my friend. "Are you sure you're okay?"

She shooed me away with a wave of her hand, but she didn't answer my question.

Chapter Thirteen

Briar Hollow, Jinx

So far I've let Festus handle the narrative. Everything that happened in the Spica mountains began with his BlackTAT mission. Now it's time for me to jump in. My participation in the expedition caused the first disagreement of my married life.

When Glory and I returned from the 16th century, I expected my new husband to be over-protective. I also knew I'd have to nip his hypervigilance in the bud before the mindset became a *thing* between us.

My disappearance scared Lucas and made him feel guilty. We euphemistically refer to the portal event that threw me and Glory back to Elizabethan England as an "accident." The truth is that my husband's uncle, DGI Director Morris Grayson, sabotaged the matrix in an effort to get rid of me.

I stood between Morris and his plans for Lucas's future as the heir to the Grysundl throne, a position Lucas didn't want then and most certainly doesn't want now.

Morris took the coward's way out. Rather than face the

consequences of his misdeeds, he committed suicide, thus adding to the burden of guilt Lucas already carried.

My husband's line of self-torture goes like this. *"If I'd done what Uncle Morris wanted, Jinx never would have been in danger, and he would still be alive."*

Survivor's guilt isn't rational; it just *hurts*.

Lucas and I shared a joyous reunion, but I instantly felt a new fear in the man I love, an awareness of life's fragility that hadn't been there before. Over time that fear could cripple our relationship—if we let it.

After my talk with Festus in the alcove, I went back to the subterranean apartment Lucas and I now call home. The set of rooms originally occupied one of the top floors of the DGI building in Londinium, but the fairy mound obligingly moved the dwelling to Briar Hollow when Lucas and his uncle fell out over our relationship.

We declined the fairy mound's offer to put the apartment back after the wedding. The current arrangement gives us the best of both worlds. Windows that somehow still look out on Londinium, and a front door that opens onto the constant bustle of activity in the lair.

I changed a few things about Lucas's apartment, but not as many as you might think. The dark oak paneling and green club chairs flanking the rock fireplace suit us both.

The brass hat tree *had* to stay. It's a daily ritual for my fedora-wearing guy to fling his 0.22 pound brown Borsalino toward the rack, nailing a perfect landing on one of the hooks every time.

We have a standing bet that after the first miss, I get to choose his next hat style. So far, to his horror, I've suggested a cowhide Stetson and a French beret as possible alternatives.

As we settled into married life within the safe confines of the store walls and the fairy mound, Lucas and I worked on living in the present while planning for the future. His uncle's death also left my husband with a heightened awareness of the importance of family ties.

One evening, cuddling in front of the fire, Lucas said, out of the blue, "I'd like to name our son Lestyn after my father."

Turning to look up at him, I said, "Do you know something I don't know?"

He laughed. "No, I've just been thinking about it for when we start a family."

"Lestyn is a good name," I agreed. "If we have a girl, I want to name her Adeline Kathleen."

"After Adeline Shevington and your grandmother?" he asked.

I nodded. "Adeline was the last Sinclair Witch of the Oak," I said. "I want to honor that. What do you think?"

"We can call her Addie," Lucas grinned. "I like it."

For every happy, relaxed exchange we shared, I still felt the weight of worry in Lucas's gaze as he watched me. There was love there, too. That made me happy, but the anxiety tinged with over-protectiveness grated on my nerves by week two.

I'd been in a suffocating relationship. I made it clear to Lucas before we became engaged that I wouldn't do that again. He understood my feelings and agreed we would enjoy a life of shared adventures free of even the most well-intentioned attempts to control one another.

That, however, was before his uncle engineered a portal "accident" that sucked me and Glory into alternate time.

Over the intervening weeks, I followed the BlackTAT research closely and wandered into the war room several times a day, for a specific reason. I intended to go with them on their first mission in the Middle Realm.

Festus got it. I could see the comprehension in his eyes. I'd done this amazing thing returning the Rivers of Time to the In Between, and now I was supposed to sit at home keeping the books for the store and serving coffee to our patrons? I don't think so.

I stopped short of telling the werecat I planned to ride shotgun out of respect for Lucas. As my husband, he deserved to hear the news first and from me.

Returning to our bedroom, I shoved three of my five cats out of the way and got under the covers. Winston, who insists on sleeping over Lucas' head, eyed me in the dim light. When I put a finger to my lips, the cat nodded slightly and went back to sleep.

In his sleep, Lucas reached for my side of the bed. I scooted into his embrace and dozed off, strategizing ways to break the bad news to my husband the next morning. In my imagination, I presented a logical case, which he accepted reasonably, and all was well.

The actual conversation didn't go quite so smoothly.

Pausing, razor in hand with shaving cream covering his cheeks, Lucas said, "No."

I will give the man credit. It took him roughly a nanosecond to realize what he'd done.

"Let me rephrase that," he said quickly. "I'd rather you not go gallivanting off on a BlackTAT mission with Festus and the gang."

Choosing to ignore his initial authoritarian reaction, I said, "I'm sure that's what you would prefer, but that doesn't change anything. Honey, you can't keep worrying that every time I'm out of your sight I'm in terrible danger. You married the Witch of the Oak. I'm not going to sit home and knit socks just because you put a ring on my finger."

The razor stilled again. "You know how to knit?"

Smiling in spite of myself, I said, "Not the conversation we're having, mister, and yes, I know how to knit."

"I'll be damned," he said, dragging the blade over the

stubble covering his cheek. "The things a man learns after he says 'I do.'"

Nice try, but the charm wasn't going to work.

"You need to talk to someone, Lucas," I said seriously. "I'm not a psychologist, but I know you need help. My disappearance. Your uncle's death. Carrying trauma like that will hurt you . . . it will hurt us. I'll go with you when I come back. We'll work on this together."

My eyes met his in the mirror for an instant before his concentration shifted entirely to the last few strokes of the shave. I leaned against the door jam and watched in silence as he methodically rinsed off the razor, dried his cheeks with a towel, and slapped on aftershave.

Taking a deep breath, he said, "How long will you be gone?"

"A few days."

"If Festus is in charge, why do you need to go?"

Pushing upright, I said, "Do we have to do this?"

The struggle that played across his features made my heart ache. I could see him weighing and discarding responses. Finally he settled on, "It's too soon."

I went to him then, lacing my arms around his neck. "Five years would be too soon for you. My magic re-opened those lands for exploration. I have a vested interest in reassembling the Temporal Arcana."

His jaw set in a stubborn line. "What vested interest?"

Trying for a light, jesting tone, I said, "Oh, you know, nothing major, just the stability of time across the three realms."

Lucas opened his mouth; I read the words in his eyes and stopped him before he could speak.

"Don't ask me not to go," I said urgently. "Because if you ask, you won't like my answer. Please don't let this be our last conversation before I leave."

He looked down, swallowed hard, and said it anyway. "Please don't go."

Fighting back tears of my own, I said, "I'm sorry, honey."

With a short, jerky nod, he said, "I had to try."

"I know you did," I replied, leaning in to give him a kiss. His mouth met mine with something like desperation.

When we parted I whispered against his lips, "Stop. I'll be fine. We have to get past this hurdle. Come on. Let's go out and have breakfast."

"Give me a few minutes," he said in a thick voice. "Okay?"

"Of course," I assured him, kissing him again. "Take all the time you need."

When I let myself out our front door, I was surprised to find Rodney waiting for me. Leaning down, I extended my hand and let him run up my arm, expecting him to head for his usual position on my shoulder. Instead, the rat stopped mid-way to my elbow, balancing on his hind legs.

"Morning, Little Dude," I said. "You need to see me?"

Rodney nodded and pointed into the stacks.

"You want to show me something?"

Another nod.

"Okay," I said moving in the direction he indicated, changing course with each gesture of his pink paw.

We wound through the collection for twenty yards or so when Rodney signaled me to stop in front of a shelf that held what looked, on first examination, like a fat toothpick with a glob of ketchup on the end.

"What's this?"

He gestured for me to look closer. I raised my hand and said, *"Et illustrant mea."*

The air over the object solidified and formed a lighted magnifying glass. The "toothpick" was a wand with a red stone at the tip and a glowing dragon etched in the shaft.

Studying the tiny implement with fascination, I said, "Did you find it in the archives?"

Rodney shook his head and began one of his lengthy, pantomimed monologues.

"Knasgowa gave it to you? Why?"

The rat shrugged.

"Why did you bring it to me now?"

He stuck his paw under the magnifying lens and pointed at the dragon.

"That wasn't there when she gave it to you?"

Confirming my understanding with a thumbs up, Rodney "said" he thought I should see the wand before I went with Festus to the Middle Realm.

"How do you know I'm going on the BlackTAT mission?"

Cocking his head, Rodney gave me a look that required no translation. *"Duh."*

"Maybe I should have gotten *you* to talk to Lucas," I muttered, reaching for the wand. To my astonishment, I couldn't pick it up.

"How did you get this down here?" I said. "It weighs a ton."

Rodney frowned and grabbed the wand, shaking his head. *"No, it doesn't."*

"Fine," I said. "You carry the wand. Let's leave it here for now though. I'll put a cloaking spell on it while we have breakfast."

The rat's face brightened at the mention of food.

"Yeah," I said. "I thought you'd like that."

After I cast the spell, I held out my hand. This time Rodney ran straight for my shoulder. The scent of bacon and eggs wafted in from the lair. Pangs of hunger and nausea chased each other in my gut. That's what I get for arguing with my husband and dealing with mini wands on an empty stomach.

Chapter Fourteen

Briar Hollow, Festus

Glory's face went green when I padded into the lair in mountain lion form. She gave me a strangled, "Good morning, Dad," and took a step back.

"What's the matter with you?" I asked, trying to soften the basso big cat rumble. "You've seen me this way before."

Embarrassment turned her complexion chartreuse. "I know," she stuttered, "but I forget you're so big and strong."

That was the right response.

"Quit looking like I'm going to eat you," I said, giving her a shoulder bump. "I'm not interested in pickles for breakfast."

The good-natured ribbing relaxed her. "Don't you like eggs and gherkins?" she giggled.

"I do not. Have you eaten already?"

"Goodness gracious, no! I have *stacks* of letters to get through. Rodney was supposed to come down early to help. He must have overslept. Have you seen him?"

"Nope," I said, hopping onto my favorite chair at the table. A plate of steak and eggs materialized on the placemat. Darby can be an annoying neat freak, but he knows how to run a kitchen.

The deep bowl of black coffee beside my plate gave off a heavenly aroma. Taking a healthy slurp, I felt the caffeine hit my system. Strong enough to put whiskers on your muzzle.

As I lapped up a whole egg, a voice called out. "Yo, McGregor! Leave a hungry coon some chow."

Rube's black-masked face popped through one of the treehouse windows.

Taking a second slug of coffee, I replied, "Get your butt down here if you're hungry. It's every mammal for himself."

The raccoon swung the side door open and shoved a wheeled bag onto the cargo platform. Releasing the winch, he ratcheted the luggage to floor level and slid down the rope after it.

Within seconds he trundled in, dragging the bag and flexing his free paw. "Almost got a rope burn. You're looking sharp, Big Tom."

Acknowledging the compliment, I nodded toward the luggage. "That's all you're taking?"

Rube climbed into a free chair and helped himself to scrambled eggs and bacon from one of the overflowing platters. "You told us to pack light."

"I know what I told you," I said, "but since when do you listen? Generally you take at least one bag exclusively dedicated to food."

Slathering butter onto a piece of toast, Rube said, "I got everything I need, all organized and even freaking *alphabetized*. Special delivery from Coon Preppers R Us."

Greer's arrival interrupted the exchange before I could ask him what the hell he was talking about.

The baobhan sith's outfit occupied the sweet spot where African safari guide meets ninja warrior. The combination of khaki and black suited her perfectly—especially the tall boots encasing those long, slender legs. A wicked looking knife in a sheath at her belt added the finishing touch.

"Good morning," I said as she poured herself a glass of juice. "What's with the lovely and lethal look?. You headed off on a mission with Lucas?"

She sat down and unfolded her napkin. "No, I am headed off on a mission with you."

A serving of French toast arranged on a bone china plate shimmered into place in front of her along with a steaming cup of coffee—cream, no sugar.

"*Suh-wheet!*" Rube said. "And *day-um*, Red. Pardon the drool, but you are *hawt*."

The baobhan sith smiled indulgently. "Thank you, Reuben. Gallant as always."

He ducked his head. "Aw, shucks, Red. Don't humble late a guy this early in the morning."

Biting through my steak bone for emphasis, I said, "*Humiliate*. Not that I mind your company, Greer, but when did you decide to come along?"

"In the night," she said cryptically. "Reuben, pray enlighten us. What is a 'raccoon prepper'?"

Wiping butter off his facial fur, Rube said, "I got enough chow in this here bag to last for days. Coon Preppers offers raccoon-specific MREs. Good nutrition is inter-algebra to my superior skill set."

"The word," I said, "is *integral*. I can't believe I'm asking this, but what kind of MREs are 'raccoon specific'?"

Eager to demonstrate, Rube slid out of his chair, flipped the bag over, and unzipped the lid. Silver envelopes divided by tabs packed the interior.

Running one black finger along their edges, he pulled out a single MRE.

"This is Menu Eight," he said. "Roadkill Ragu. It's all about the sauce. Hides the gamey flavor. You got your crackers and cheese appetizer and a big ole chocolate brownie for dessert. I like that one hot, but now this . . .," he extracted a second envelope, ". . . is Dumpster Dijon with a side of Fried Cheeto Delight . . ."

I held up a paw. "We get the idea. You do know there will be food on the *Tempus Fugit* already?"

"Well, yeah," Rube said earnestly, "but I'm an epic curator."

"*Epicurean*," Greer and I said at the same time, and then we both laughed.

The raccoon frowned, swiveling his head between us. "What?"

"As usual," Greer said, wiping her eyes, "you are an utter delight, Reuben."

We were still trying to regain our composure when Chase came in from the connecting corridor to his cobbler's shop. He stopped to kiss Glory before joining us.

"Well," he said, pouring his coffee. "I see everyone's in a good mood. Dad, do you need a hand getting your gear to th*e Tempus Fugit*?"

"I won't turn down free labor," I replied. "Why are you going to the Middle Realm?"

"Business," he said, digging into a stack of pancakes. "I made a pair of boots for Miranda, and now I'm getting orders like crazy from the other pirates."

Although Chase will step in and help me in my role as Guardian when I need him, he prefers to live a "normal" human life—or at least as "normal" as a werecat can manage.

"That's outstanding, son," I said. "When we get back I'd love to see what you're working on."

Word to the wise. Your kids *never* get too old to appreciate parental interest.

We were still talking boots when Jinx walked out of the stacks with Rodney on her shoulder. She grabbed an enormous bear claw pastry from the sideboard and sat down.

"Morning, everyone."

A chorus of greetings answered her.

"So Festus," she said, "what time do we leave for the Middle Realm?"

She caught me mid-swallow. When I quit choking, I said, "Wait. *What?* You're coming, too? What does Lucas have to say about this?"

From the doorway, the man answered for himself.

"Lucas says my wife is an independent entity. She makes her own decisions. Hate to say 'good morning' on the run, but the Blacklist vault inventory won't check itself."

He grabbed a breakfast taco and a thermos of coffee that had conveniently appeared in mid-air over the table. Shoving his fedora back, Lucas bent to kiss his wife.

"Be careful out there, and call me if you get good mirror reception."

Jinx raised a hand and ran it along his jaw. "I will, and thank you."

I've been married. Something about their exchange told me he hadn't been so agreeable when he first learned about Jinx's plans. Did Greer's decision to come along have anything to do with that?

Almost as if he heard my thoughts, Lucas looked over at the baobhan sith, took in her attire, and visibly relaxed. "You're going with them?" he asked.

"I am, laddie," she replied. "Did you think I intended to bury myself under inventory reports with you?"

If Jinx heard the unspoken "take care of my wife" command in the exchange, she didn't let on.

So far my party had gone from four to six, but there were

more surprises ahead. When Tori heard Jinx intended to come with us her response was immediate and decisive.

"Oh, *hell* no. You think you're going to go traipsing off to the Middle Realm without me after what you put me through with that lost in time stunt? Think again."

My reaction to that declaration was equally pointed until Tori fixed me with a glare and asked, "Which part of 'ride or die' friend do I need to explain to you, Festus?"

In all fairness, we did force Tori to stay in Briar Hollow and preserve the appearance of normalcy in the store while the rest of us worked on getting Jinx and Glory home. I understood why she wasn't willing to let her best friend out of her sight quite yet, but that wasn't the whole of it.

I suspected Jinx was participating in the expedition to put a stop to her husband's hovering. She brightened when Tori said she was coming along. After the anxiety Jinx had exhibited the night before, if she needed some BFF time, I wasn't going to get in the way.

For appearance's sake, however, I grumbled, "Fine, McGregor, party of *seven* for the Middle Realm, your table is ready," before I stomped off to the war room.

Silly me for thinking we'd stop at only *three* extras.

A couple of hours later, when Chase had all our gear loaded on a rolling cart in front of the portal, I noticed Rat Boy sitting on Jinx's shoulder.

"*What*," I said, pointing a claw in his direction, "is *he* doing here?"

"Rodney's going, too," Jinx said.

Curling my lips back to show my fangs, I snarled, "*Holy stinking hairball!* This is not a garden party."

Jinx planted her hands on her hips. "Don't you show your teeth to me, Festus McGregor. Rodney won't be any trouble. He's going to ride in this."

She pointed to a nicer version of Rube's waist pack belted around her middle. This one featured alternating mesh panels and clear plastic panes.

"How is that flimsy thing supposed to keep some hungry *nonconformi* from making a snack out of Rodney?" I demanded.

"Go on," Jinx said. "Try it."

I drew back my right paw and slapped at the pack only to hit a wall of solid air around Jinx's midsection.

Ignoring the stinging in my pads, I refused to give ground. "Boundary magic. Big hairy deal. That just means when something tries to eat you *both*, I have to risk my hide saving you, too."

Bristling, Jinx said, "For your information, I don't need..."

Rube put two fingers in his mouth and let out with an ear-splitting whistle.

"Lighten up, the both of yous," the raccoon ordered. "You ain't never turned down a chance to play hero once in your nine lives, Festus, and ain't nobody stepping on your femalism principles, Jinx. How about we kick the tires, light the fires, and blow this pop stand?"

Everyone held their breath waiting for me to reply. In the end, I decided this wasn't the hill to die on for the day.

Eyeing the raccoon sourly, I said, "Did the Wrecking Crew watch *Top Gun* again?"

"We sure did," Rube said. "Wanna hear my rendition of *Great Balls of Fire*?"

Helpful as always, Tori said, "I do!"

"No," I said, "you do *not*. Rat Boy's in."

The sound of wings forestalled further conversation; Jilly and Lucy landed on the cart handle.

"Sorry," Jilly said, "we seriously over-roosted. I see our party has grown."

"It has," I groused, "and we need to get the hell out of here before anybody else decides to tag along. Attendant, the wharf at Cibolita—dockside to the *Tempus Fugit*."

The portal matrix flickered to life. I went through first, with the others in tow. Chase and the cart brought up the rear.

Emerging through the membrane, the smell of saltwater and fresh air immediately filled my nostrils. A flock of gulls swarmed over a nearby fishing boat, snatching remnants of the morning's catch the sailors flung into the air.

Chase looked around the busy waterfront. "It's remarkable how quickly the port has come back to life since the Sea of Ages filled," he said.

Lucy ruffled her wings. "I like it. Londinium can be stuffy. Cibolita feels new and exciting."

"You detect the air of rebirth," Greer said. "The people of Cibolita feel reinvigorated after centuries of literal drought."

From the deck of the *Tempus Fugit*, Miranda called, "And we thank the gods the waters flow once more."

Squinting because of the morning sun, I spotted her silhouette against the flawless sky. Standing on her vessel wearing a navy frock coat with brass buttons, Miranda Winter cut a rakish, commanding figure.

"Ahoy, Captain Winter," I said. "Permission to come aboard?"

"Permission granted, Master McGregor, and welcome," she replied merrily. "We look to have fair winds and following seas."

I had no idea what that meant, but our resident pirate seemed delighted.

Accepting the invitation, Jilly and Lucy flew up the gangplank and landed on the railing. Jinx, Tori, and Greer went next. When we reached the deck, Rube and I positioned ourselves to watch as Chase strained on the incline with the cart.

Unable to resist giving him grief, I said, "Boy, are you getting enough exercise?"

The mild taunting worked. He put his back into the effort and, with a final shove, the cart rolled aboard.

Puffing from the exertion, he asked Miranda, "Where should I stow this?"

Removing the ship's control box from her coat pocket, the captain touched a button. The cargo hatch slid back and a flat platform rose level with the deck.

"Roll it onto the lift," she said, "and lock the wheels."

Caught up in the nautical theme of the moment, Chase replied, "Aye, Captain."

Before my son returned to dry land, we exchanged a fist-to-paw bump.

"Stay safe out there, Old Man."

"Don't you worry about me, Boy. Worry about keeping your own nose clean."

"I'll do my best, but I am a McGregor."

"And don't you be forgetting it."

The back and forth may not sound sentimental, but for us it was a warm leave taking.

Chase stood on the dock with a gathering crowd as Miranda weighed anchor and deployed sail.

Watching the canvas fill, I said, "Wait a minute, the wind is from the wrong direction."

Grasping the ship's wheel firmly, the captain said, "I told you I engineered a few modifications. The *Tempus Fugit* makes her own wind now."

"That," I said, "will come in handy considering we have to sail up a waterfall."

I was enjoying our majestic departure when the sound of claws on the teak deck signaled Rube's presence.

"I shoulda brought that sword Lucas made me wear at the wedding," he said. "Then I could look like one of them movie pirates."

"Be glad you got through the ceremony without cutting off your own tail."

Never drop a quarter into a loquacious raccoon. "That reminds me of a story," Rube said. "I knew a guy, who knew a guy, whose second wife's third cousin got his tail snapped off in a varmint trap."

Rolling my eyes, I asked, "Is this a long story?"

"I don't know about long, but it's inspire rational."

"*Inspirational*," I said. "I will regret this, but how does some raccoon getting his tail lopped off qualify as inspiring?"

Growing serious, Rube said, "Bob made medical history. He was the first raccoon in the world to have a custom-fitted prosthetic tail."

"*Stop*," I said, raising one paw. "Just *stop*. We're not out of the harbor, and you're already telling ridiculous stories."

Rube shook his head. "Be that way, but if you get your butt in a crack and wind up without a tail, you're gonna wish you had listened."

"I'll take the risk."

By the blessings of Bastet we enjoyed a compelling voyage—so compelling Rube entertained himself the whole way taking pictures of dolphins along the bow with his iPhone.

We approached the River of Virgo in late afternoon. Miranda called us to the quarterdeck before initiating the ship's ascent.

"You'll have a better view from here," she said. "Brace yourselves. We're about to get airborne."

Once again relying on the all-purpose controller, Miranda raised the *Tempus Fugit* off the surface. Going to the rail, I watched diamond-bright streams of water pouring off the hull and peppering the sea below.

The ship rose slowly through the spray-dampened air until we hovered directly opposite the main stream. The captain changed the direction of the wind catching the sailcloth and sent us into the channel.

As we passed through the jagged hole in the sky, I examined the edges of the aperture. The transitional structure reminded me of gouged plastic on our side, but appeared seamless and smooth from the Virgo perspective.

I looked back toward Cibolita through a brilliant double rainbow. Jilly landed beside me. "Do you know the symbolism?" she asked.

"No."

"The first bow represents the world and all its materialism," she said. "The second signifies the realm of the spiritual. We're entering a river associated with an intensely introverted astrological sign."

Since no one could overhear us, I said, "Honey, could you give me that in English?"

She chirped in amusement. "We're in deep waters, Festus. Deeper than the river flowing beneath the hull."

"You do know I'm a cat, right?"

"Of course. Why?"

"Cats don't like water. Especially *deep* water. All that astrology stuff belongs in the litter box."

Swiveling her head, Jilly gave me an avian half smile. "Too bad, darling, because we're swimming in metaphysical unknowns now."

Chapter Fifteen

Aboard the Tempus Fugit, *Jinx*

The boundary spell had a double purpose: keeping Rodney safe *and* sheltering the unknown artifact entrusted to him by Knasgowa. The Cherokee witch—my grandmother by several "greats"—gave the rat the wand for a purpose which seemed to be awakening.

Rodney's native curiosity aside, he insisted the wand had to come with me, but the implement wouldn't budge for anyone but him. That's a long way to say a brilliant rodent and a mini magical stick had me, the Witch of the Oak, over a barrel.

Compared to the relative boredom that had dogged me since my return from the 16th century, the morning portal transit to Cibolita lifted my spirits immediately. The exotic atmosphere of the port city appeals to me.

Lucas and I have had several romantic dinners in the Middle Realm over the past few weeks. As Acting Director of the DGI, my husband has become well known in Londinium.

Seemingly oblivious to our newlywed status, Fae politicians at all levels make a habit of talking to him in public. He accepts the interruptions as an annoying consequence of his job, but we both put a premium on preserving the privacy of our date nights.

Cibolita provides the perfect answer. The newly transformed town crackles with infectious energy. We both love the sights and smells of the open air markets and the variety of food and drink available in the city's restaurants and vendor carts.

We've also visited the *Tempus Fugit* and gotten to know Miranda better. Now in possession of the Copernican Astrolabe, the pirate can't help but play a significant role in the reassembly of the Temporal Arcana and the reintegration of time travel into Fae society.

I feel a kinship to the Temporal Captains of the Coast and the people of Cibolita, as both the Witch of the Oak and the person responsible for opening the Rivers of Time. Far from being off-putting, the vague air of frontier lawlessness there makes me more determined than ever to explore and understand the expanded dimensions of the In Between.

On the day of the expedition's departure, when the *Tempus Fugit* moved away from the dock, I walked to the stern to watch the city recede in the distance. After several minutes, Tori joined me.

Standing side by side at the rail, I said, "You really didn't have to come along, Mama Hen."

"Yes," she answered, "I *really* did. What makes you think I want to deal with your mother again if something happens to you? Besides, I'm getting sick of staying at home and running the store while you traipse off to parts and times unknown."

A pang of guilt shot through me. "I've never meant to leave you behind. It's just how things have worked out lately."

"You didn't leave me anywhere," Tori said agreeably. "I knew I needed to be in Briar Hollow to keep the rumor mill in check, but Beau can cover for us for a few days. If the town gossips start in, so be it. I've been needing to get out of town and see all of this for myself."

That surprised me. Tori has been dating my brother for some time. I assumed they'd been to the Middle Realm together. "Haven't you and Connor had some dates in Cibolita?" I asked.

"Yes," she said, "we have, and every single one has marked the adoption of yet another homeless *nonconformi*. I'm sorry I ever complained about you coming home with stray cats."

I laughed. "Love of animals runs in the family."

"True," she agreed, "but the dogs and cats you and your father adopt don't talk, can't change forms, don't emit poisonous substances, and do not require substantial additions to the Shevington stables."

Connor serves as mayor of the Otherworld city of Shevington, founded by our grandfather (again with several greats tacked on), Barnaby Shevington.

"According to my brother," I said, "we are no longer supposed to refer to that particular facility as 'the stables.' He prefers Shevington Exotic Species Sanctuary."

Tori rolled her eyes. "I know. He pitched that idea at the last general faculty meeting at Shevington University. The Sanctuary is a joint project with the Department of Ethnobiology, but the whole thing's a cover story for your brother to have an academically passable excuse to bring home more exotic critters."

Still laughing, I said, "You two couldn't be more perfect for one another. Do I need to remind you that *you* are the one who brought home all four of *my* cats?"

"My place didn't allow animals at the time," she said defensively, "and I knew they were all perfect for *you*, which they are. And they like your new husband."

"Yes, they do," I said, the pitch of my voice going quiet.

Tori's best friend senses instantly went on high alert. "Did you and Lucas argue about you coming on this trip?"

Wincing at the combative characterization of my exchange with my husband, I said, "'Argue' might be too strong a word. Let's go with 'disagree.'"

Pitching her response in a low voice so the others wouldn't hear, Tori said, "He was scared to death when you disappeared. He's not over it yet."

"I know that," I said, not bothering to hide my frustration, "but he has to get *over* the experience. I'm not going through a replay of what I went through when I dated Chase."

Tori made a tsking sound. "Different men. Different situations."

"Fair point," I retorted, "but *same* woman."

Turning around and leaning against the rail, Tori crossed her arms over her chest. "You've changed a lot since this all started, Jinksy. Remember the morning you found out about your magic? You told me you ran out on the sidewalk in your pajamas convinced you were having a bad dream."

I remembered alright. The whole town thought I'd lost my mind, and I wasn't so sure they weren't right. "Having my dead Aunt Fiona show up in the kitchen was something of a shock."

"When we get back," Tori said, "we should take a day and spend it with her in Shevington. I miss her cookies."

The thought of sitting in Fiona's cozy kitchen with plates of warm oatmeal cookies and glasses of cold milk made me feel uncharacteristically homesick for simpler days.

"Sometimes I miss how innocent our lives used to be," I admitted, as a pod of dolphins broke the water's surface alongside the ship. "But then I remember how much I love the life we have now. Disagreeing with Lucas was part of protecting that."

Tori nodded. "How did the two of you leave it?"

"I think we're okay," I said, trying not to sound as uncertain as I felt. "He was obviously glad to find out Greer decided to come along for the ride."

Eyeing the baobhan sith who was talking with Miranda at the ship's wheel, Tori said, "Do you think Lucas asked her to join the expedition?"

Shaking my head, I said, "No, he didn't have time. He looked genuinely surprised when she said she was coming."

"Maybe everybody needed to get out of town," Tori suggested, glancing down at the pack at my waist. Rodney had unzipped half of the top flap and stuck his head out to watch the dolphins. "Even Little Dude here."

"I'm not sure this is a sightseeing trip for Rodney," I said, looking to the rat for permission. "Can I tell her?"

He nodded, and I ran down the details of the morning episode with the miniature wand.

When I finished, Tori asked Rodney, "Did Knasgowa tell you what she wanted you to do with the wand?"

Rodney raised one paw over his lips and made a locking motion.

Not believing what I was seeing, I said, "Wait a second, Buster. You didn't tell me the part where you're holding out on me."

He shrugged, pointed at his wrist, and shrugged again.

"You know something, but it isn't time to tell us?" Tori asked.

The rat gave her a thumbs up.

"Let's make sure we're all running in the same wheel here," I said. "Does anybody else know about the wand?"

He shook his head.

Tori and I exchanged a look. "Well," she said. "We trust Rodney and we trust Knasgowa. I guess that's going to have to be good enough for now."

I considered telling Tori about the cryptic message from my grimoire, but before I could start, Miranda called us up to the quarterdeck. The *Tempus Fugit* was about to make her ascent to the River of Virgo—through a double rainbow no less.

When I turned away from the rail, I staggered under a wave of dizziness. Rodney grabbed the pack's zipper and hung on for dear life until Tori caught my elbow and steadied me.

"Hey!" she said, alarmed. "You okay?"

Shaking my head to clear it, I swallowed hard against a rancid, nauseous bubble in my throat. "*Whew!*" I said, blowing out a shaky breath. "I guess I don't have my sea legs yet. I thought I was going to be sick there for a minute."

"That settles it," Tori said as we started across the deck. "You're sleeping in the bottom bunk tonight. I did not sign on to be in the pathway of barf."

As my stomach roiled again, I said, "Me either. I probably should have eaten more for breakfast. I'm fine. Just motion sickness. It'll pass."

Inside the pack, I felt Rodney's paw patting my stomach in a tiny, touching gesture of comfort. He didn't tell me until much later that at the exact moment the nausea hit, the dragon on the wand emitted another burst of flame.

Chapter Sixteen

Abandoned Building, Edgar

The rhythmic scratching of the nib hypnotized Edgar, transporting him out of his surroundings and into the landscape of reflection. There, he forced himself to confront the consequences of his choices and behaviors.

After a lifetime of denying and justifying his failings, Edgar faced the implications of years wasted to melancholic self-absorption.

In periods of notoriety, he'd displayed arrogance; in less fortunate times, self-pity. From his days as a student at the University of Virginia to his abortive military career, Edgar'd laid his misfortunes at the feet of others, bemoaning the injustice of his mistreatment at their hands.

He placed a disproportionate amount of blame on his cold and distant stepfather. The man's dismissive assumption that Edgar lacked worth gave the young man an excuse to underperform. His criticism allowed Edgar to assume the stance of victim.

He gambled away the money his stepfather gave him for his

education. He drank when he knew he possessed no head for intoxicating beverages—and, yes, he visited the opium dens—but never to the point of addiction as some charged.

Examining these immature vices from the perspective of a soul clawing his way back to lucidity, Edgar recognized the exquisite pain underlying each decision.

He saw himself running a desperate race against unrelenting reality. He had given his life over to childish fears, not the maturing discernment of a man.

For the duration of his existence, he imagined the Angel of Death to be hot upon his heels. He came to believe from the age of two forward that the people he loved died *because* he loved them.

He nursed the secret fear that had Virginia not married him, she would have lived into happy old age. But to hold such beliefs was to give himself powers reserved only for the Deity. For all his hubris, Edgar had never aspired to divinity.

Lenore told him he must read his words aloud. "Give your characters life!" she counseled. "Set the scene free to play out before your visage. Every word you set down in ink yearns to dance with its fellows."

So Edgar did just that. He summoned his devils and invited them to dance by the pale light of the moon.

> *My sweet little wife—my Sissy—first coughed blood while singing. I no longer recall the tune, but I shall never erase from my mind's eye the horror of the crimson drops sprayed across her white lace handkerchief.*
>
> *But I did not bring the affliction upon her, and would have done anything to alleviate her fear and suffering. Yet, recoiling from her illness, I left her alone far too often and I sought the company of other women—most frequently for the monetary relief their station in life offered my diminished material condition.*

Edgar paused to lean his head against his hand, stunned by the torment those few admissions evoked. The discomfort of the exercise threatened to derail his purpose, but more rested on the task at hand than his emotional comfort.

With studied resolve he collected himself, dipped the pen, wiped the excess against the rim of the inkwell, and went on.

That foretelling of fate occurred in 1842, but I must direct the attention of this self-examination three years earlier when, by chance, I tipped my hat to a handsome woman dressed in black upon a New York street.

It was an act of courtesy to which I gave no passing thought. Though I admit to the tendency of observing attractive women in public spaces, I did not on this occasion entertain such notions.

To my surprise, that evening, in Fanny Osgood's parlor, I met the same woman formally—a golden-haired beauty who would, for the ensuing five years, become my muse and my love—my Lenore.

I kept company with her outside the bonds of my marriage, even after Sissy fell ill and suffered so keenly. For that, I have no defense. But how could I fail but be drawn to Lenore? No person, male or female, spoke of the act of writing with the insight and imagination she displayed.

In Lenore, I found a working companion who comprehended the cost of the labor of authorship, a woman who appreciated the rigorousness with which a writer must repeatedly test his mettle.

In her estimation writing assumed the level of a metaphysical enchantment. She spoke of words as if each possessed within itself a unique life spark, an animus that, when connected to its fellows, contained the seeds of genesis.

Once in a moment of gaiety, I accused her of the practice of witchcraft. Turning eyes on me that were the color of the sea at dawn—azure, flecked with gold, and restless like the waves—Lenore answered in a fashion that astonished me.

> "Do not make sport of witchcraft, Edgar. What Mr. Emerson calls the Oversoul, others know to be magic. None of us are so fortunate as to understand every miracle of the natural order, most especially not the myriad miracles that occur when pen meets paper."

Quoting Lenore's words summoned her voice into the fevered cauldron of his brain and set his hand to tremble with such violence that ink splattered the page. The harsh cries of the raven echoed in his ears, "Nevermore. Nevermore. *Nevermore!*"

The pen slipped from his fingers as Edgar balled his hands into fists and struck the desk. "No!" he cried. "*No!* Seneca said it is a place, not a pronouncement—a *place!* Nevermore is a *place.*"

Shoving his chair back, Edgar moved to stride vigorously across the room, but the sole of his shoe slipped on the papers littering the floor. He flailed wildly, but found no handhold to stop his fall. He landed on his back crying out when his head bounced sharply against the wooden planks.

Later, Edgar would remember that he stared at the ceiling, blinked in a futile attempt to clear his vision and the silence the ringing in his ears, and then slipped into the peaceful nothingness of unconsciousness.

Chapter Seventeen

Aboard the Tempus Fugit, *Jinx*

After our vessel came on level with the main body of the river, Miranda steered the ship several hundred yards upstream, dropped anchor, and tossed a lead line over the side to take a depth sounding.

Observing her motions with a critical eye, Festus said, "That fancy remote control of yours can make this thing fly, but it won't tell you how deep the water is?"

Miranda gave the werecat a sidelong glance. "Very funny. There are some things I prefer to do the traditional way. The *Tempus Fugit* has a shallow draft. I don't think running her aground would serve our greater purpose."

Festus said exactly what I was thinking. "How the hell do you run a *flying* ship aground?"

The captain set about methodically coiling the lead line. "All accounts suggest we'll be sailing through uninhabited countryside, but those voyages took place centuries ago. How do we know settlements haven't sprung up since? And if they have, are the settlers Fae *nonconformi* or human? I figure staying waterborne gives us the best chance to lay low."

Rube nodded appreciatively. "You gotta give her the win on that one, McGregor. Fae ain't gonna blink when a boat comes flying by, but humans? They're all about torches and pitchforks."

Conceding to the wisdom of Miranda's strategy, Festus said, "I stand corrected."

Confident that the ship could safely navigate the main channel, Miranda raised the anchor and filled the sails. As the *Tempus Fugit* moved upstream, the captain did take out her control box.

With a few clicks, she raised poles from the decking and strung a tarp to create a shaded area. We had confirmed one fact about the territory so far; it was tropical as in *damned* hot.

During the first hour of the voyage, we unpacked the gear and settled into our cabins. Jilly and Lucy bunked together across the corridor from Festus and Rube, while Tori and I had the space adjacent to the captain's cabin.

Greer said she would spend her nights on deck reading, baobhan sith code for "keeping watch."

In honor of our first evening onboard, Jilly, Lucy, and Festus made a shifter committee decision to show up for dinner in human form. When Tori and I went on deck, we found the werecat dressed in light khakis and a broad-brimmed hat. He was standing below the canopy using binoculars to scan the shoreline.

I picked up a second set of glasses resting on the table and conducted my own reconnaissance.

A variety of monkeys swung through the jungle canopy, keeping track of the ship's progress. I saw colorful birds, including some parrots, and spotted at least three crocodiles slipping into the dark, muddy water.

Rube dragged a box beside us to give him enough height to

watch the banks without getting close to the rail. He'd seen the crocodiles, too.

"I ain't gonna be surprised if the *Creature from the Black Lagoon* comes crawling outta that soup," the raccoon observed darkly. "This looks like the freaking heart of the Amazon."

"Have you been to the Amazon?" I asked.

"No," he replied gravely, "but we got the *National Geographic Channel* on the cable package in the treehouse. Same diff."

To think all those explorers bothered going in person to wind up in some cannibal's cooking pot.

When Lucy and Jilly joined us on deck, we gathered in a loose circle of camp chairs. Gesturing toward the binoculars, Jilly asked what we'd spotted on shore.

"Monkeys and parrots," Festus replied.

Her expression brightened. "Well," she said, "that's good news. Now we can make contact with the natives.

She let out with a series of caws and whistles I wouldn't have expected a human throat could produce.

"I'm impressed you can do that without being shifted," I said.

"Years of practice," she assured me. "It's not easy to get the inflection right on the high notes."

When a tentative squawk issued from a tree overhanging the river, Jilly replied with what even I understood to be an invitation.

A large macaw with a brilliant scarlet head and a magnificent tail flew under the canopy and landed on the edge of the table. The sharp hooked beak clacked a few times before the newcomer delivered a protracted monologue in what sounded like Common Avian.

Jilly responded in the same tongue. The animated exchange proceeded at a rapid clip, far too fast for my rudimentary understanding of the language.

Leaning toward Lucy, I said, "Do you understand them?"

"Yes," she said. "The bird's name is Aria. Jilly is asking her if we'll encounter any people between here and the Spica tributary."

"And will we?"

Lucy listened for several seconds and then said, "According to Aria there are people living in the Spica Mountains, but not before. Her personal flight range doesn't extend that far, so she's passing on what she's heard from birds living upstream."

With a final cordial barrage of squawks, the macaw flew back toward the bank. Jilly confirmed Lucy's translation, but with a cautionary note.

"We can't make any concrete decisions based on a strange parrot's word, but Aria swears there are no settlements nearby."

Lucy looked up at the ship's rigging. "Somebody should climb up to the crow's nest with the binoculars to confirm that."

After a beat, Rube said, "Well, you're the crow on the team. Get at it."

"I am a *raven*, not a crow," Lucy said. "Either Jilly or I could shift and fly up there, but we couldn't very well take the binoculars with us, now could we? You know, feathers not fingers?"

The raccoon ripped open the sack of chips he'd scrounged from the galley. "My bad. Guess that leaves you, Big Tom. Good climbing."

With studied nonchalance, Festus crossed his arms. "I have a bad hip."

Rube chewed contemplatively, scattering a rain of crumbs over his chest. He turned bright black eyes on us. "How about one of you gals?"

Tori and I both shook our heads.

"Too bad," he said between bites. "It woulda been good to get a better look around."

In the silence that followed, realization dawned slowly in his furry brain. When his brow furrowed, I knew he'd put it together.

"You ain't thinking *I'm* going up there, are you?"

"That's exactly what we're thinking," Festus said. "You have hands. You can carry the binoculars. You climb things all the time."

Rube started backing up, leaving a trail of crumbled potato chips in his wake. "I climb trees what are rooted in solid *ground*. I ain't going up no moving pole in the middle of a boat with crocodiles in the water. I fall in, I'm croc chow. Period."

"Then don't fall," Festus said pleasantly.

Rube turned toward Greer. "Red, help me out here."

The baobhan sith flipped the page in her book. "You are the logical choice, Reuben. The attributes of your species afford you greater agility than the other members of the team."

"I ain't agile," he protested. "Ask anybody. I trip over my own feet all the freaking time."

"Quit your stalling, and start climbing," Festus ordered. "The sooner you get up there, the sooner you can come back down."

The raccoon went, but he bitched all the way up the mast.

Shielding her eyes and watching his progress, Miranda said, "I don't blame him. Before I made captain, I hated taking my turn in the crow's nest. The view's great, but you should never look down.

On cue, Rube let out with a stream of profanity.

Miranda snickered. "He looked down."

Rube might not have liked the assignment, but he stayed in the crow's nest long enough to complete a 360-degree sweep of the countryside. When the raccoon descended the mast, he dropped and kissed the deck, rattling off a litany of thanks to the Trash Gods.

"Can the drama," Festus said. "What did you see?"

Getting up and dusting off his belly fur, Rube said, "You

mean other than them carne-voracious swimming lizards? There were some big bird-looking things flying way off toward the mountains, but I couldn't really make 'em out. Too far away. I gotta get me some Roadkill Ragu. That was a traumat-i-cizing experience."

Miranda steered the *Tempus Fugit* into a calm eddy and dropped anchor for the night. Then she laid out a spread of fruit, cold cuts, bread, and cheese. We ate as the sun set, and the jungle came alive with night sounds.

When a big cat screamed in the distance, I saw Festus's eyes flare.

"Anybody you recognize, McGregor?" Rube asked, working on his third MRE. I made out the label in the dim light—Teriyaki Trash Delight.

The werecat shifted restlessly. If he'd been in feline form, his ears would have gone flat against his head. "Some kind of leopard, I think. Not a shifter, but after tonight, I'm staying on four legs just in case."

Jilly laid a soothing hand on his knee. "Lucy and I both want to be in our feathers, too. Tomorrow we can take turns flying into the trees, conversing with the natives."

Festus had better sense than to tell her no, but he did say, "Not too far in, and stay together, okay?"

"Okay," she said, giving his knee a squeeze. "But I can out-fly anything this jungle can throw at us."

They smiled at each other. "I have no doubt," Festus said, "but humor me."

"How come ain't none of you people interested in humoring *me*?" Rube grumbled, dribbling teriyaki down his chin. "Didn't one of you blink about sending me up that pole."

"*Mast*," Miranda said, making herself a second sandwich. "It's called a mast."

"Pole, mast, *stick*, I ain't going up there again."

Festus gave him a good natured cuff on the ear. "Get over it, already. We weren't going to let you be crocodile chow."

"Oh yeah? What was gonna stop me from going over the side if I fell?" Rube demanded.

"This," Miranda said, thumbing a button on her box. A faint glowing web slowly materialized around the hull. "Safety net. Falling overboard isn't an option."

Rube's head swiveled between the net and Festus's impassive face. "Did you know about the catch-a-coon contraption, McGregor?"

"Of course, I did," the werecat lied.

"I ain't buying a word of it."

"Yeah," Festus grinned, "but you'll never know for sure, will you?"

When Rube went below decks to retrieve yet another MRE, I said, "Festus, that wasn't nice. You should apologize for scaring Rube like that."

"I *should* do lots of things."

"Festus," Jilly said. "Jinx is right."

The corners of his mouth drew down. "I'll say something to him before we go to bed."

"Promise?" Jilly asked.

He didn't want to, but the werecat promised. I like Jilly anyway, but if she can locate and tap into an unknown compliant streak in Festus McGregor? Now we're talking *serious* magic.

Chapter Eighteen

Aboard the Tempus Fugit, *Festus*

We left Greer and Miranda topside talking. Everyone scattered to their respective cabins, which allowed me and Jilly to steal a private moment in the passageway.

She gave me a quick kiss. "Remember your promise. Say something nice to him."

I rolled my eyes, but said I would.

Inside our quarters, I shifted back to mountain lion form and stretched out on the bottom bunk. Without saying a word, Rube scaled the ladder to the upper bunk with an oversized bag of pistachios clutched in one paw.

Within seconds, cast-off husks started to rain over the edge with just the right amount of spin to land on my fur.

"You're on my last nerve cell," I growled when a spitty hull came to rest on the tip of my nose.

"Oh," Rube said innocently, "you awake down there, McGregor?"

I batted the pistachio off my muzzle and counted to ten

before I answered. "Okay, *fine.* I didn't know about the net, but I knew you weren't going to fall."

To my knowledge, raccoons don't toss hairballs, but Rube did a good impression. "Oh really. How did you figure that?"

Lobbing a complete curve ball in his direction, I replied, "Because if I didn't respect your professional abilities, I wouldn't work with you."

That got me dead air.

Snickering, I said, "Didn't expect me to say that, did you?"

"Naw, I honest to the Trash Gods didn't. Sorry about the husks. Night, McGregor."

"Night, Rube."

"Festus?"

"Yeah?"

"You ain't no slouch yourself."

Satisfied that I'd kept my word to Jilly and truly made up for any hurt feelings on Rube's part, I settled in for the night.

Down the corridor, a faint buzz of conversation emanated from the cabin Jinx and Tori shared. It didn't surprise me that they were staying up late; it had been a while since their last road trip.

The indecipherable rise and fall of voices blended with the lapping of the river along the hull and the backdrop of a jungle night. The effect lulled me to sleep, secure in the knowledge that over my head the baobhan sith would stand guard until the dawn.

Hours later, the tearing of a foil pouch being ripped open awakened me with a start. Rube sat on the floor beside his suitcase pouring water into an MRE.

His good humor fully restored, the raccoon greeted me with a toothy grin. "Morning, McGregor. Want a Survival Scramble?"

"No thanks," I said stretching and scratching behind my ears. "I smell coffee."

"Yeah," Rube agreed. "I heard Miranda's boots out in the passage at the crack of daylight. We've been underway since the sun came up."

Until he mentioned it, I hadn't realized the *Tempus Fugit* was moving. "Anybody else awake?" I asked.

"I think all the girls is up there on deck. The dames got us guys seriously outnumbered."

"What's wrong? You can't handle six to three odds?"

"Me?" the raccoon said, his grin growing wider. "I ain't the one offering apologies 'cause my girlfriend told me to."

Flattening my whiskers, I said, "On second thought, I wonder how Survival Scramble would taste with coon bacon?"

"You're all talk, *Big Tom*," Rube said, slapping his paw on the deck for emphasis. "I got myself a parrot-pecked partner in crime."

Stepping off the bunk and drawing myself to my full height, I said, "For your information, I am your *boss*, not your partner. I'm going topside to find that coffee."

"Yeah," Rube said, "that's right. Better get your tail up there and check in with Jilly. Tell her I'll vouch for you being a good little kitty cat last night."

Making a point of ignoring him completely, I exited and climbed the stairs to the main deck. Greer, Jinx, and Tori sat under the canopy having breakfast. Without being asked, the baobhan sith fixed a plate for me and poured coffee in a cereal bowl.

"Thanks," I said, taking the first delicious caffeinated hit of the day. "Where are Jilly and Lucy?"

"Out there," Tori said, gesturing toward the jungle with her fork. "They're mingling with the feathered locals and gathering intel."

Fixing my eyes on the bank with thinly disguised concern, I said, "How long have they been gone?"

"One or both of them check in every half hour," Jinx assured me. "You missed Jilly by five minutes. She's fine."

When I turned to answer, the sight of her breakfast plate stopped me short. Two pieces of dry toast? Generally Jinx can put away eggs and bacon like a truck driver and heaven help the stray bear claw that winds up on her plate.

"What's wrong with you this morning?" I asked, staring at the dessicated bread slices.

"Turns out I get sea sick," she admitted, "and I need to lay off the pastries anyway. My jeans are getting tight."

Rodney, who was sitting beside her plate, stood up and flexed his muscles, turning sideways to show us his trim stomach.

"Yeah, yeah," I grumbled. "We know. Thirty miles a night in your wheel. Show off."

Behind us I heard Rube's claws coming up the stairs. "Morning, ladies and rats!" he said, crawling on the serving table and surveying the food. "What's for breakfast? I'm starving."

"Liar," I said. "You had a Survival Scramble MRE in our cabin."

"Which," he said, spearing a link of sausage with a fork, "was *first* breakfast. Now I'm on *second* breakfast. Ain't you never read *The Hobbit?*"

Still annoyed by the teasing I'd endured in our cabin, I said, "You are the only mammal I know who could find a way to use literature as an excuse for being fat."

Completely unfazed, Rube said, "You bet your yeller butt, I can. What good's a solid education if a guy can't use it to improve his standardization of living?"

Before I could correct him, a shadow swept over the deck. The raccoon looked up, yelped, and dove under the table. Rodney followed Rube's line of sight and made a hasty retreat into Jinx's waist pack.

It registered on me briefly that the rat seemed to be having a hard time getting inside the pouch before my full attention became fixated on the air space above the ship.

The creature hovering over the *Tempus Fugit* could have made short work of the canopy, Rube's hiding place, most of the ship's rigging, and *us* for that matter.

From somewhere under the tablecloth, Rube's indignant voice penetrated my thoughts. "This caper weren't supposed to involve flying lizards, McGregor. You didn't say *squat* about no freaking *dragons*."

Looking toward the quarterdeck, I saw Miranda working the controls on her all-purpose box. The wind in the sails died followed by the rattle and splash of the anchor.

"I didn't say *squat* about dragons you striped moron, because I didn't *expect* dragons," I said. "Not to mention that this trip was *your* idea. Why didn't *you* know about the dragons?"

Greer rose from the table; the vampire actually took the time to *fold* her napkin. "Moot points at this juncture of affairs, gentlemen," she said.

One minute the baobhan sith was with us under the canopy, the next she was standing beside Miranda. The pirate removed one of the pistols tucked in her belt and handed it to Greer.

Squinting against the sun, I watched the rhythmic beat of the dragon's extended wings and thanked Bastet I had shifted to my larger form.

Compared to the big European dragons and the North American dragonlets, the beast was roughly the size of a draft horse. Substantial enough to eye me as a potential *hors d'oeuvre*, but small enough that I could put up some fight on the way down the damn thing's gullet.

"Do you recognize the species?" Jinx asked.

"No," I said. "Too small for *Draco Europa Giganticus*, too big to be a dragonlet."

The yellow dragon glowed in the morning light as it lazily circled the ship's mast. Branch-like fringes dotted with purple sprouted along the creature's spine and wings. They all but obscured the rider, but I could make out a confident figure wearing gold leathers dyed to match the dragon's hide.

"She's beautiful," Tori said.

"Which one?" Jinx asked.

"Both of them. What do we do now?"

I looked at Jinx. "You're the Witch of the Oak."

Her eyes widened. "*You're* the head of BlackTAT."

Miranda settled the matter for us. Planting her hands firmly on her hips, the captain called out, "*Hey!* You up there. Something we can do for you?"

The dragon came round the stern and hovered in front of Miranda and Greer. In the back of my mind, I took note of the welcome breeze flowing across the deck generated by the powerful strokes of the creature's wings. The humidity wasn't doing a damn thing for my fur.

"Are you from the Otherworld?" a female voice called out.

"We are the crew of the *Tempus Fugit* out of Cibolita in the Middle Realm," Miranda replied.

"How did you ascend the waterfall?" the rider asked.

"We'll answer your questions," the captain said, "but why don't you come aboard so we can talk instead of shout?"

The girl laid a slender hand along the neck of her dragon. Its small ears swiveled toward her, signaling what I assumed to be a silent consultation.

After a moment the rider nodded and said, "Thank you. We accept. Stand back, please, so Giallo has sufficient room to set us down."

The dragon—Giallo—furled its wings and came in for a landing, hindquarters first. With solid footing attained, the beast's body lowered toward the deck. To my surprise, the front claws promptly tucked under the scaly chest in cat-like fashion.

European dragons have heads like horses. This animal appeared almost aquatic. Its snout extended in a long, narrow line running toward a blunt, flared point. Smoke curled from the oval nostrils.

The dragon's green eyes looked out from either side of a boxy forehead trimmed with a red crest. The expression conveyed no threat, only calm curiosity.

The girl slid out of the saddle, the soles of her boots hitting the planks with a ringing authority.

Miranda, who had come down from the quarterdeck to meet her, stepped forward and extended her hand. "I'm Captain Winter, mistress of the *Tempus Fugit*."

"My name is Blair McBride and this is Giallo. Are you here to find us?"

The pirate and Jinx both looked to me to supply an answer, but for once, I had zip. Nothing about this trip fell under the heading of "expected," which left me unusually slow on the uptake. The instant I had that thought, our situation got stranger.

The wind changed. My nose picked up the unmistakable scent of tiger.

Blair McBride was a werecat—with a pet dragon.

Chapter Nineteen

Deck of the Tempus Fugit, Festus

Every culture has rules about good and bad behavior. Mine told me I couldn't blurt out Blair's shifter identity. First, to do so would be gauche as hell, and second, "outing" a fellow werecat was a poor way to handle first contact.

I had maybe two seconds to calculate the etiquette algebra before Jinx gave me a shooing "go on, you do it" gesture. My mind registered the odd expression on her face, but why wouldn't she look odd? A dragon had landed smack in the middle of our peaceful breakfast.

Setting my whiskers at a firm but friendly angle, I stepped forward.

"Hi," I said, "I'm Festus McGregor. We're a search and recovery team sent out by the Ruling Elders to locate a group of artifacts called the Temporal Arcana."

It was a good opener—friendly, honest, packed with information. Blair didn't hear a word.

She furrowed her brow and gawked at me. "You're a werecat."

So much for my concerns about etiquette. "Yes, I am."

Not much to argue with there, but Blair managed to counter my statement anyway. "But you're not a tiger."

I wanted to say, *Did the lack of stripes give me away?* Instead, with infinite patience, I went with, "In my large form, I'm a North American Cougar."

Her next statement abruptly smacked me into awareness.

"You're shifted during the day."

Of all the werefeline species, tigers have the strongest instinct for solitude and introversion. Modern weretigers manage the trait, but stuck up in the Spica Mountains off a lost temporal river, I doubted Blair had any opportunity to embrace social evolution.

The young woman wasn't being rude; she was embarrassed. *I* was embarrassing her—making her feel more or less like a clothed person who wandered into a nudist colony by mistake.

"My apologies," I said. "I know weretigers prefer to shift at night in private."

Getting Jinx's attention, I raised my eyewhiskers. I needed her to take over for a few minutes. She got the message.

"Hi, Blair, I'm Jinx Hamilton, Witch of the Oak. Why don't we sit and talk while Festus goes below to change?"

Twin crimson patches appeared on Blair's cheeks. Regardless of where she'd been raised, the young woman recognized her social *faux pas*. One shifter *never* tells another shifter how to manage their form.

"Mr. McGregor," she stuttered, "I am so sorry. That was rude of me...I...I..."

Holding up one paw to stop the flow of words, I said, "I'm not offended. The humidity in this place is kinking my fur anyway. I'm perfectly happy to go bipedal."

At that, Blair nodded sympathetically. Fur management issues are a universal bonding topic for werecats.

Heading down the stairs, I heard Jinx introducing the rest of our party to Blair. When I nudged the door of our cabin open with my nose, the litter of cast-off hulls on the floor gave me a brilliant idea.

I could shift *and* throw the rest of Rube's pistachio stash out the porthole since I was about to have opposable thumbs at my disposal—Festus McGregor for the win.

Dressing quickly, I returned topside to find the group seated under the canopy. A pitcher of iced tea had appeared in the middle of the table.

I'm sure you're expecting me to describe some kind of big diplomatic conclave, but that's not how the rest of the morning unfolded. At the time, with a scant understanding of how time flows along the River of Virgo, I took Blair to be a few years younger than Jinx and Tori.

The dragon rider couldn't contain her animated excitement at meeting us. Everything we said and did touched off a fresh round of culture clash revelations with Blair launching flurries of questions.

I arrived at the exact moment she held her tea glass up to the light and stared at the ice cubes with rapt fascination.

"My father told me that water can become solid," she said, her voice suffused with wonder, "but I never expected it to be so ... so ... "

"Cold?" Rube offered. "Living in a steam box like this joint, a guy with an ice machine could make a freaking fortune. Now, cold being the opposite of hot, let's get back to talking about *him*."

The raccoon pointed accusingly at Giallo who was enjoying a sun bath on deck. The dragon's nostrils produced rhythmic smoke puffs that might have been sooty snores.

"So you're like one hundred total percent certain he's got a handle on the fire thing *and* that he don't eat raccoons?" Rube demanded.

Still enraptured by the cold drink in her hand, Blair glanced toward Giallo who snorted but didn't open his eyes. "He did catch the stables on fire once," she admitted, "but he was very young. He's much more careful now."

"*Careful* being a good thing," Rube said emphatically, "since we're sitting on a wooden tub. No offense intended, Your Pirateness."

"None taken," Miranda replied drily.

Rube nodded and kept going. "So I'll take that as a *no* on burning the boat down. What about the eating raccoons part?"

Blair looked at Rube with a bemused expression. "Giallo never saw one of your kind until today. You appear to be related to the jungle coatimundi. If so, he tells me that he finds the texture of your species coarse and unpalatable."

Completely ignoring that he'd been given the answer he wanted, Rube slapped his paw on the rail.

"Geez, *Lou-eeze!* First them midget dragons in Shevington tell me I'm *stringy* and now that flying barbecue grill over there says me and my kind is 'coarse.' I got coatimundi cousins and there ain't nothing wrong with our family textiles."

Jinx and Tori couldn't control themselves a minute longer. Both burst out laughing. The smile that had been tugging at the corners of Blair's mouth spread across her face.

Rube knew exactly what he was doing—putting everyone, most especially Blair, at ease. It was working.

"He means 'texture,'" Jinx said, wiping away tears of mirth. "Rube has a hard time with insults to his quality as an entrée, even when it means he's in no danger of being eaten."

The raccoon put his paws on his hips and faked a huff. "Sue me. I got a sensitive nature."

That touched off a fresh round of laughter loud enough that

Giallo opened both his eyes and his mouth. Even with the increasingly cordial tone of the conversation, I took note of the size of the dragon's teeth as somewhere between impressive and *damn*.

Blair inclined her head toward her mount and said, "*Giallo!* That is *not* nice!"

Instantly suspicious, Rube said, "What ain't nice?"

The young woman tried to compose a diplomatic translation. "He offered to . . . uh . . . *sample* your texture if that would make you feel better."

Rube's eyes narrowed. "Very *freaking* funny, Captain Iguana. You ain't the first lizard that's offered to take a bite out of me."

Giallo's heavy frame shook with laughter. He lifted his foreleg and held a foot out in Rube's direction.

"What's he doing?" the raccoon asked.

"Offering you his friendship," Blair said. "Giallo wants to shake your paw as a pledge never to do you harm. A clasping of the hands is a tradition among the riders in our flight."

Rube had no problem talking a big game from fifteen feet away; physical contact, however, wasn't in his plan.

"Uh, that's okay. I'll take his word for it," the raccoon said, backing up a few paces.

Time to pull rank. If I had to shift in the name of good relations, Rube could mammal up and shake a dragon's paw.

"Don't be ridiculous, Rube," I said. "Handshakes are a tradition in our world, too. Don't be rude. You're not trying to offend Giallo, are you?"

Rube shot me a murderous glare, but he started to mince forward. I was tempted to shout "boo!" just to watch him jump out of his fur. Giallo's body language betrayed his barely contained mirth as well, but the dragon held still, purring as a reassurance of his benign intentions.

When their paws finally touched, Rube's ears shot up. "Holy

stinking Dumpster Gods," he said, "how are you doing that?"

Swiveling in our direction, the raccoon added, "He's talking —*inside* my head."

Suspicion confirmed. Dragon and rider shared a mental link, one Giallo seemed prepared to extend to the rest of us.

"Giallo speaks telepathically," Blair explained. "His kind possesses no other form of speech."

Since I hadn't heard the dragon's voice, my feline curiosity got the better of me. "What did he say?" I asked.

If I'd been on four legs, what happened next would have sent *me* jumping into the rigging with my fur standing on end.

"I would not hurt the small one. He amuses me."

Okay, good that Giallo spoke to me; bad that he startled me. I take pains to cultivate my image as a suave, sophisticated cat of mystery. There was only one acceptable reaction—act blasé.

"You may think he's funny now," I assured the dragon, "but wait until you've listened to him for an hour or two. You'll rethink that texture aversion."

Clearly everyone heard Giallo, which meant the whole group was now looped in with no need for further second-hand translations.

Giallo's willingness to communicate with us erased any lingering doubts Blair might have had and she said as much. "You must all be trustworthy, or Giallo wouldn't let you hear his voice."

"A policy of which my mother would approve," Jinx said. "Even big fire-breathing dragons should be careful about talking to strangers."

"We have never had a reason to be cautious of strangers since we've never seen anyone from outside the Spica Mountains," Blair said. "Well, with the exception of one hermit in the jungle, but he's harmless. Please, can you tell me, how long have we been here?"

"You don't know?" Tori asked. "How is that possible?"

"Time can't be measured accurately in these lands," Blair said. "Sometimes it moves rapidly, at others it freezes. We accept a 'day' for whatever length of light we receive."

Miranda reached into the pocket of her vest and pulled out a gold pocket watch. When she opened the case, her eyebrows arched. Without a word, she laid the timepiece on the table. The hands revolved at a rapid clip, "hours" passing in seconds.

None of us were unfamiliar with the relative nature of time. Days in the Otherworld are longer than those in the human realm, but for simplicity sake, we use the same numerical dates for the passage of years.

I looked over at Greer. "Is there a precise date for the imposition of the Agreement?"

The baobhan sith shook her head. "The segregation was accomplished in successive waves. Human historians place the beginning of their Reformation at 1517."

Sometimes you have no choice but to rip off the bandage. "Give or take a decade or so," I told Blair, "you've been here 500 years."

The young woman took the news well—better than Jinx did.

"Miranda," Jinx said in a strange voice, "when you told Festus it might feel like we've been gone for months, is the opposite possible, too?"

The pirate frowned, "You mean could long stretches of time pass without our noticing?"

Jinx nodded.

"From what Blair has said, I suppose that's possible," the captain admitted. "Why?"

Without a word, Jinx pushed back her chair and stood up. Rodney's waist pack had slipped below her now bulging belly. By my guess, the Witch of the Oak was nine months pregnant.

Chapter Twenty

Deck of the Tempus Fugit, *Jinx*

Festus tells me I know how to steal a scene. According to him, my instant pregnancy thoroughly eclipsed the impact of Blair and Giallo's earlier arrival aboard the ship.

My memories of that day are a chaotic mix of terror and joy. The clear perceptions I do retain are now tightly interwoven with things I didn't understand at the time—chief among them the insight that Addie, my daughter, started calling the shots the instant she came to life within my body.

Addie compelled me to join the BlackTAT expedition. Tiny and already breathtakingly powerful, she knew exactly where and *when* to make her entrance in the world.

I should have put it all together. Pistachio ice cream and cherry pie? Talk about denial.

But honestly, when I left Briar Hollow, I didn't know I was pregnant. If I had known, I would have stayed at home with Lucas, ensuring that we experienced the birth of our baby together.

My first suspicion that something wasn't right coincided with the wave of dizziness that hit me before the ship ascended the waterfall.

Like most kids, I grew out of car sickness by the time I reached my teen years, and I've spent hours on boats with my father. Sea sickness wasn't the culprit.

The first night aboard the *Tempus Fugit* my sleeping mind conjured the vision of a toddler who walked into the cabin and stood beside my bed saying, "Mommy, wake up. Wake up, Mommy. It's time for me to be born."

Jerking back to consciousness in the dim light with my heart hammering in my chest, I thought, for the barest instant, that I heard a second rhythm—the vague, distant thump of a new life.

When I adjusted to the light, I saw Rodney inside his pack, suspended from a peg on the wall. The rat's eyes questioned me, *"Are you okay?"*

Putting a finger to my lips, I nodded, and gestured to my head making awkward, confused gestures designed to convey the message *"bad dream."*

Nodding, Rodney climbed out of the pouch, gathered his body, and jumped the distance to my pillow. Kneading the surface with his paws, he stretched out next to my head and laid a cool paw against my burning face.

That had to be the problem. The humid, warm jungle night. The explanation lulled me back to sleep, but in the morning when I started to dress for breakfast, I couldn't snap my jeans.

Thankfully, Tori had already left in search of coffee.

"Everybody bloats when they travel," I told Rodney, passing a hand over the recalcitrant fastener and muttering, *"capitulum convenire"*—expand to fit.

A breakfast of dry toast and plenty of water would take care of the problem. My mother and Aunt Fiona swear by dry toast as a cure for everything from typhoid to an impending cold.

But the home remedy didn't save me. Mid-way through the group's conversation with Blair, Rodney squeezed out of the waist pack and looked at me with open alarm. I remember shaking my head imperceptibly, but I felt what he saw—my continually expanding abdomen.

I laid a hand against my belly and concentrated as hard as I could on an elasticity spell. That's all that saved me from bursting out of my jeans.

Then Blair asked how long she and the other dragon riders had been in the Spica Mountains and I clued in. The child inside me was growing in response to the shifting nature of time on the River of Virgo.

I admit it; I panicked.

With no other way to vocalize what was happening to my body, I stood up, eliciting a stunned silence followed by a cacophony of responses.

"Holy *freaking* Trash Gods!" Rube exclaimed. "You got a bun in the oven."

Tori gasped, "Jinksy, what the *hell*?"

And then, from Festus, "How is that even possible?"

That snapped me back. Training my attention on the werecat, I said testily, "*Seriously,* Festus? I need to explain the mechanics to *you*?"

"No," he said emphatically, holding up both hands to fend off a potential torrent of unwanted information. "The mechanical part I get, but you weren't pregnant half an hour ago."

Out of nowhere, a digging pain slammed into my rib cage. I exhaled sharply, wrapping my arms protectively around my belly. Greer, of all people, appeared at my elbow. The baobhan sith encircled me with a strong, cool arm and eased me back into my chair.

Looking in her steady gaze, I asked in a frightened voice, "What was that?"

"Your child kicking," Greer replied with a warm smile. "It means only that she is healthy."

Reaching blindly for Tori, I felt my best friend's fingers entwined with mine. "How do you know it's a girl?" I asked.

Greer squeezed my shoulder, "Listen," she commanded. "Listen with your powers."

Stilling my mind, I focused past the cries of the jungle birds, beyond the water lapping against the hull, and through the chaotic emotions of my companions. I went inside, to the still center of my being where the deepest awareness resides. There, for the first time, I heard my daughter's voice.

Tears filled my eyes. "She's laughing," I whispered.

A paw came to rest on my knee. I looked down into Rube's black-masked, grinning face. "Ain't nothing better than a baby kit giggling," he assured me. "Means you got a real little rascal in there. Congratulations, Jinx. This is freaking *awesome*."

"Thank you," I said, sounding as dazed as I felt.

Tori's hand tightened on mine. "Do you need to lie down?"

I shook my head. "I can just hear what Mom would say to that. 'You're pregnant; you're not dying.'"

"Atta girl," Tori said, holding my gaze. The look said, *"I don't know what the hell's going on, but we've got this."*

You have no idea how much I needed that look.

Gathering my focus, I turned to Blair. "Have you ever seen this before?"

"No," she said, "but there are stories of women in the First Flight who came here unaware they were with child. They experienced accelerated pregnancies. It happened to some of the dragons, too."

"Your whelp's heart beats strong and true," Giallo said. *"Fear not for her safety."*

Jilly and Lucy chose that moment to return to the *Tempus Fugit*. The wereparrot landed on the back of one of the empty chairs. When she saw me, she lost her footing, quickly spreading her wings to catch herself.

"Well," she said. "We appear to have missed a great deal."

"Ya think?" Tori said. "The dragon uses telepathy, by the way."

"Of course he does," Jilly said sardonically.

Most of what transpired over the next few minutes lingers in my brain as a confused blur. There were more introductions for Blair's benefit, I remember Miranda putting my feet up in one of the chairs as I stared at my puffy, over-sized ankles.

For some reason the pirate captain's solicitous ministrations made me think of Lucas. That's when I started to cry—and I don't mean pretty crying.

Burying my head in Tori's shoulder, I sobbed my heart out.

Festus made some crack about hormones, which only made me cry harder, but slowly Tori's voice penetrated the fog of my misery. "Jinksy, honey, what is it?"

Alternating between hiccuping and coughing, I managed to say, "Lucas. He's missing everything," before dissolving into fresh wails.

Without a word, Greer called on her preternatural vampire strength to pick me up and carry me below with Tori and Rodney trailing behind.

Festus is going to have to tell you what happened next, because I proceeded to have a complete breakdown. Don't worry. I got my head back in the game, but not before I experienced nine months of hormones assailing my system in a matter of hours.

Most women have nine months to negotiate the path to motherhood. It happened to me in a day—a very *long* day—or whatever passed for a day on the River of Virgo.

I ceased to be the powerful Witch of the Oak. Well, that's not entirely true. Older practitioners routinely scold me for being restrained with my magic. I lived the first thirty years of my life as a human; I tend to default to human solutions—but not that day.

Frightened and overwhelmed by impending motherhood, I made no effort to contain my powers. No object in the room was off limits. I shattered a port hole and sent a wash basin hurling toward the cabin wall, rescued at the last minute by Greer's lightning reflexes.

When I levitated the bed off the decking, Tori grasped both my hands and flooded my being with her cool, grounding magic. It helped, but nothing took away the pain.

Trust me on this. When you're in labor, you couldn't care less about breaking furniture. You don't care about dragons on the deck, wonky time rivers, and missing temporal artifacts.

In between contractions that seemed to last forever, I cursed every stinking spell-slinging practitioner in my life for failing to teach me the one incantation that mattered—the blessed magic of the epidural.

Chapter Twenty-One

Abandoned Building, Edgar

Instead of lapsing into restful darkness, Edgar felt the weight of gravity pull him steadily downward. He could have fallen for a moment or for an eternity. Slowly, however, he noticed light edging the outer limits of his perception and something moving forward from the shadows.

His old friend, the raven Seneca, glided toward him. The bird alighted on a tree branch that appeared at exactly the second his talons reached for purchase.

"Hello, Edgar," Seneca said nonchalantly. "You look well."

Momentarily taken aback, Edgar felt the flush of annoyance wash over him. "That's all you have to say to me?"

"What would you have me say?"

Rising to a seated position, Edgar probed gingerly at the back of his head. "I don't know," he said, "but I should think my exile might warrant a more effusive reunion."

"As you wish," Seneca said amiably. "You look *very* well."

Still searching for a scalp wound, Edgar scowled at the

raven. "How can I look well when I've just knocked myself unconscious?" he demanded.

Watching him with something akin to amusement, Seneca said, "You won't feel anything back there, you know. You're not really here. Actually *here* isn't here either, but you most certainly are not present—or at least the corporeal aspects of you."

Wincing at the bird's repetitious convolutions, Edgar said, "I assure you that regardless of my form, my head does most assuredly hurt."

"It will hurt a great deal more when you awaken," the bird assured him, "which will occur shortly. We can only converse while you are insensible, so let us attend to our business."

"What business would that be?"

"The business of ensuring that you take the necessary steps to free yourself of your current circumstances."

Crossing his arms over his knees, Edgar asked stubbornly, "Why have you never come to me before?"

"You have never lapsed into unconsciousness before," Seneca said reasonably, "nor has an opportunity arisen for your liberation to be realized."

Staring at the bird with open consternation, Edgar said, "Why did you not tell me that I could communicate with you from an insensate state?"

"Because," Seneca said, fixing a single disapproving eye on Edgar, "I did not think it wise to advise you to knock yourself in the head whenever you wished to have a conversation."

"I would have done more than that to share words with a fellow human being," Edgar snapped.

The raven tilted his head and something like amusement glinted in his eyes. "Perhaps you have failed to notice this salient fact, Edgar, but I am not human."

In spite of himself, Edgar laughed. Then, for reasons not

entirely clear to him, he said, "You are a bird now, but you were once man, were you not?"

"I was."

"How did you come to be as I have always known you?"

"I ran afoul of the politics of Nevermore."

Throwing his hands up in consternation, Edgar said, "Have we not spoken in riddles long enough? What is Nevermore? More to the point, *where* is Nevermore?"

"Nevermore," Seneca said, "lies beyond the land of Tír na nÓg and through the Never Wood. It is bounded on the opposite side by the Never Sea and lies under the dome of the Never Sky. It is Lenore's true home and the place of her unjust incarceration."

Hope lightened Edgar's features. "She is not dead?"

"No," the raven replied, "and I sincerely apologize for telling you otherwise. I worked at the behest of Reynold Isherwood in those days, but my obligation to him ended rather tidily when an ill-tempered sorceress burned him to a crisp in the Tower of Londinium."

That revelation unexpectedly brought tears to Edgar's eyes. Swallowing hard against the lump in his throat, he asked softly, "Did Reynold suffer?"

Seneca blinked several times and cocked his head. "Forgive me," he said. "That was both callous and insensitive. I failed to consider that you might retain sentiment for the man, even after he sent you into exile."

Twin rivulets ran down Edgar's cheeks. "Reynold was good to me in many ways. He encouraged my career and gave me many excellent compositional exercises to hone my skills."

The raven clasped the branch more firmly in his talons, cleared his throat, and leaned forward. "Edgar," he said, "those were not exercises. The topics Reynold set before you for precision crafting were well-conceived literary weapons designed for deployment against Nevermore during the War of Bibliophile Aggression."

"Now I know you are a figment of my imagination," he said. "Such a thing is not possible."

"I assure you it is quite possible," the bird said, "but our window of opportunity has begun to close. All will be explained once you free yourself from this jungle. You have already begun to consider an exit strategy, have you not?"

"I have. Will I be successful?"

"Yes," Seneca replied. "You will be aided by a collection of confederates who will, to your perception, seem quite strange. Believe me that regardless of their form, those who offer the hand of assistance to you are to be trusted. Do not allow yourself to be guided by fear. Be bold, Edgar, if you wish to be free."

Fighting a rising sense of panic at the thought of being alone again, Edgar cried, "Wait! Please! You must tell me more. Why would Reynold involve me in a war without my knowledge?"

Seneca paused and looked into the darkness as if listening to a far distant voice. "I know, Brother," he said, addressing the void. "Give us a few more seconds."

Then he turned back to Edgar. "Reynold made you aware of the Otherworld, but he did not explain the outlier kingdoms, entities that did not join the Confederation of Magical States. Nevermore is one such kingdom. Lenore violated the rules set down by her brothers, the Master Publishers."

Edgar pulled himself onto his knees. "Yet again you speak in riddles. Literary weapons? Master publishers? How am I to believe any of this?"

"You already believe in scriptomancy, Edgar," Seneca said. "Think. You saw Lenore work her sorcery. She was sentenced to a life without pen and paper. Otherwise, she would have used her powers to reach you already."

"What is scriptomancy?"

"The magic of writing, Edgar. Turn your mind backward. You witnessed the castings that brought the scenes she composed to life."

An image rose unbidden in Edgar's mind, an afternoon when he called upon Lenore, several drinks toward intoxication. Her maid showed him to the parlor where, for a split second, he imagined tiny figures waging a battle across the papers covering Lenore's desk.

When a rocket launched from the defending side and hurtled toward the attackers, Edgar gasped. Lenore slammed her pen upon the desk and turned in her chair. The figures were gone.

His eyes locked with Seneca's "That," he whispered, "cannot be."

"That which cannot be," Seneca replied, beginning to fade into the darkness, "is precisely what I find most often to exist. I will see you soon. Join . . . with . . . *Tempus Fugit.*"

Edgar awakened with a start, bolting upright only to groan as the room spun around him. Pain shot through his head. When he put his hand to his hair, it came away covered in blood.

Using the desk for balance, Edgar struggled to his feet and staggered to the wash basin. He wet a towel and pressed it against his throbbing head.

"Time flies?" he whispered. "Why would Seneca tell me to join the flight of time?"

Edgar flinched when a shadow darted across the wall followed in rapid succession by six more. Moving cautiously to the window, he saw a line of the demons . . . no . . . the *dragons* flying in formation toward the river. This was no regular patrol.

Emboldened by his conversation with Seneca, Edgar snatched up the field glasses and hurried downstairs, ducking into the jungle and taking the path toward the river. By his count at least a dozen of the creatures were making for the waterway.

His headache forgotten, Edgar scaled the same tree he'd previously used as an observation post. Lifting the glasses, he studied the behavior of the dragons. They seemed to be flying in a grid formation.

Lost in thought, he watched them for what might have been two hours in the passing of normal time. Then, he spotted a lone yellow dragon flying over the clouds from down river. The beast hovered high over his fellows for several minutes. The riders kept their focus on the jungle below and appeared not to notice.

When the yellow dragon turned and headed back down the river, Edgar trained the glasses on the creature's retreating form —and that's when he saw it: a three-masted schooner moving slowly toward an encounter with the search party.

By some device, the riders also spotted the ship. After a scramble of shouted but unintelligible orders, they maneuvered their dragons into a line across the stream and waited.

When the vessel rounded a bend in the stream, the wind in the sails died. A single dragon rider advanced and addressed the tiny figures on the deck.

Edgar took the glasses away, rubbed at his eyes, and focused again. There was a dragon rider on the ship and behind her on the deck, the yellow dragon.

Within seconds, two riders peeled away and headed cross country toward the mountain fortress. The remaining dragons split into two groups of five flanking the ship, which got underway again with full sails deployed.

As Edgar continued to stare, the pendant on the ship's mast snapped taut so that he could read the words.

Tempus Fugit.

Chapter Twenty-Two

Deck of the Tempus Fugit, Festus

Rube waited for Greer to carry Jinx below before he let out with a low whistle. "Geez *freaking* Lou-eeze!" he said. "Did anybody see *that* coming? 'Cause me? I totally did *not* see that coming. I mean we ain't had time to give her no baby shower or nothing."

Right. Because breeches of social etiquette topped our inventory of current problems. "You're babbling," I told the raccoon. "Don't make me come over there and smack you."

He gave me a round-eyed look. "Maybe smacking me ain't such a bad idea. Could be that last MRE I ate was bad and this is all, like, a hallie-lucinda-nation."

"Nice theory, genius," I replied. "None of the rest of us ate an MRE, and we all saw the same thing."

A burst of profanity from below deck made everyone jump.

The women exchanged a knowing look. "She's in labor," Jilly said. "We have to make a decision. Shouldn't we turn the ship around and go back to Cibolita?"

"You can't do that," Blair said urgently. "Returning to your timespace could harm the baby."

That didn't jive with the girl's previous statements, and I said so. "You told us you've never seen one of these rapid-fire pregnancies. Now you're saying you have?"

"No," Blair said, "but I have read the journals of the First Flight riders. The expectant mothers who tried to return to the Otherworld lost their babies from the stress of the time transition."

So much for an orderly retreat. "Ideas?" I asked the group.

"We could stay at anchor here," Jilly suggested. "Wait for the child to be born and then head back."

A crash sounded beneath our feet followed by a violent splash. Leaning over the railing Miranda said, "Port hole. She blew it clean out of the frame. Witches in labor have trouble controlling their powers."

"What do you know about witches in labor?" I asked.

"I get around," the pirate assured me. "If Jinx has a long, difficult labor, her telekinesis could damage the ship. We need to move her to a setting she can't destroy—or sink— with her magic."

Giallo, who had been silent through the big pregnancy reveal, said, *"Time flows fast today. The Citadel is within reach. Marta can deliver the whelp."*

"Who's Marta?" Jilly asked.

Blair smiled. "My friend. Really my second mother. She will know how to help the Witch of the Oak."

Nothing about Blair or her dragon had touched off major warning bells with me, but I was a long way from agreeing to take Jinx into an unknown stronghold to give birth to the next Daughter of Knasgowa.

"If I agree to that," I said, "and that's a big if, I'm going to need more information first. I'm sure you have questions for us as well. Let's all sit down and take a beat here. Greer and Tori will take care of Jinx."

I didn't mention that Greer would hear every word of our conversation and that I would be seeking the baobhan sith's opinion before making a decision about our next move.

Blair sat down in the chair closest to Giallo and opened the discussion with a blatantly obvious statement.

"You weren't prepared for the temporal inconsistency here, were you?" she asked.

"Why do you say that?" Miranda said.

"Because you wouldn't have allowed a pregnant woman to make the voyage if you had known the risk," Blair said. "The Otherworld no longer remembers the dragon riders."

She had already guessed the truth. Trying to soften the blow wouldn't help.

"It's more a matter of your having been erased than forgotten," I said. "The Ruling Elders destroyed the records pertaining to the dispersal of the Temporal Arcana. We came up here on a hunch."

"What hunch?"

I explained the Virgo symbols Rube found and how he tied the information to the Spica Mountains on Daniel Winter's chart.

"If the Elders destroyed all the records," Blair said, "why didn't they do the same with the documents that contained the Virgo symbol?"

Rube, who had produced a sack of pretzels, munched contemplatively. "The Virgo stamp was mini-school," he said. "Super tiny, like a drop of ink that wasn't supposed to be there. First few pages, I ignored it, but then that same dot kept showing up in the same place, so I blew it up with my phone camera."

Blair frowned. "You did what?"

Wiping off his paws, the raccoon dug his iPhone out of his waist pack and demonstrated.

"The sorcerer who created this device must be powerful indeed," Blair said.

"You ain't gonna believe it," Rube said, "but the humans came up with this one."

Blair shook her head. "Everything you're telling me is so incredible. My father tried to educate me about the Otherworld and the Human Realm. He always believed that our Flight would be recalled, but reading about Fae culture in books is not the same. I don't know what . . . er . . . *who* you all are."

"Well," I said, "you know I'm a werecat. Greer is the baobhan sith."

When Blair's face registered confusion, Rube said helpfully, "Red's a Scottish vampire, but don't worry. She only chows down on salesmen at conventions once or twice a month."

The dragon rider blanched at the word "vampire," but managed to keep herself together, turning next to Miranda.

"Elf," the captain said simply. "Plain old elf, with a few strains of this and that thrown in for flavor."

After Lucy and Jilly identified themselves as avian shifters, I explained that Jinx and Tori were Fae witches, although Tori works primarily in alchemical studies.

That brought Blair forward in her chair. "Oh! There are so many people at the Citadel who will want to talk to her. Many of our riders are amateur alchemists. Ongoing education is a major part of drakonculture."

Lucy cocked her head to the side. "Drakonculture? There's a whole culture associated with dragon riding?"

Blair's face registered shock. "The Ruling Elders erased all memory of drakonculture as well?"

"Any knowledge we have of dragons exists primarily in legend," I told her. "There are half a dozen or so surviving examples of *Draco Europa Giganticus,* and we have dragonlets in North America, but no creatures that match Giallo in size and conformation."

Over the next few minutes, I delivered a tight synopsis about how the Rivers of Time came to be reopened, and I produced my letter of marque from the Ruling Elders. The document granted me the power to negotiate for, confiscate, or if necessary, seize any timefaring artifact we located.

Blair studied the wording. "The First Flight's specific mission during the Great Dispersal was to transport the Hourglass of the Horae."

Finally, some operational forward motion. We had an artifact in our sights. "How many riders were in the First Flight?" I asked.

She lifted her chin proudly. "More than a hundred."

"How many are there now?"

Giallo answered. *"No more than five and twenty,"* he said. *"The alteration of the river signaled a coming change, but our leader, Master Kian, resists."*

Resistance. Rarely a good word.

"What do you mean 'resists'?" I asked.

"With your arrival comes an end to our purpose in this place," the dragon said.

In other words, no one would be offering us the keys to the Citadel.

I looked at Blair. "You said your parents were First Flight riders. They know about the Otherworld. Will they help us negotiate with this Kian?"

When Blair hesitated, Giallo said, *"Adair and Esme faced their final flight as one."*

An awkward silence descended on the group until Rube climbed down and went over to Blair.

He put a hand on her knee. "I'm awful sorry, Dragon Lady.

My folks is gone, too. You don't never quit missing them, but it gets better. Promise."

Tears filled Blair's eyes. "Thank you ... "

"Rube," he said, "my pals call me, Rube."

Blair laughed, scrubbing at her wet cheeks with the back of her hand. "You're sweet."

Grinning, Rube patted her knee again. "Something else this bunch don't always appreciate. You gotta stick around, Dragon Lady. Team Coon could use a smart dame like you." He looked over at Giallo. "You, too, Captain Iguana. Excepting the part about you being a dame, which you ain't."

I'll give the Trash Panda credit. He knows how to lighten the mood.

After a minute, I asked Blair, "How long has it been since you lost your parents?"

"Five rainy seasons."

"Does that mean five years?"

"Here," Blair said, "a 'year' means nothing. In the beginning, the First Flight tried to use the Otherworld system to measure time, but no two days passed in the same way. Now we rise with the sun, sleep when our bodies need rest, and use the arrival of the rains as temporal markers."

"You said the First Flight accepted exile to guard the Hourglass of the Horae," I said. "That's no longer necessary. You can all return to the Otherworld and become part of Fae society again."

Blair shook her head. "Master Kian will have something to say about that."

Extending her wings and ruffling her feathers, Jilly said, "I don't know about Master Kian, but according to the local parrots there are multiple dragons flying search patterns upstream."

My eyebrows went up. Apparently my girlfriend had never

heard of burying the lede. "You're just now getting around to mentioning that?"

Jilly clacked her beak. "In case you missed it, we arrived at roughly the same time Jinx stood up and revealed her pregnancy. You had enough on your hands. The search parties are miles away. Executing a flight grid makes for slow work. There's time before they arrive."

From the guilty look on Blair's face, I suspected I already knew the answer to my next question, but I put it to her anyway. "What are they looking for?"

"Us," she admitted. "Giallo and I aren't supposed to be here."

Chapter Twenty-Three

Deck of the Tempus Fugit, *Festus*

A pregnant witch in uncontrolled telekinetic labor *and* a rogue dragon rider. Thankfully rules don't mean much to me. BEAR operational protocols offered zero guidance for dealing with either problem.

I also wasn't in the mood for more surprises. Making direct eye contact with Blair, I said, "You asked if we came looking for you. I told you the truth. How about repaying the favor?"

A red flush spread over the girl's cheeks, but she didn't evade the question. "Master Kian forbade me and Giallo to patrol the River after the flow changed directions. We defied his orders and investigated anyway. We had no idea we'd find you here."

Miranda instantly hijacked the conversation.

"Wait. The river did *what*?" the captain demanded. "Start at the beginning and tell me everything."

When the temporal rivers burst through the sky into the Middle Realm all kinds of wild theories circulated about the behavior of the waterways on the other side of the openings. I didn't waste my time, reasoning the answer would be different for each one.

Miranda had a more pressing motivation. She wanted the information to ensure the accuracy of her navigational charts, but also to inform future expeditions along other temporal streams.

Knowing that we might be entering areas where the inhabitants could be stirred up from a river upending itself would definitely influence our mission prep.

I let Miranda monopolize the conversation and gather the necessary intel, while I considered the more immediately useful insight in Blair's statement.

Master Kian was a control freak, which made him highly susceptible to manipulation at the paws of someone skilled at pulling his strings.

Cats are all about string pulling.

When Miranda finished, I cleared my throat to get Blair's attention.

"We have to find a safe place for Jinx to have her baby," I said. "There are dragon riders between us and this Citadel of yours. You know these people. I'm open to suggestions."

The girl gazed upriver. "Kian already knows Giallo and I broke our patrol pattern. We could try to divert the search party, but in the end, the consequences will be the same. The Flight will find your vessel. I think it would be better for us to be here when the riders arrive."

"Agreed," I said. "Will Kian be with the search party?"

Blair shook her head. "No. His dragon, Emrellon, injured a wing and hasn't fully recovered. You won't meet Kian until we reach the Citadel."

"We have charts of the river drawn by Miranda's great-great-grandfather," I said. "They suggest we're a day or two away from the Spica tributary. Is that a reliable estimate?"

I jumped when Giallo's answer rumbled through my thoughts.

"The flow of time has increased. We will arrive when the sun sits low on the horizon. Sooner if you make good speed."

A renewed round of crashes and vocal commentary issued from the direction of Jinx's cabin. The *Tempus Fugit* rocked in the water and the sound of groaning lumber made the hairs on the back of my neck stand up.

Rube let out a low, impressed whistle. "*Day-um!* I didn't know Jinx knew them words."

"You haven't heard her mother let loose," I said. "Miranda, step on it. We need to get Jinx on dry land before nightfall."

The captain answered with a curt nod, turned on her heel, and took the steps to the quarterdeck two at a time.

"Exactly how much trouble have you and Giallo created for yourselves?" I asked Blair.

The girl shrugged. "Kian will be angry. He prefers absolute obedience, but to be honest, I'm not sure our future lies with the Flight. Kian may be able to deny that things are changing, but Giallo and I can't—especially in light of all that you've told us."

The dragon stood and stretched, flexing his wings and twisting his neck until it popped. *"I will fly to my brothers and sisters,"* he said. *"Many of the dragons also question Kian's judgment. I will tell them of you."*

I was hardly in a position to order Giallo to stay onboard, but I also didn't want us to be partners in a full-scale revolt against Kian—at least not until we recovered the Hourglass of the Horae.

When I voiced my concern, the dragon responded with an observation that would prove to be both astute and accurate.

"Weak men fear irrelevance," Giallo said. *"Your presence manifests Kian's deepest fears. Even the most careful diplomacy will not change that."*

Rube held up one black paw. "Question. How tall is this Kian guy?"

"About my height," Blair said. "Why?"

The raccoon and I exchanged a knowing look. Blair stood five foot four—maybe five five.

"Sounds like to me he's got himself a Napoleon Bones-apart complex," Rube said, putting one paw under his waist pack and attempting a faux French pout.

Blair frowned. "I don't understand."

"Short guy trying real hard to act tall," Rube replied sagely. "It's like one of them condensation things."

"Compensation," Giallo said.

The dragon caught on fast.

Rube's assessment might be vaguely ridiculous coming from a critter who strains to make two foot one on tiptoe, but the raccoon probably wasn't wrong.

Behind me I heard booted footsteps on the stairs. Greer emerged from the hatch.

"How is Jinx?" Jilly asked. "She's in labor, isn't she?"

The baobhan sith nodded. "Yes, but delivery is not imminent."

"With all that racket she's been making?" I asked. "Are you sure?"

"Yes," Greer replied cryptically. "I am sure. The child is not yet ready to see the world."

I learned a long time ago not to question Greer's vampiric powers. For all I knew, she'd had a conversation with the baby in the womb and asked about the time of delivery.

"You heard what we've been discussing?" I asked.

The baobhan sith nodded.

"Are you good with all of it?"

"Yes," she said, "we must meet Master Kian eventually. Tori has managed to calm Jinx for now, but as her labor progresses, I fear Jinx will seriously damage the ship. The Citadel will be a safer place for the birth to occur."

The rattle and clang of the anchor chain echoed across the water. Over our heads, the sails snapped and filled. As the *Tempus Fugit* lurched forward, I called up to Miranda, "I'm assuming you have no problem with sailing right up to Kian's front door?"

The captain gave me a slow, sly grin. "Wouldn't that be the kindest thing to do?" she asked innocently. "Why make him wait to discover his cherished sense of authority isn't absolute?"

Giallo let out a burst of flame that sent Rube diving for cover. Even as I recoiled from the heat, I realized the dragon was laughing again.

"Turn your approval down a few degrees," I said. "Rube's right. Wooden ship. Fire. Bad combination."

The blast furnace receded. *"Apologies. I relish the prospect of Kian learning that lesson."*

With that, the dragon stood on his hindquarters and pushed off the deck, moving with the fluid, economical grace of a ballet dancer. He cleared the rigging with two powerful wing strokes, rapidly gaining altitude and speed.

Rube's jaw dropped. "Ain't you scared riding him when he does that, Dragon Lady?"

Blair watched Giallo's rapidly diminishing figure with unabashed affection. "Never," she said. "There's no greater sense of exhilaration than sitting astride a dragon in flight. Would you like to go up with us sometime?"

Instead of sputtering out a string of negatives, the raccoon surprised me. "I'll take it under consider-estimation."

"Maybe you did eat a rotten MRE," I said. "Unless my ears deceive me, you just said you'd think about taking a ride on a dragon."

Rube looked offended. "You ain't the only one who can evolvulate, you know."

"I'll bet you a case of Roadkill Ragu you never *evolve* enough to make a dragonflight," I countered.

"Throw in a case of twinkies and you're on."

"Done."

We sealed the deal with a spit handshake that touched off some unnecessarily pointed commentary from Lucy about gross male bonding rituals.

Jilly saved the conversation from taking a dive into a gender norm debate. "We should get airborne, too," she said. "The more eyes in the sky, the better."

"Hang back when the search party shows up," I said. "If this meeting goes south, we may need you out there in the jungle."

Flexing one claw, Jilly said, "We're already outnumbered."

"Outnumbered, maybe, but not outwitted."

When the two birds headed for the jungle, Greer and I moved toward the canopy. The instant I smelled the remaining breakfast food, my stomach growled. I'd barely had three sips of coffee before Blair and Giallo appeared over the ship, and nothing to eat.

Greer claimed her seat, first sipping at a fresh cup of tea. She watched in silence as I filled a plate. When I joined her, I said, "You've seen dragon riders before." It wasn't a question.

"I have," Greer said, "centuries ago. They were once great Fae warriors."

"Why have I never heard about this?"

The baobhan sith shrugged. "We had no reason to speak of it. The only surviving remnants of drakonculture lie amid the ruins of Drake Abbey in the Middle Realm."

During the tenure of the Agreement, the Middle Realm was theoretically sealed off, but that didn't stop Greer from maintaining a mostly business relationship with Fer Dorich, the

Godfather of the In Between. I trusted her to have inside information.

"Why was the abbey abandoned?"

"The dragon riders were rumored to have quit the abbey of their own accord," Greer said. "Blair's story invalidates that interpretation."

I started to raise a hind paw to scratch my whiskers but stopped before I dislocated a hip. The human form doesn't lend itself to feline moves.

"The dragon riders wouldn't be the first group to get a raw deal courtesy of the Ruling Elders," I said. "Those guys don't always represent our brightest and best."

"They are politicians," the baobhan sith said. "Whether Fae or human, the profession erodes common sense in direct proportion to the length of their public service."

No argument from me on that analysis.

"We can't forget that we're here to locate elements of the Temporal Arcana," I said.

Greer raised her tea cup, pausing to look at me over the rim. "We cannot forget that we are here to protect the Witch of the Oak."

Typically I don't react well to people who decide to school me on my job. "You have an objection to multi-tasking?"

"Studies suggest that dividing one's attention degrades performance," she said mildly.

"*Human* studies. I think we can manage to take care of Jinx *and* snag the Hourglass of the Horae."

"Master Kian will not simply hand it to you. Have you crafted a plan?"

"Yeah," I said, spearing a sausage. "We're going to play it by ear."

Rube, who had happily seized the chance for his third—or maybe fourth—breakfast shook his head. "Pardon me for saying that strategy ain't instilling no particular confidence in me, McGregor."

Great. Now I was getting lip from the Trash Panda section. "Why would that be, Striped Tail?"

"'Cause," he replied, reaching for a knife, "I been to karaoke night at the Dirty Claw."

Resigning myself to negotiating the raccoon's latest twisted logic detour, I said, "What does that have to do with anything?"

Slathering enough butter on a biscuit to shoot my cholesterol up 200 points, he said, "'Cause playing it by ear ain't gonna do you or us no good when you can't carry a tune in a bucket."

"You have a better idea?"

"As a matter of factual point, no," he said. "But I say we follow the big lizard's lead."

I frowned. "Giallo?"

"Yep," Rube said, brushing crumbs off his chest. "Sure as dumpsters is sticky and road kill stinks, Captain Iguana's up to something."

Chapter Twenty-Four

The Skies Over the River of Virgo, Giallo

Giallo surged through the humid layers of air hanging above the river. His flight pierced the clouds, carrying him into the high cooler spaces. Only then did he set his course downstream. The yellow drake didn't need his eyes to find the searching dragons nor did he want the eyes of their riders to find him.

The fate of the Flight sat poised at a critical juncture. The next series of decisions were best left to drakonkind. Too many among the riders, including Master Kian, seemed to forget the underlying principle of the relationship between their species—free will.

No dragon had ever been domesticated or broken. The Fae sat astride their backs because the dragons *allowed* it. They *allowed* themselves to be husbanded into a smaller form. They *allowed* the protracted exile in the Spica Mountains.

But if they *allowed* Kian's shortsighted fears to determine their future, the fool would doom them all to extinction.

Giallo flew to meet his brothers and sisters to seek a consensus. Once the dragons agreed to a plan, they could guide their Fae partners.

He began that process aboard the *Tempus Fugit* when he disclosed his telepathic abilities to the newcomers. By displaying his trust, Giallo dispelled any suspicions Blair might harbor toward the werecat McGregor and his companions.

Like all dragons, Giallo recognized the dissonance of lies. He heard none as he pretended to doze on the ship's deck.

The Ruling Elders sought the return of the Temporal Arcana; Giallo intended for them to have the Hourglass of the Horae and more.

The night before, Eingana confided to him that in the dreams she shared with their child, the whelp yearned to hatch.

By tradition, Eingana held the gender of their child in secret, but she smiled and nuzzled Giallo when she said, *"Our whelp is like you, husband. Strong willed."*

"Then let us hope the whelp also listens to your reasonable voice, my love."

"My comforting purrs and entreaties to remain within the shell will not work much longer, Giallo," she warned. *"The child yearns to meet the world. You know the force of that desire."*

Giallo did know. He remembered his excitement when muffled sounds penetrated the thin shell of his own birth egg. As his mind awakened and he ranged the dreamscape with his mother, Giallo learned the first lessons of drakonkind.

Increasingly the shell that protected and nurtured him became an unwelcome restraint. His son or daughter had begun to experience the same feeling.

In contrast, the Fae mind developed in turgid stages. Blair retained no perceptions from within her mother's womb and possessed only cloudy images before the first year of life. She could not relive the moment when she first saw the sun or felt her mother's tender caress.

Dragons relished every second of being from the first to the last, understanding that regardless of the span of years attained, no treasure surpassed the preciousness of life's spark.

Unable to measure time accurately without clever devices, the Citadel riders failed to grasp the true length of their residence in the Spica Mountains.

The ignorance McGregor and the others displayed about drakonculture confirmed what Giallo already knew. The Otherworld no longer remembered the alliance between his kind and the Fae.

They had forgotten that in the days of the Tuatha Dé Danann the great creatures reached out to the Elvish races before slowly extending their friendship throughout Fae society.

The dragons searched for candidates with the innate talent to form a mental bond. In partnership with those pioneering riders, Giallo's ancestors helped to found drakonculture.

While their distant cousins, the European dragons, lounged in solitary caves hoarding treasure, the working dragons populated the mighty drakon abbeys scattered throughout the Middle Realm.

Giallo's line descended from the dragons of Drake Abbey. He felt a responsibility to see that once great mother house restored. The alteration of the River of Virgo and the arrival of the *Tempus Fugit* would have been enough to convince Giallo that what had been a dream was now his destiny, but then he heard the heartbeat of the witch's child.

The baby Jinx Hamilton carried was to the dragons born.

As he neared the patrols flying grids beneath the clouds, Giallo made his presence known to his brothers and sisters.

The dragons shared a collective awareness and social structure apart from the bonds they forged with their riders, one that did not rely on the slow convention of speech.

With flashing images, Giallo shared the form and texture of

the encounter aboard the *Tempus Fugit*. He opened his feelings about the unborn whelp in Eingana's egg and his new knowledge concerning the Fae child waiting to meet the world.

Then he put an elemental question to his fellow dragons. *If we do not act, how will our kind survive?*

Multi-layered concerns and reactions flowed back from a dozen voices. Eager, curious, cautious, and daring all at once.

Do the strangers bring word of the other flights?
How can Kian deny the authority of the Elders?
Is this not the day for which we have waited?
Does the witch know her daughter is dragon born?
And finally:
What do you ask of us, Giallo?
The drake's reply carried conviction and confidence.
When I move to secure our future, Kian will order the riders into the skies to stop the visitors. In that moment, I ask only that you refuse to take flight.

~

The Deck of the Tempus Fugit, *Festus*

Blair and Miranda worked through a complicated set of temporal navigational computations to arrive at an estimated time of arrival at the Citadel.

"We can make better time than Giallo suggested," Miranda said at last. "Two hours to the tributary and then another forty-five minutes to reach the port beneath the Citadel."

That last bit surprised me. "You have a port?" I asked Blair.

"'Port' may be a bit grandiose," she replied. "Workers dismantled the supply ships that accompanied the First Flight and used the timbers to construct the fortress. They preserved the docks for the fishing boats that augment the Citadel's food supply. The craft confine their activities to the tributary. They're too small to navigate the main river."

Out of nowhere, Rube hit my chest like a guided missile and yelled, *"Incoming!"*

The force of the airborne raccoon knocked me clear as Lucy shot over the bow, coming in for a beak-jarring landing.

Panting from the exertion, the raven gasped out, "Jilly's right behind me."

"Why do I think I'm not going to like this?" I said.

"Because you won't," Jilly answered as she glided past, extending her wings to alight on the nearest chairback. "There are a dozen dragons waiting around the next bend."

Rube clapped a paw over his mask and groaned, "That ain't good. Where's Captain Iguana when we need him?"

"*Here*," Giallo said, his voice penetrating all our thoughts at once.

Looking up, I spotted the drake. His wings lay folded against his body as he dove through the clouds.

Somewhere near my knees Rube gulped. "He's got brakes, right?"

"Bastet's whiskers, I hope so," I breathed, stunned by the dragon's physical power and the sheer velocity of his flight.

Even Greer, the imperturbable baobhan sith, paled as she watched his plummeting descent.

Blair, on the other hand, regarded Giallo with a mixture of love and awe. "Just watch," she murmured.

Giallo waited until the last moment to unfurl his wings and coil his body backward, throwing out his hind legs to make contact with the deck. The force of the landing rocked the *Tempus Fugit* in the water.

"Show off," Blair said, going to the dragon and running her hand along the length of his snout.

Only seconds passed, but I suspected the two of them shared

a private exchange before Blair broke away and spoke to me. "The waiting dragons will escort us to the Citadel."

"That don't sound like no welcome wagon to me," Rube observed.

Giallo's rough chuckle rumbled across our thoughts. *"Do not fear my brothers and sisters. Unlike Kian, they seek truth."*

The assurance eased some of my worry, but not enough to throw caution to the winds. "Jilly, Lucy, get back into the jungle and stay there."

Without warning, Jilly flew toward me. I barely had time to raise my arm to give her a perch before we were beak to nose. "We won't be far away," she said softly. "Take care of yourself."

"You, too," I said, holding her gaze for a long moment before she took off with Lucy close behind.

Clearing my throat, I said to Miranda, "Turn up the wind. I don't like tentative arrivals."

"Me, either," the captain said, moving to stand at the ship's wheel with the rest of us arrayed behind her in loose formation.

When we cleared the bend in the river, we saw them. A suspended line of waiting dragons, winged jewels in tones of vermillion, sage, indigo, azure, ginger, and amethyst.

Hyperboles and hairballs are different sides of the same disgusting coin, but I agreed with Rube when he whispered, "By the Trash Gods! Ain't they beautiful?"

They were—a beauty that transcended their colors and tight aerial alignment. The creatures conveyed a timeless majesty that stretched far beyond the origins of the Fae.

Miranda brought the ship to a stop less than a hundred yards from the riders. A youngish man with reddish hair astride the azure dragon nudged his mount forward. "Blair McBride, Master Kian commands your presence at the Citadel."

The slender girl's voice rang across the water. "Tell Kian I return to the Citadel in the company of new friends sent by the Ruling Elders to end our exile."

Up and down the line heads swiveled in confusion, but the dragons remained completely serene.

"Kian will demand proof," the red-headed youth said at last.

"He shall have it," Blair replied.

The boy hesitated. "Will you fly with me to the Citadel to deliver this news?"

"No," Blair said. "I will not. Giallo and I stand with the newcomers. Now make way so that we may pass."

Her bluff worked. The line parted with five dragons each taking up position on either side of the *Tempus Fugit*. The rider who had spoken for the group and the woman on the sage drake headed upriver.

"Dragon Lady," Rube said quietly, "you do know you just threw down a cutlet, right?"

"Gauntlet," Blair replied without missing a beat.

"Cutlet, gauntlet. Either way, there ain't no turning back now."

Chapter Twenty-Five

The Tempus Fugit, *Festus*

With the ship underway again, Greer and I went to Jinx's cabin to bring her up to speed. I didn't expect to find the Witch of the Oak in any shape to weigh in on mission decisions, but if I didn't at least try to keep her in the loop, I'd hear about it later.

We paused outside the door. Deferring to the baobhan sith's superior hearing, I whispered, "What's going on in there?"

"Tori is using the psychic connection they share to help Jinx manage the contractions and keep her energies at a more stable level."

"Maybe we shouldn't disturb them."

Greer arched an eyebrow and gave me a wry smile that left me squirming before she said a word. "Why are males so ludicrously uncomfortable at the conclusion of a process in which they play an instigating role?"

Faced with going into the room with a witch in labor or talking reproductive psychology with a vampire, I rapped lightly on the door.

Tori answered. "Come on in, you big fraidy cat."

I pushed the door open, but not before hissing at Greer, "Would it have *hurt* you to tell me she could hear us?"

The state of the room left me speechless. The place looked worse than the Wrecking Crew treehouse after a marathon poker game.

When the porthole blew out, several planks of paneling went with it, leaving a splintered, gaping hole to the outside that now shimmered with translucent barrier magic. Debris littered the floor, and I spotted a handful of cotton swabs driven clean through the top of the table.

Tori sat in a chair by the lower bunk holding both of Jinx's hands. The women's eyes were closed. Rodney sat on the pillow next to Jinx's head, running one paw comfortingly through her hair. He waved his free paw at me; I waggled my fingers in response.

The mother-to-be looked better than I expected, but Tori couldn't hide her exhaustion. Heavy black shadows under her eyes stood out starkly against deathly pale skin. For a second I thought Jinx was asleep until she grimaced and shifted in the bed.

"Greer," she said hoarsely, "please take over here and make Tori rest and get some food."

Tori's jaw set in a stubborn line. "I'm not leaving."

The baobhan sith laid a hand on her shoulder. "We will stay with Jinx until you return. She will have greater need of you in the hours ahead."

She didn't like it, but Tori relinquished her position and headed up top. When the baobhan sith took Jinx's hands, green fire flared in the vampire's eyes and a wind I couldn't feel moved through her thick russet hair.

Jinx instantly looked like a dose of good drugs had just hit her system. "You're stronger than Tori," she murmured.

"Not stronger," Greer said, "only different."

After a few seconds, Jinx blinked to sharpen her focus and looked up at me with sleepy amusement. "It's not contagious, Festus. Sit down."

Perching gingerly at the foot of the bunk, I said, "Bastet knew what She was doing when she gave this job to women. Men could *not* do this."

"Men can't *do* the common cold," Jinx said. "What's been going on up there?"

Whatever Greer was doing, Jinx not only followed what I had to say, she asked several probing questions. The conversation seemed to be distracting her, so I answered at length, trying to paint a vivid word picture of the morning's events. In the end, though, we needed to confront the question of where her child would be delivered.

Drawing in a long breath, I plunged forward. "So, kiddo, here's the long and the short of it. We have to get you off this ship before this child is born because you might sink us."

Jinx blinked. "Did you just call me 'kiddo'?"

I grinned. "I am 70 years and change older than you."

She chuckled. "You're one in a million, Festus."

Faking a scowl, I said, "Just a million?"

The light-hearted exchange allowed Jinx to drop her brave face. When she spoke again, her voice quivered, "I don't want my baby born in a strange place."

My heart went out to her. She'd been hit by a maternal freight train with zero time to adjust. Rodney reacted much the same way, nestling against Jinx's chin to offer as much comfort as his tiny body could provide.

"I know, honey," I said softly, "but we don't have a choice. We need this ship to get home. Miranda checked out that groaning lumber sound we heard. She found—and patched—a leak in the hull."

Jinx started to cry. "I didn't mean to do that."

Rodney instantly began to wipe away her tears with his tiny pink feet. I wanted to wrap the poor kid in a protective, fatherly hug. Jinx and Chase were doomed as a couple from day one, but if things had been different, I would have loved to have this exceptional, kind-hearted young woman for a daughter-in-law.

"Of course you didn't mean to," I assured her. "We know that. Remember that promise I made to you back home? I won't let anything happen to you or your baby, Jinx. You know that. You have my solemn word on Knasgowa's grave."

Jinx nodded and swallowed hard against the lump in her throat. "I want Lucas."

"Then let's get this baby into the world and get you home to him. Deal?"

"Deal," she said. "Do what you think is best. I trust you, Festus."

When her eyes drooped closed, I stood up and moved to face Greer. Mouthing the words, I said, "We need to talk. Privately."

The baobhan sith nodded. The wind returned and green embers glowed in the depths of her gaze. The muscles in Jinx's face went slack. Rodney sat up and carefully moved across her chest, inviting himself into our conversation.

"She is asleep," Greer said. "But I cannot keep her in this state long for fear of harming the child."

Pitching my voice low, I said, "How long do we have before this kid gets here?"

"The child will wait."

That was cryptic, even for the baobhan sith. "Say again?"

"The child says she will wait until her mother is in a safe place."

So. My suspicions were correct. "The baby really is talking to you?" I asked. "With words?"

The light in the baobhan sith's eyes darkened to emerald.

"She both speaks and listens. This is no ordinary child, Festus. She is exceptional, even for the daughter of a tree witch. She is eager to enter the world within the walls of the Citadel among the dragon riders."

"Why?"

"That," Greer said quietly, "is not for me to say."

Rodney held up his paw.

"You have something to add, Short Stuff?" I asked.

He pointed at the waist pack hanging undisturbed on its peg. I reached over and took it down, unzipping the top. Rodney dug around inside, opened a hidden pocket, and pulled out a fat toothpick with a red end.

"What the hell is that?" I asked.

The rat made a motion describing a magnifying glass. "Do I look like a witch?" I said. "How am I supposed to magnify that thing?"

"You don't have to," Greer said. "I can see the object quite well. It is a wand, with a dragon etched on the shaft."

Rodney nodded vigorously, pointed to Jinx's swollen belly, and went through a complicated series of gestures.

"The wand belongs to the kid," I translated. "Knasgowa gave it to you. The dragon on the shaft showed up before we left. What in the name of Bastet's litter box is all that supposed to mean?"

He shrugged.

"You're a big help," I groused. "Don't show that wand to anybody, okay? We have enough problems."

Making a locking gesture over his lips, Rodney slid the wand back in the pocket.

After the exchange with Greer and Rodney in Jinx's cabin, I

didn't exactly enjoy the rest of our journey to the Citadel camped out on deck with an umbrella drink.

We were on our way to confront a control freak dragon master and turn his fortress into a maternity ward.

"Yeah, Kian? Hi. Festus McGregor here. The Ruling Elders sent me to take your pet time artifact. In the meantime, can our pregnant witch use your fortress as a delivery room? Thanks, man. Really appreciate it."

Jinx's unborn child seemed to be calling far too many of the shots in this whole caper for my comfort, *and* ten big ole flying lizards flanked the ship with an eleventh napping near the bow.

If I'd been free to shift, I probably would have used the deck boards for a scratching post to work off some steam. Instead, I was left to pace restlessly.

When Greer emerged from below deck, she intercepted me near the foot of the main mast. The position allowed us to speak quietly while still keeping an eye on the dragons flying high to port and starboard.

"Were you in feline form," the baobhan sith said, "I would be tempted to ask who stepped on your tail."

"Very funny," I growled. "Right now I wish I had a tail. Being bipedal this long makes me antsy."

Point of order, I wouldn't recommend growling at vampires unless you consider them to be close friends. The grumpier I get, the more amusing the baobhan sith finds me. My jugular vein was safe.

"Facing Master Kian on two legs presents the better option," Greer said. Then lowering her voice, she added, "Especially assuming he mirrors the true form of his riders. That appears to be a minor detail Blair neglected to mention. You smell them, too, don't you?"

That *minor* detail was a whopper. All the dragon riders were weretigers. In Blair's defense, she probably didn't mention it because to her tigers flying around on dragons wasn't odd at all.

"I didn't pick up their scent until they moved alongside the ship," I admitted. "Why would an entire dragon flight be made up of weretigers?"

That wasn't a rhetorical question. Greer had several centuries on me age-wise. I figured she might know something I didn't. As usual, the baobhan sith didn't disappoint.

"You are too young to have traveled in the regions once referred to as the Orient," she said. "During the Inquisition, I found Europe tiresome. All those pious torture chambers and public burnings. For much of that time I resided in China."

Searching my memory and running the dates, I said, "Didn't the Inquisition last 700 years?"

"Give or take a few decades," Greer replied. "I returned to the West as needed. When Ferdinand and Isabella began the Spanish Inquisition in 1478, however, my visits became more sporadic."

When you pose a question to a really old Fae, you always risk protracted history lessons prefacing the main point. I tried to nudge her along. "What does that have to do with weretigers and dragons?"

"Zhu Jianshen, the Chenghua Emperor, was the ninth ruler of the Ming Dynasty," Greer said. "The imperial concubine, Consort Wan, dominated his court until her death in 1487. The Lady Wan even went so far as to keep the birth of the crown prince from the Emperor. She hid the child from his father for five years. I found her quite fascinating."

I started to say "I bet you did," and caught myself. You can only push vampiric good graces so far. "This Lady Wan was a weretiger?" I asked.

"No, but she had an appetite for the . . . *company* . . . of weretigers."

That made me want to clap my hands over my ears and chant "lala lala lala la." Even international cats of mystery fear the perils of "too much information." I went with a knowing nod that encouraged Greer to keep talking.

"In Chinese belief the Tao embodies the duality of the Universe. The coiled, patient power of the tiger and the bold, open energy of the dragon symbolize the concepts of Yin and Yang. When combined, their union heralds well-being and good fortune."

Cocking an eyebrow, I said, "They get along well?"

The baobhan sith laughed. "Yes. In the legends, the first dragons sought out the most compatible Fae species with whom to form a bond. I would surmise weretigers emerged as especially strong candidates."

I wasn't sure how that insight might help when we faced Master Kian, but any information was better than none. "Anything else?"

Greer looked toward Giallo's reclining form. "According to Lady Wan, the most powerful connections were those forged between a weretigress and a male dragon. Perhaps this explains why Kian seems threatened by Blair and Giallo."

Don't talk in front of a "sleeping" dragon if you don't want him to join in the conversation.

"The drinker of blood understands," Giallo said.

When the baobhan sith didn't react to the statement, I took a chance that I was having a solo communication with the drake.

"Can you hear me?" I thought.

"Yes."

"When I explain that I have the authority to take the Hourglass of the Horae, will Kian hand it over?"

"No, but you shall have it all the same. Be flexible, werecat. Watch and listen. You will know when to act."

Try as I would, I couldn't get Giallo to say more, but Rube's words came back to me, speculating how much the dragon wanted to leave the Spica Mountains—*"he ain't gonna much care what it takes to pull that off."*

The raccoon was right. Giallo was up to something, and he'd just told me to be ready when he made his move.

As Miranda guided the *Tempus Fugit* out of the main stream and into the tributary, the narrowness of the waterway forced our dragon escorts to assume a higher altitude, which in turn gave us some breathing room.

Scanning the jungle, I caught glimpses of Lucy and Jilly in the canopy.

After our conversation, Greer went back to reading her book, rather than returning to Jinx's cabin. To the casual observer the baobhan sith looked unflappable and vaguely bored, but I knew those sharp vampiric senses remained on high alert. If the situation went south, she wanted to be on deck and on hand.

The captain manned the ship's wheel with Blair nearby. Rube camped out on the deck playing solitaire, drinking orange soda, and rhythmically dipping chips into an oversized jar of salsa he'd retrieved from our cabin.

"You told me you only packed MREs," I said.

Shifting the queen of hearts onto the king of spades, the raccoon said, "Custom-built suitcase. It's got a false bottom for medicinal snacks."

"Chips and salsa are medicinal?"

"Well, *duh*."

"And why exactly do you need medicine?"

He looked at me like I'd lost my mind. "We ain't all got iced catnip for blood, McGregor. I'm freaking *nervous*, okay?"

"You don't look nervous."

"Which would be because I'm taking my meds," he said, dunking another chip. "Sometimes I swear to the Trash Gods you was dropped on your head when you was a kitten."

Muttering invectives about mouthy stripe-tailed vermin, I went over to Miranda. "How much longer?"

Blair answered. "Not long. You can see the uppermost levels of the Citadel now."

Squinting in the direction she pointed, I made out rows of openings at the top of a dark rock face forward and to our left.

"What are those arches?"

"Landing pads," Blair replied. "Dragons and their riders share quarters. The river will turn two more times and then the docks will come into view."

Below us on the main deck, Greer heard the girl's words. The baobhan sith marked her place, put the book down, and climbed the steps to stand with us.

"Okay, listen up everybody," I said. "We need to be on the same page before we get to the Citadel. Blair, how is this meeting likely to go down?

"I expect Kian to be waiting on the dock," she said. "He will have ordered the remaining riders of the flight to be aloft at the base of the cliff in a display of manpower."

Rube gathered up his cards, stuffed them in his waist pack, and finished off the salsa and chips. "So," he said, brushing his paws together, "we gonna get tossed in a dungeon or what?"

"Hardly," Blair said. "He'll make a show of wanting to see your letters of marque. Kian isn't a fool. He won't turn away a representative of the Ruling Elders nor will he deny aid to a distressed witch in labor, but he will put on a show before he says yes."

"Great," Rube said, "a poser. But he'll wind up caving?"

"He will," she said. "After he agrees to letting the Citadel healers help the Witch of the Oak, I imagine Kian will offer you the hospitality of the fortress for dinner and lodging—and then do everything he can to keep the conversation away from the Hourglass of the Horae."

"That's fine," I said. "We'll take him up on everything except the rooms. I know Tori. She won't leave Jinx's side. Greer, you stay with them and keep an eye on Rodney. The rest of us will come back to the *Tempus Fugit* at the end of the evening. Understood?"

Everyone nodded. I knew Tori would guard Jinx like an overprotective werebadger, but with Greer's night vision and lightning reflexes I could be assured they'd both be safe—plus she could get them out of the fortress if need be.

Greer keeps a particularly handy trick in her bag of vampiric skills: the flight of the baobhan sith. It's about as smooth as riding an F-5 tornado but effective as hell with unlimited mileage.

That left one question unanswered. "What about you, Blair?" I asked. "What happens to you once we dock at the Citadel?"

The girl set her jaw. "It doesn't matter what happens with Master Kian. When you leave the Spica mountains, Giallo and I want to go with you."

For the record, I didn't realize what I was signing on to when I said yes.

Chapter Twenty-Six

The Tempus Fugit, *Festus*

Blair knew her boss well. When we rounded the second bend, a short, stocky figure stood at the end of the wooden pier, legs planted wide in a pugnacious, authoritarian stance.

"See," Rube said, elbowing me in the knee. "Total Bones-apart complex."

A dozen dragon riders hovered their mounts above and behind Master Kian, shielding the face of the Citadel with their bodies. On cue, our escorts peeled off and assumed position in the formation.

Blair moved to stand beside us. "Are you okay with this?" I asked.

"Yes," she said. "I know what I have to do."

"But ain't those people friends of yours?" Rube asked.

She nodded grimly. "The two riders flying each end of the wing are my *best* friends, Maeve and Davin."

The raccoon looked up at her. "It ain't easy leaving your pals, Dragon Lady."

"If I know them as well as I think I do," Blair said, "they'll make the right choice."

When shifters are in human form, we feel the vestigial reactions of our alternate selves. Her words made my fur stand on end.

"We're not here to start a full-scale revolt," I reminded her.

She confronted me with an intensity I didn't expect. "You would turn them away if they asked for your help in leaving this land?"

People who stand up for their buddies rank high in my estimation. "No, I would not," I said, "but hold off on the insurrection until we're on our way out the door."

Blair inclined her head in acquiescence, which did nothing to keep me from worrying about what she and Giallo might get it in their heads to do next.

"So," I said, "twenty-two in the air. Giallo is twenty-three. How many more dragons in the flight?"

"Two," she said. "Giallo's mate, Eingana—she will be coming with us when we leave—and Kian's injured drakaina, Emrellon."

"Understood. What about Eingana's rider?"

"Miriam died in an accident before the last rainy season," Blair replied. "Eingana has not chosen a new rider."

We fell silent a hundred yards from the pier. Miranda docked the ship and expertly tossed the mooring line toward one of the cleats where the cable looped itself in place.

When she deployed the gang plank, I squared my shoulders and walked down to meet Kian. Greer and Rube came next, followed by Miranda and Blair.

Kian met me halfway. "Welcome to the Spica Citadel," he said. "To whom do I have the pleasure of speaking?"

All feline species are capable of territorial aggression, a tendency exacerbated by the solitary nature of all tigers.

Weretigers are not an exception, but in theory their cat brain can be influenced by their human mind.

Honestly, I could make the same set of statements about the nature of mountain lions. But of the two of us, I was betting on Kian being the one to turn our first meeting into a hissing, trash talking alley cat fight if I gave him the opportunity.

I know how to mark my turf without resorting to the use of bodily fluids, which I accomplished by firing a full spread of title torpedoes.

"Festus McGregor, Chief of the Werecat Clan McGregor, Guardian of the Daughters of Knasgowa, Senior Agent with the Bureau of Enchanted Artifacts and Relics, and Head of the Blacklist Temporal Arcana Taskforce. These are my associates, the baobhan sith Greer MacVicar, Senior Agent with the Division for Grid Integrity; Reuben Stripedtail, Senior Recovery of Magical Objects Specialist; Captain Miranda Winter, Mistress of the *Tempus Fugit* out of the Middle Realm port of Cibolita; and I believe you know Blair McBride. The Witch of the Oak, Jinx Hamilton, and the Alchemist Tori Andrews are below deck. The Witch of the Oak requires the assistance of your Citadel."

Kian looked like I smacked him in the whiskers. After several seconds he awkwardly extended his hand. "An honor Chief McGregor. Kian Abercrombie, Master of the Spica Citadel."

When I shook his hand, I throttled back a notch. "You can call me Festus."

Regaining some of his footing, Kian said, "Festus, may I ask how one of my riders came to be in your company?"

"Blair and Giallo happened upon us while they were patrolling the River of Virgo," I said smoothly. "They were kind enough to escort us to your doorstep."

Overhead dragon wings moved restlessly, but I kept my eyes

on Kian. The guy was mad enough to chew nails, but he had to play diplomat.

"How . . . *hospitable* . . . of them both," he said tightly. "Blair, I think you and Giallo can return to your posts now."

Blair let several tense seconds pass before she answered. "Master Kian, I resign my commission with the Citadel Wing and pledge allegiance to the Witch of the Oak and her companions."

Medically speaking, I don't think it's healthy for a guy as stout as Kian to turn the color of an eggplant. "You can't resign your commission," he snapped. "You are to the dragons born."

She stayed cool as catnip on a winter morning. "It is for that reason that I have chosen to sever my relationship with the Flight. Giallo and I believe the future of drakonculture lies beyond this place."

That was enough to unleash Kian's temper and his bad judgment. "I will not allow you to abscond with one of my drakes."

Giallo uncoiled from the deck and landed on the pier. I was proud of Rube; he never flinched.

The planks bowed under the dragon's weight and percussion waves radiated across the harbor. One of the hovering dragons snorted fire and another flapped its wings violently.

None of the dragons took kindly to Kian's claim of ownership over Giallo.

The yellow drake's thunderous words penetrated all our thoughts, leaving no one in doubt about his feelings regarding the Master's proprietary attitude.

"A dragon belongs to no man, Kian Abercrombie. Claim you otherwise?"

The Master faltered, casting a nervous glance toward the members of his flight and their mounts. "I misspoke," he stammered. "I meant to say that we would grieve the loss of your comradeship, Giallo."

The dragon exhaled a cloud of soot. *"A wise retraction."*

With that he extended a foreleg to Blair who climbed aboard, settling smoothly in place behind his massive head.

Without another word, the drake sprang from the pier. He angled past the Flight and headed along the face of the mountain before settling on a landing pad in the upper tier.

I let the effect of the exit linger before saying pleasantly, "Now that we have that out of the way, let us return to the matter at hand, Kian. The Witch of the Oak requires your assistance."

No longer confronted by a bellicose fire-breathing beast, Kian's native arrogance returned. "Your group has already caused discord in my ranks. Why should I extend the hospitality of this Citadel to a Tree Witch who will not even show her face in greeting?"

Before I could pin the pompous twerp's ears back, an old woman did it for me.

"Kian Abercrombie!" she said. "How dare you insult the Rightful Companion of a Mother Tree?"

She waved her cane to clear a path through the small knot of curious onlookers gathered on the shore and stumped toward the Master. I could see in Kian's body language that he'd received more than one dressing down at this woman's hands.

When she confronted him head on, the Master affected a fake smile tinged with unctuous concern. "Marta, you should not over-exert yourself."

"Judging from the expansion of your waistline, Kian, I doubt your familiarity with exertion," she retorted. Then, turning to me, she asked, "What ails the Witch of the Oak?"

Bowing respectfully from the waist, I said, "Madam, she is with child. Her delivery draws near, but she displays symptoms of telekinetic labor. We require a secure location so that she may give birth in safety."

Kian couldn't help himself. "Your ship isn't safe?" he asked testily.

Marta wheeled on him again. I wouldn't have been surprised in the least if she'd thwacked him with her cane. "Have you ever witnessed a witch in telekinetic labor?" she demanded.

Jinx blames the baby for what happened next. A long, moaning wail pierced the air before descending into deliciously colorful bursts of profanity.

Rube grabbed his iPhone and managed to record the last few seconds.

"What do you think you're doing?" I said under my breath.

"We got the fourth annual Cuss-a-Coon Charity Marathon coming up," he whispered loudly. "I'm entering that in the 'Caught on Tape For Freaking Real' event. *Day-um!* I am totally walking away with the five-star dumpster gift certificates this year."

"I'm so happy we could arrange that for you," I growled. "Now put that damn thing away and act like a professional."

If Kian picked up on the exchange, the cannon balls prevented him from reacting.

The *Tempus Fugit* carried four eight-pounder deck guns, which Miranda admitted she liked more for their decorative effect than any real need of weaponry. If you're not up on your nautical ballistics, which I wasn't until I came under actual fire, the "eight pounds" refers to the size of the big cast iron spheres that started bouncing off the pier.

Okay, most of them bounced. Several others pierced the boards and kicked up sprays of river water—which conveniently doused Kian, leaving him dripping with silent outrage and rapidly dissolving dignity.

"I believe my point regarding telekinetic labor has been made," Marta said in a lecturing tone. "I'll send for a stretcher."

Greer who had been silent and still—except for batting away

a couple of the projectiles that came too close to her vampire self—spoke up. "There is no need. I will carry the Witch of the Oak."

One minute the baobhan sith was with us on the pier, the next she was gone. When she reappeared, Jinx was in her arms. Tori followed with a bag and Rodney's pack around her waist.

When they came down the gangplank, Jinx made eye contact with Kian. "Thank you for your hospitality. I apologize for our abrupt arrival."

Any man in his right mind knows better than to insult a pregnant woman in front of witnesses. Kian played it smart. He went down on one knee and said, "*Quercus de Pythonissam*, you honor us with your presence. We are at your service."

As Greer and Tori followed Marta down the pier, I smiled at Kian, "I think we got off to a bad start. Maybe we should go somewhere and talk."

The master stood, struggling to regain a shred of his cherished authority—a tall order since he looked like (apologies to Rodney) a drowned rat.

"Of course," he said stiffly. "Please join us for dinner. I will have rooms prepared for the night."

"Thank you," I replied graciously. "Dinner sounds lovely, but we prefer to sleep aboard our vessel. Now tell me about this magnificent fortress."

Forced into the role of unwilling tour guide, Kian dismissed the hovering dragons with a wave of his gloved hand and started a bone dry recitation of the First Flight's history.

Between Blair's well-played declaration of independence and those cannon balls, we had more than achieved our goal of putting Kian off balance. Now, we had to keep him that way until we could get the hell out of the Citadel with a newborn baby, a renegade dragon rider, and a confiscated time artifact.

As Kian and I started up the long stone steps toward the

front entrance to the fortress, I caught sight of Jilly perched in a nearby tree. Using her wings as semaphore flags she asked, "Having fun yet?"

In the interest of our relationship, I chose not to reply with the first hand gesture that came to mind.

Chapter Twenty-Seven

The Spica Jungle

Edgar kept the field glasses trained on the schooner, temporarily oblivious to the risk of discovery he faced. When a flash of sunlight on the lenses blinded him, however, Edgar suddenly became cognizant of his vulnerability.

Falling backwards through the thick leaves, he caught hold of the trunk and cowered there fighting to regain his composure. Only when he felt confident that his carelessness had not betrayed his position did Edgar inch forward again to study the people onboard.

To his surprise, he realized the person standing at the wheel who appeared to be the ship's captain was a woman in pirate garb. She conferred at intervals with a man pacing the deck near the masthead.

Edgar noted he moved with a slight limp, yet still conveyed a feline-like grace. The silver streaking the man's temples and his collegial interaction with the captain suggested some degree of seniority.

An exotic, red-haired woman in trousers and knee boots

emerged from below deck. As she moved to join the limping man, her compelling beauty made Edgar's breath catch in his chest.

The fourth person on the deck was one of the riders from the Citadel. She kept to the bow near her yellow dragon who dozed in the sun. That left only a raccoon lounging against the railing eating thin, crisp bread from a brightly colored bag

When the older man spoke to the raccoon—and the raccoon appeared to *answer*—Edgar made a supreme effort to remind himself of Seneca's words and to draw resolve from them.

"You will be aided by a collection of confederates who will . . . seem quite strange . . . do not allow yourself to be guided by fear. Be bold, Edgar, if you wish to be free."

When the schooner turned into the tributary, Edgar came down from the tree and shadowed the ship's progress. By sticking to the underbrush and lagging slightly behind, he could watch everything that transpired while remaining hidden.

Every few paces, he cast a nervous eye toward the Citadel, a structure he'd never approached even a single time during his exile. An imposing line of dragons shielded the installation, their numbers swelling with the addition of the creatures escorting the ship.

"They are not demons," Edgar muttered to himself like a mantra. "They are *not* demons."

When the *Tempus Fugit* docked, Edgar hid among an outcropping of boulders and watched through the field glasses as the man with the limp confronted a stout figure Edgar took to be the leader of the dragon flight.

From that vantage point, Edgar witnessed the yellow dragon's forceful reaction to the exchange and the creature's surging ascent toward the summit with his rider onboard—and Edgar saw cannon balls lift from the deck under their own power and rain onto the pier.

That final, dramatic event visibly—and literally—doused the leader's sense of purpose. Dripping and embarrassed, he assented to allowing the redhead to carry an injured or perhaps ill woman into the Citadel, trailed by a blonde female Edgar had not seen before.

As the dragons peeled away to their alcoves and the onlookers dispersed, Edgar considered the evidence at his disposal. Nothing in the body language of the participants suggested trust on either side.

Perhaps the newcomers had no choice but to ask for help for their friend. Had they placed themselves in danger to aid her? If the visitors were in trouble, would they not be more inclined to help Edgar if he positioned himself to be of assistance to *them*? A benign *quid pro quo*?

Emboldened by his conversation with Seneca, Edgar resolved to follow that strategy. But in order to be on hand when an opportunity presented itself, he must do the unthinkable—draw even closer to the dragons' lair.

The Citadel, Jinx

Before we reached the Citadel, Festus attempted to coach me on the importance of immediately getting the upper hand with Kian. He suggested, in a roundabout way, that I might want to play up my condition for the dragon master's benefit.

Festus will never know how close he came to losing one of his nine lives over that suggestion. I can state unequivocally that there is zero need—as in *none*—to "play up" a contraction.

Thankfully my daughter remained remarkably quiet within

my body until we drew nearer to the Citadel, but once the fortress came into view, I felt her rising excitement and impatience.

At one point I laid a hand on my belly and said, "You're wearing me out, little girl."

The restless activity stilled.

"Thank you, baby," I whispered. "You won't have to wait much longer, okay?"

Tori mopped my sweating brow with a cool cloth. "Is she listening?"

I nodded. "Yes, but she's in a hurry to get here."

"And I'll bet you're ready for her to get here," she said, packing what amounted to an overnight bag for our stay in the fortress. "Hang in there."

When Greer appeared at the door of the cabin and told me she planned to carry me off the ship, I started to protest. The idea of being carted around by the baobhan sith like a sick toddler rankled me, but when I tried to stand, I couldn't pull it off.

The vampire lifted me into her arms. I gave in to how scared, overwhelmed, and exhausted I truly felt. My head dropped onto Greer's shoulder and I closed my eyes.

"Do not be afraid," she said quietly against my ear. "I will protect you and your child."

"Me, too," Tori said, laying her hand reassuringly on my shoulder. "Let's do this thing."

I managed a weak nod. From that point, getting Kian to greet me formally on one knee as the Witch of the Oak was my last active contribution to the mission. Any action I took after that came from a higher operational imperative: motherhood.

From the pier, we followed the old woman named Marta into the fortress. I took in the crumbling, softening lines of the structure and noted evidence of the fortification's creeping decay.

Blair had told us the truth. Kian was holding on to a self-proclaimed empire in decline. No wonder she and Giallo were prepared to rebel rather than sit by and watch the last remnants of drakonkind die.

We passed through a pair of wooden doors reinforced with iron bands and outfitted with heavy but rusty locks. The blessed cool of the stone interior enveloped us.

As we moved deeper into the mountain, all sounds except the footfalls of our group died away. Torches in wall sconces created wavering, surrealistic light.

The broad hallway gave Tori room to walk beside Greer. "Didn't Errol Flynn make this movie?" she asked me.

The reference to the Golden Age of Hollywood we were taught to love by our movie buff moms put a smile on my face, but it also made me long for my mother.

"I wish they were here," I whispered hoarsely.

My best friend didn't need to ask which "they" I meant.

"Me, too," she admitted. "Don't ever tell her I said this, but I wouldn't mind Mom ordering me around right about now."

At the end of the passage, Marta opened the door to a plain but pleasant room. There was no furniture beyond a bed and a couple of chairs. Nothing fragile to break. I was shocked, however, to see a large window looking onto a calm jungle pool.

"I thought we were inside the mountain," I said as Greer laid me on the mattress.

"We are," Marta replied. "You are not the only practitioner of magic to have been within these walls, Witch of the Oak."

The woman's lined, soft face and warm eyes drew me to her. "Jinx," I said, returning her smile. "My friends call me Jinx."

Marta took my hand in hers and patted it softly. "Do not be afraid, Jinx. I have helped many babies to start their life's journey."

"Were any of them witches?"

"I did not always live in the Land of Virgo, child. I have counted many sorts of people among my friends, Fae and humans alike. All will be well."

When Marta left the room to gather supplies for the delivery, Tori pointed toward the window. "Do you see them?" she asked.

"See who?"

Going to the pane, she pointed to an area of the adjacent jungle canopy. I made out a black bird and a flash of red. "Jilly and Lucy?" I asked.

"Yes," Tori said. "I think this window is enchanted to show the view from the front of the fortress."

"It's good to know they're . . . "

My words died on a sharp gasp of pain.

Greer held her hand out to me. I reached for the baobhan sith with bone crunching strength. She didn't even blink, but I apologized anyway.

"You can not hurt me," Greer said. "Squeeze as hard as you like."

I accepted the offer. The contractions were getting harder and frighteningly close together, Without warning my telekinesis kicked in again. Both chairs slammed into the far wall and splintered.

"Okey dokey then," Tori said. "I guess we stand."

Rodney, who was sitting on Tori's shoulder, started to run down her arm and come to me.

"No!" I barked.

The rat stopped, hurt and astonishment registering on his furry features.

"Sorry, Rodney," I panted. "Please stay in the pack. I don't want to hurt you by accident."

Tori opened the pouch. He hesitated then reluctantly ducked inside, immediately pressing his paws against the clear plastic front and keeping his eyes glued on me.

When the zipper closed, the boundary magic sprang to life. No matter what I might fling about the room, none of it would hurt my tiny friend—or my larger friend who was taking care of him.

"You don't have anything to worry about, Jinksy," Tori said, with a tad too much self-assurance to be convincing. "I've seen all the best birthing scenes in the movies. I've got this."

I stared at her with open disbelief. "Oh, really," I said. "Give me an example."

She looked like a deer caught in the headlights. "Miss Melly," she stammered. "In *Gone with the Wind*."

Clenching my teeth I said, "'I don't know nothing 'bout birthin' no babies' is *not* my idea of a comforting reference right now."

"Oh," she said, "uh, yeah. Uh. Hold on. I'll come up with something better."

As beads of sweat started to roll down my face, I said, "Just be here. You have to remember everything so you can help me tell Lucas."

Tori caught hold of my free hand and held it tight. "I *am* here. I'm not going anywhere."

Marta reappeared, checked me out, and announced, "This baby is in a hurry. It's time to push, Jinx. *Push.*"

A new mother once told me that the sensation of giving birth amounted to shoving a watermelon through the eye of a needle. You look for all the leverage you can find.

I grabbed hold of the headboard to do as Marta ordered and instantly found myself deep inside a psychometric vision. Every woman who had lain in that bed and brought a baby into the world stood by my side.

They cheered me on, screamed and cursed with me, took my pain into their bodies and shared their own.

Just before the last wrenching effort that birthed my daughter, fireballs erupted in the air around the bed. They shot toward the walls, striking and erupting in showers of hot sparks.

Marta didn't bother to look up. I heard her voice, low and sing-songy, crooning to the baby. Then a cry split the air. Marta cut the cord and held up not the red, wrinkled, bloody newborn I expected, but a clean, pristine infant.

The old woman laid the child in my arms. All around the bed translucent fantasy dragons manifested in flight, diving and swirling in time with my daughter's flailing fists and merry laughter.

Then Rodney was on my chest holding out the miniature wand to the baby. Everything fell into place when the implement expanded to fit her hand. This was what Knasgowa intended.

Grasping the wand with a confident giggle, my daughter began drawing looping circles in the air. Streams of shooting stars burst from the wand's tip and started chasing the baby dragon brigade.

"That's your kid alright," Tori said ruefully, but she was grinning from ear to ear. "She's gonna be a handful."

"More than you may be able to predict," Marta said. "This child is dragon born."

At the time I didn't know what the phrase meant and I didn't care. I was holding the most beautiful, perfect child in the world in my arms. I loved her instantly and ferociously.

"Have you picked a name?" Tori asked, sitting down next to my pillow and staring at the baby with loving eyes.

"Adeline Kathleen Grayson, but we're going to call her Addie."

"Hello Addie," Tori said leaning closer. "I'm your Aunt Tori and that's your Aunt Greer. We're going to be very important people in your world."

That touched off another round of merriment from the little one.

"You like your name, don't you?" I cooed.

Addie looked up at me with bright intelligent eyes and said, "*Like!*"

Positive I hadn't heard what I thought I heard, I looked at Tori who chose the perfect movie reference for the moment.

"Houston, we have a problem."

Chapter Twenty-Eight

Spica Citadel, Festus

Don't think for a minute I liked sending Jinx into the Citadel even with Greer for protection. I listened to Kian and made polite noises, but my friend and her child remained front and center in my thoughts.

Now, understand I didn't want to be *in* the room when she gave birth, but honoring the tradition of men my age I would have *absolutely* paced outside the door.

In my day fathers-to-be didn't do the Lamaze thing and, bipedal abilities aside, I am a cat. We tend to go off and handle such matters alone and in our own way. Chase's mother, my late wife Jenny, didn't want me underfoot the day he was born.

When the midwife called me into the room, Jenny introduced my son to me as a human child and then, enveloping him with her shifter magic, transformed him into a mountain lion cub and then the cutest Russian Blue kitten you've ever seen.

Afterwards, I hit my favorite werecat bar, The Dirty Claw, handing out cigars and buying creamed whisky for the house.

I know it's not progressive, but in my head, women give birth and their men go get drunk in celebration.

So yes, while we waited, I tended to business—in large part so we could get Jinx the hell out of there and back to her husband and family.

After interminable lectures about arcane architectural details, Kian finally led us to his study, an indicator that the cards were about to meet the playing surface.

The dragon master arranged himself behind a massive oak desk while Rube, Miranda, and I sat across from him in torturous high-backed chairs.

Rube took in the arrangement that emphasized Kian's self-importance and ensured the discomfort of his guests. The raccoon turned his head and gave his ear a vigorous scratch to hide an eye roll and mouthed the words, *"What a jackass!"*

Among his myriad talents, Rube happens to be an excellent judge of character.

Kian took a protracted and pretentious amount of time to read my authorization to assume custody of the Hourglass of the Horae. When he finished, he looked up and said, "No."

I didn't expect cooperation, but I also didn't anticipate open defiance.

"You understand that my task force operates by order of the Ruling Elders?"

Kian spread his hands wide and smiled as if to say, *"What can I do?"*

"The Ruling Elders dispatched your dragon flight. You retain custody of the Hourglass of the Horae by their permission alone. I am rescinding that permission."

The Master shook his head with feigned regret. "Chief McGregor, you are not, yourself, a member of the Ruling Elders nor do you carry correspondence from the mother house of my order. Without verifications from my superiors that you are who you say you are, I cannot release the artifact."

In the chair next to mine Miranda leaned forward resting her arms on her knees. "You mean your superiors at Drake Abbey?"

This time Kian offered us a genuine smile. "Why yes! You are familiar with our mother house?"

"I am familiar with the *ruins* of your mother house," the pirate said flatly. "There's nothing left of Drake Abbey but crumbling walls and piles of stone on the far side of the Sea of Ages."

That shocking news temporarily deflated the Master's superior attitude. "Drake Abbey has fallen?" he asked in a stunned voice. "What about the other houses? Where is the center of drakonculture now?"

When we dropped the same bombshell on Blair, I tried to soften the blow. This time I ripped the bandage off—not out of any ill feeling for Kian, although I had plenty of that brewing in my system. There was just no way to make the truth easier.

"Drakonculture no longer exists in the Otherworld."

A reasonable man might, upon learning he and his riders were the last of their kind, be more inclined to cooperate. Kian swung hard in the opposite direction, drawing even deeper into defensive self-importance.

"If that is true," he said, "I have no choice but to assume I am the last legitimate dragon master. In the absence of confirmation of the story you present, Chief McGregor, I will not relinquish the Hourglass of the Horae.

He used lots of words to say a simple thing: *McGregor, you're lying.*

When I bristled at the implied insult, Rube laid a restraining paw on my arm.

"Ain't bureau-crazy a bitch?" he said, hitting the Master with a full dose of fake sympathy. "All them rules and ports of call you gotta follow. We didn't mean to cruise in here throwing cannonballs and ruining your day with bad news. How about we hit the chow line and jaw about all this stuff later?"

The entertainment value of watching Kian sort out Rube-speak for "bureaucracy" and "protocols" allowed my temper to cool a few notches.

"An excellent suggestion," I said. "We've been living on ship's rations. I'd love a good meal."

Kian jumped at the chance to abandon his role as negotiator and take on the guise of convivial host. "Of course!" he exclaimed, springing out of his chair. "I have been *unconscionably* rude."

Ushering us into the adjacent corridor, the master said, "The evening meal won't be served until the sun drops lower in the sky, but let us adjourn to the dining hall. The kitchen staff will prepare a light repast in the interim."

We followed Kian down two levels, our footsteps echoing in the mostly empty fortress. He showed us into a grand banquet hall that now housed a sad collection of trestle tables grouped in a bedraggled clump under the vaulted windows.

The three of us made ourselves at home while Kian went in search of someone to boss around. I glanced outside and spotted Jilly on the balustrade. She waved a wing in my direction and flashed a quick semaphore message.

"*All quiet out here. U ok? Jinx?*"

Using a protracted nose scratch to mask my answer, I signaled, "*Yes. No word on baby.*"

"Geez, McGregor!" Rube said, glancing around to see if anyone was watching. "Was you raised in a barn? No booger picking at the table! It ain't polite."

"I am not picking my nose, you moron," I hissed, jerking my head toward the window.

When the raccoon spotted Jilly, he picked up a paw to wave,

but quickly converted the gesture into a combing motion over his ears as Kian re-entered the room.

Two servants followed the master carrying trays of bread, cheese, and fruit. Rube's nose twitched in anticipation of the food and my stomach growled. We really were hungry.

Slices of succulent mango and sweet, syrupy figs paired perfectly with thick slices of bread still warm from the oven and good, sharp cheddar. With mugs of dark ale to wash the food down, I almost forgot my growing distaste for the supercilious dragon master.

We were discussing the Citadel's brewery, a pet project of Kian's, when Marta entered the dining hall. I could tell from her beaming face that the delivery had gone well.

By the time the old woman reached the table, I was on my feet. "She had the baby?" I asked. "Are they okay?"

"Yes and yes," Marta assured me. "The Witch of the Oak is asking that you all come with me to meet her daughter."

Turning to Kian, I said, "Will you excuse us?"

Honestly, the guy couldn't wait to be rid of us for a few minutes. He even looked the other way when Rube rolled two slices of bread and a hunk of cheese in a cloth napkin and tucked them in his waist pack.

As we fell in step behind Marta, I asked the raccoon, "Why didn't you steal the silverware while you were at it?"

"Ain't my pattern," he replied complacently. "Wouldn't look good with my Grand Baroque."

"Wait a minute," Miranda said. "You have a set of Grand Baroque silverware?"

"Working on it," Rube said. "Next time we go to Claridge's in Londinium I'm going for the soup spoons. Wanna help?"

While the pirate and the trash panda discussed pilferage, I focused on our surroundings.

From the dining hall, Marta took us into the main foyer

before turning left down a long, straight passageway. We had a clean shot from Jinx's room to the front of the Citadel. Good information to keep in mind if a hasty exit became necessary and Greer couldn't use the flight of the baobhan sith.

I was so preoccupied formulating Plan B—and C and D—I almost ran into Marta when she stopped before a closed door and tapped lightly.

Jinx answered. "Come in."

Marta stepped aside and we entered single file. I noticed two shattered chairs lying across the room, but someone had brought in replacements. Greer sat in one of them, but Tori was at the foot of the bed leaning against one of the posts.

Jinx greeted me with a beaming smile. "Hey!" she said. "Come meet my baby."

Rube didn't wait for an invitation. He scaled the bedspread and ambled straight across Tori. "Aw, man!" he said. "Check it out! You had a girl kit, Jinx."

"I noticed," Jinx laughed. "Addie meet your Uncle Rube."

The baby looked at Rube and burbled, "Puppy?"

"Naw, not puppy," he said. "Raccoon."

"Racky-yoon!" Addie cried merrily.

"Close enough, kid," Rube grinned. "Close enough."

He took the whole exchange as if talking with a newborn infant was the most normal thing in the world; it left me frozen mid-stride and speechless. Granted I only had one kid, but as best I could remember, they don't come out talking.

"Should . . . should she be doing that?" I finally managed to stammer.

Jinx looked at me with equal parts alarm and delight.

"Addie," she said, "this is Uncle Festus. He doesn't think you should be talking yet and he's right. What do you have to say about that?"

The little girl looked at me and her whole face lit up. *"Kitty cat!"*

The baby's ability to discern my shifter species while I was in human form rattled me more than the talking. "What else is she doing?" I asked.

"Addie," Jinx cooed. "Show the kitty cat your dragons."

Raising one chubby fist with Rodney's miniature wand, now the size of a pencil, gripped in her fingers, Addie produced a flight of pink dragons that, unless I'm mistaken, were dancing the fandango—and punctuating the beat with rhythmic bursts of flame.

I sank down in the chair beside Jinx. "She's beautiful. . . and . . . talented."

"I know," Jinx said, turning worried, pride-filled eyes on me. "I have absolutely no idea how we're going to contain her when we get back home—and Festus, we have to get there as soon as possible. Marta thinks she has an explanation for what's happening with Addie."

Thank Bastet someone did.

"The child is experiencing accelerated growth from the temporal instabilities here in the mountains," Marta explained. "The effect should have stopped when she was born, but it did not."

If we were working against a wonky clock, I needed at least an approximation of how fast the hands were spinning. "Can you guess how old she is now?" I asked.

The answer came from an unexpected quarter. "Babies start forming simple words at roughly six months of age," Greer said.

Everyone stared at the baobhan sith like she'd grown a second head.

"Geez, Red," Rube said. "Not meaning no offense, but you ain't exactly the motherhood type."

"Perhaps not," she replied complacently, "but I am quite

capable of conducting research into childhood developmental milestones."

Jinx frowned. "Why would you be researching childhood development?"

"When I became aware of your pregnancy, I thought the information might be of use."

"When," Jinx said, "*exactly*, did you become aware of *my* pregnancy?"

"The evening you chose to consume blood red pie and that disgusting green ice cream in tandem."

Coming to Greer's defense, I said, "That was kind of a dead giveaway. Anybody would have guessed you were having a craving, Jinx."

The baobhan sith didn't take the out I offered. "I seldom operate based on guesswork," she said. "I heard the baby's heartbeat."

Jinx's jaw dropped. "You didn't think you should mention that to me?"

"I did not," Greer replied. "The child clearly had begun a predestined course that was meant to culminate in this fortress."

Marta nodded sagely. "I am not surprised. Addie is dragon born. She would want to be as near the creatures as possible when she entered the world."

"Hold on," I said. "Everybody just slow down. We have a kid that's growing up too fast, *and* she has some special connection to the dragons?"

"She is one of the chosen," Marta said, "and Kian must not be made aware of this fact."

"Why not?"

We all jumped when Giallo's stentorian voice entered our minds simultaneously.

"He cannot know because he would seek to keep the child here in hopes she will bond with my whelp."

"Oh man," Rube said, "you got a bun in the oven, too, Captain Iguana? I ain't drinking the water around here, that's for dang sure."

Jinx had a less sanguine reaction. "I'd like to see Kian try to keep my child."

If anything, the Witch of the Oak has always been reticent about using her powers, but becoming a mother changed that. Her eyes flashed with blue light, and a gust of wind rippled over the bedclothes.

"Okay, okay, Mama Bear, simmer down," I said. "Let's deal with these problems one at a time. Marta, have you ever seen a child grow this fast?"

"Yes," the old woman replied. "Some of the babies born shortly after our arrival in the mountains matured rapidly through the first weeks of their lives—or what we understood then to be weeks."

"How much did they grow?" Jinx asked.

"Most approximated the size of a five year old when the process stopped."

"Five *years!*" Jinx cried. "We can't wait until she's as big as a five-year old! Lucas missed her birth, he can't miss *five years* of her childhood. Festus, please, you have to do something."

Giallo spoke again. *"Come to me, werecat. I have a plan."*

Chapter Twenty-Nine

Citadel, Festus

Good ROMO agents learn to accept that no mission ever comes off as planned. I may not have wanted to start an insurrection against Kian, but now that I'd met the man, I also knew he wasn't fit to safeguard the future of the surviving dragon riders.

The fortress housed two precious artifacts: one physical and one cultural. In retrieving the Hourglass of the Horae, I couldn't look the other way and in good conscience allow the destruction of drakonculture.

Taking the meeting with Giallo meant throwing in our lot with the dragons.

I looked across Jinx's bed at Greer. "What do you think?"

The baobhan sith regarded me with cool eyes. "From the moment Blair and Giallo landed on the deck of the *Tempus Fugit* this moment could not be avoided."

"Rube?"

The raccoon grinned. "I told you Captain Iguana was up to something. Might as well go find out what."

"Miranda?"

"Kian showed his true attitude toward the dragons on the docks," the captain said. "He thinks he owns them. He doesn't. Giallo is getting ready to show him that. I say we stay on the side of right."

That left Jinx and Tori. "Do either one of you have anything you want to say?" I asked.

"You know what I want," Jinx said. "I want to go home."

At that, Addie waved her mini wand and created a perfect representation of the lair back in Briar Hollow in the air over the bed. "Home," she said. *"Dada!"*

Tori nodded. "What she said."

"Okay, we talk to Giallo. Marta how long before Kian gets suspicious and comes looking for us?"

The old woman laughed. "The Master prefers to lie down in the afternoon. He missed his nap thanks to your arrival. I venture to say he's snoring on the couch in his study. He won't rouse until the dinner bell sounds. There is time enough."

I could have used a nap in the sun, too, but that didn't seem to be on the agenda.

"Okay, let's divide and conquer. Greer and Tori, you stay here with Jinx and Addie. Miranda, go back to the dining hall. Try to give Jilly and Lucy an update through the windows. Do you know semaphore?"

The pirate cocked an eyebrow. "I captain a schooner, Festus. What do you think?"

"Sorry. Marta, will you take me and Rube to meet with Giallo?"

"My pleasure," she said. "We'll use the servants' stairs. They lie hidden behind the main walls and have been largely abandoned. No one will see us."

"Perfect."

I held out my hand to Jinx. She clasped my fingers tightly.

"You have a beautiful daughter," I said. "She's all you need to think about right now. Let us worry about the rest. Okay?"

She nodded, her eyes shining with tears. "I'm sorry, Festus. I know I'm not much help right now."

"You just had a baby. Nobody expects you to help. Get some rest."

As we left the room, I heard Addie's bright voice. "Kitty cat and racky-yoon fix it, Mama."

In the space of fifteen minutes the child had gone from simple words to simple sentences. If we didn't get her out of the Land of Virgo she'd be ready for pre-school within a day.

As the door closed behind us, Rube said, "You hear that, McGregor? What the kid said? She's right. We do gotta fix this."

"We're working on it," I said. "Miranda, if Kian wakes up early, can you keep him contained?"

The captain laughed. "With one hand tied behind my back. If necessary I'll make up some reason to get him down to the pier. Hell, I'll throw him in the water to go fishing for my cannon balls if that's what it takes."

Even though the mental image of Miranda dunking Kian pleased me immensely, I said, "Let's try to avoid that last part."

"Killjoy," she accused me, as she strode away down the corridor. "You don't let me have any fun."

Watching her, I doubted seriously the man has been born who could get between Miranda Winter and her amusements.

"Okay," I told Marta. "We're ready."

The old woman grasped one of the wall sconces and pulled it forward, triggering a hidden door.

"*Suh-wheet!*" Rube said. "It's like sewer tunnels but in the walls. Us coons is all about sewer tunnels."

"A fact our noses never let us forget," I observed drily. "Lead the way, Marta."

She reached into the opening and produced a second torch,

holding it aloft to light our way as we entered the passage. After closing the door, Marta started up a circular stairway. The old woman moved with greater agility than I expected. By the third flight, I was ready for acupuncture and yoga in Londinium.

At the sixth level, Marta opened another door and we stepped into an empty set of rooms. Dust coated the furniture and cobwebs draped the corners.

"These were Miriam's chambers," Marta explained. "Eingana would not leave them after the accident. The stalls are through here."

We passed under a stone arch and into a stable. With no windows to drive away the shadows, it could have been night or day, but unlike the neglected living chamber, this area was swept clean and smelled of fresh hay.

Lanterns cast warm pools on the flagstone floor, illuminating our path to the last stall where Eingana, Giallo, and Blair waited.

The drakaina lay curled around a pearlescent egg that gleamed in the golden light. The creature's hide possessed a similar luster, perhaps a shade darker, like rich clotted cream. Her almond colored eyes gazed at us beneficently.

"Welcome to my home," she said in our thoughts. *"My mate and his rider speak well of you."*

Completely abandoning the last traces of his life-long dragon fear, Rube marched straight into the stall. "Hey, Dragon Lady," he said to Blair before holding out his paw to Eingana. "Nice to meet you, Mrs. Captain Iguana. Your old man's a good lizard. You didn't marry no bum, that's for sure—and congrats on the kid in the shell."

Eingana's sleek body shook with laughter as she reached for his paw with one taloned forefoot. *"You are Rube?"*

"Guilty," the raccoon said, giving her foot a vigorous shake. "So when's the little one gonna bust out?"

"*That,*" Giallo said, "*is part of what we wish to discuss. Eingana, this is the werecat, McGregor.*"

"Festus," I said, shaking her foot as well and trying not to react to the razor sharp talons that passed lightly over my fingers. "Please accept my congratulations as well."

The drakaina's eyes studied me. "*You,*" she said at last, "*are a good man.*"

"I try to be."

"*My mate says you will help. I believe him now.*"

"Help with what exactly?"

Blair spoke for the first time. "I told you that when the *Tempus Fugit* leaves, we want to go with you back to the Otherworld. Giallo won't leave Eingana, and she won't leave the egg. Kian has no intention of giving you the Hourglass of the Horae. Giallo has come up with a plan to take care of all those issues—tonight."

The drake shifted his body to reveal a low bench running along one wall of the stable. "*Sit,*" he said. "*Let us discuss our common problems.*"

Marta cleared her throat. "I will leave you to your discussion," she said. "When you are ready to return to your friends, I will be in the living quarters."

"You don't have to go," I told her.

The old woman smiled. "I cannot lie about what I have not heard."

As her footsteps died away, Rube and I took our seats on the bench. The raccoon immediately started digging through his waist pack.

"So," he said, pulling out the bread and cheese he'd lifted from the dining room. "Way I see it, the biggest problem we both got starts with *k*, ends with *n*, and gotta dumpster load of self-importance in the middle."

Then, just as he stuffed a hunk of cheddar in his mouth, the raccoon remembered some vestige of good manners. "You mind?"

The words came out *"Youth mindth?"*

"We do not," Giallo said.

A can of grape soda came out of the pack next. The racoon popped the tab, gulped half the contents, burped, and said, "You're the best, Captain Iguana."

I couldn't help myself. "Is that damn fanny pack bottomless?"

"First off," Rube said, breaking off another lump of cheese, "it ain't hanging off my fanny. Second, I may or may not have won a capacity spell in a poker game to which you wasn't invited."

"What did I tell you about gambling with witches?"

"You told me," Rube said, biting into a slice of bread, "that it ain't smart to do, which would be true coming from a second-rate gambler like you. Me? I got game."

Both dragons let out sooty bursts of merriment infused with sparks.

"This is why we seek your help," Giallo said.

"What is?" I asked.

"Friendship," he replied. *"You cannot understand friendship if you do not also understand family."*

"True friendship rises to the level of family," I said. "Half the time I want to wring this varmint's bloody neck, but yes, he is my friend and my brother."

Rube choked, hastily gulped more soda, and said hoarsely, "Anybody got a tape recorder? Ain't nobody gonna believe he said that."

Giallo laughed again, but then his green eyes darkened. *"We seek your friendship, McGregor, to the benefit of your family and ours."*

"I'm listening."

Giallo should have been a lawyer. He laid out a highly logical case that involved stealing the Hourglass of the Horae as a prelude to liberating Jinx and Addie—with one minor catch. We also had to stage an egg-napping.

"We wish our welp to hatch in the Otherworld," the dragon said. *"Here our son or daughter will be confined, forced to be small. Its potential will be stolen."*

"The archaic husbandry may explain why the dragons have stopped reproducing," Blair said. "If this whelp is born in the Otherworld, it could be the first of a new generation of working dragons. We want to reclaim our way of life, restore Drake Abbey, and after that, all the other houses."

I was up to my eyewhiskers in spearheading a task force to recover the Temporal Arcana for Miranda and the other time-faring mariners. Drakonculture deserved an equal chance at rejuvenation. I said just that before asking the most critical question. "How do you envision this working?"

The dragon wanted Rube to remain in the Citadel after dinner that evening. Using his telepathy, Giallo would guide the raccoon into the chamber where the Hourglass resided.

"Marta will help distract the guards."

"She left rather than listen to this discussion," I said. "How do you know she'll participate in the theft of the artifact?"

Blair, who had joined us on the bench, looked toward the direction of the living quarters.

"I've known Marta all my life," she said. "After I lost my parents, she took care of me. She didn't want to hear this conversation because she doesn't want to lie to Kian. Marta remembers him when he was younger, before he became the Master. She hopes he can change. We've worked out a way for her to help without knowing the larger plan."

Rube laid a paw on her knee. "Don't you want the old lady to come with us?"

"I do," Blair said. "I hope many people in the Citadel will join us in the Otherworld eventually, but we have to make this break first to show them the way."

She said it with the sadness of a person called to leadership who wished her life didn't have to change to uphold her principles. I sympathized with the feeling.

"How will Rube get out of the Citadel with the Hourglass?" I asked.

"The object is not large," Giallo said. *"He has but to lift the artifact and stop the flow of the grains. Time will stop. All living creatures around him will freeze. He may then move freely, exiting the fortress and disappearing into the jungle."*

Rube, who was already warming to the idea, said, "How come the Hourglass won't freeze me?"

"While you hold the object in your hand, you will not be affected."

"And the egg?" I asked. "How do we get it out safely?"

"Before Rube leaves for the jungle, he will come here. Blair will have placed our egg in a pack he can wear upon his back. At a safe distance from the Citadel, he will right the Hourglass. When the flow of time resumes, the Drinker of Blood will use the wind that is her gift to fly the Witch of the Oak to your vessel. You will sail for the main river where Rube will await you. We will follow in the skies overhead."

That all sounded well and good, except for the twenty-three other dragons at the Master's disposal.

"You think Kian will let us just sail off with the Hourglass of the Horae and a dragon egg and not put up a fight?" I said. "That's the kind of optimism that gets people killed."

"I have taken care of such a possibility," Giallo said. *"The Master will order the dragons to pursue. They will not."*

"How can you guarantee their behavior?"

"*Our brothers and sisters do not wish to die in this place either,*" Giallo said. "*We leave first, but more will follow, McGregor. Something has begun that Kian cannot stop. The path home has opened before us and we will take it.*"

Chapter Thirty

Spica Jungle, Jilly and Lucy

Jilly snapped at an insect hovering near her head and tossed the crushed remains to the side, cleaning her beak against the branch.

"*Hey!*" Lucy cawed. "What did you do that for? I told you I'm hungry."

"Sorry," Jilly said. "I forgot you're an omnivore. Bugs give me indigestion."

"This stake-out is giving me indigestion," Lucy groused, flapping a wing toward the fortress. "*They* get to sit in there and have dinner while *we're* stuck out here in the jungle."

"Does Festus look like he's enjoying himself?" Jilly asked.

The wereraven swiveled her neck to get a better view of the dining room. Festus, Rube, and Miranda sat at a table with Kian and several of his riders.

"No," Lucy admitted. "He looks like he's going to toss a hairball at any second, which makes me feel marginally better."

Jilly made a tsking sound. "Show some solidarity. Kian's been talking non-stop since they sat down. It isn't in Festus's nature to hold his tongue that long."

Lucy ran her beak through her breast feathers, then tilted her head to stare quizzically at her friend. "I like working with Festus, but I don't think I could date such a total grouch."

The wereparrot bobbed back and forth. "The sour puss attitude makes up only a fraction of the total man," she said. "He's really very sweet and gentlemanly."

Jerking her head towards the Citadel, Lucy said, "He doesn't look sweet right now."

"Because he's climbing the walls to get Jinx and her baby home," Jilly replied. "Jinx must be beside herself with joy on the one wing and panicked out of her mind on the other. Lucas doesn't even know she was pregnant. Now she's going to show up with a toddler."

Lucy shook out her feathers. "At least he'll miss the diaper changes."

Both birds sat silent for a second and then tittered with laughter. "That's not nice of us," Jilly said.

"Neither are diapers," Lucy countered.

Movement in the dining hall interrupted the light-hearted moment. As they watched, Kian stood and pushed his chair back, signaling an end to the meal. Everyone present followed his example and began to filter toward the doorways in small groups.

"Come on," Jilly said. "That's our cue. Let's get to the front of the Citadel. I told Festus we'd be nearby if he needed to signal further instructions."

Taking flight, they made for a spot they'd scouted earlier. It provided thick foliage but offered a clear view of the steps leading to the pier. The group from the *Tempus Fugit* emerged from the building with Kian in front.

At the halfway point on the stairs, the werebirds heard Rube say, "Sorry gang. I gotta see a man about a dog."

Kian looked confused. "There are no dogs in the Spica Mountains."

"It's a figure of speech," Festus explained smoothly. "It means Rube needs to relieve himself."

To emphasize the extreme nature of his condition, the raccoon crossed his legs, danced a nervous jig, and said, "I'll see you guys at the boat," before diving head first into the underbrush.

"Should we wait for him?" Kian asked.

"Uh, no," Festus said. "I think he may have . . . additional . . . business. He did eat quite a lot at dinner and, well, if you're unfamiliar with raccoon digestion . . . "

His voice trailed off and he looked to Miranda for support. "Let's just say it's unwise to be downwind," the captain said. "The stench makes bilge water smell sweet."

The dragon master's face registered horror. "I certainly hope he'll go far enough into the jungle that his . . . leavings . . . won't be an issue for those of us in the Citadel. I sleep with my windows open."

"Rube is quite considerate," Festus said, taking Kian's elbow and propelling him toward the pier. "But we should be on our way all the same."

As the group passed the tree, the werecat looked up, made eye contact with Jilly, and winked.

"See," the wereparrot whispered, "I told you he's not a grouch all the time."

"*I'll* be a grouch if Rube really is down there somewhere tending to his business," Lucy answered. "All that garbage he eats tends to ferment in there, you know."

Jilly nodded. "Fair point. We need to get back to our post

outside the dining hall anyway. That's where Rube will leave the building when he's completed his mission. When he meets up with us, all we have to do is get him to the rendezvous point and we're out of here."

"Let's not count our dragons before they hatch," Lucy advised.

"*Dragon*, singular," Jilly said, taking off from the branch. "The whole idea is for the egg *not* to hatch."

"Right," Lucy said, following after her. "What could possibly go wrong trusting a *raccoon* with an egg?"

The Citadel, Rube

Kian came back up the steps from the pier, holding a handkerchief over his nose. He glanced nervously to the left and right almost as if he expected something foul to jump out at him.

Snickering, Rube wished the team's Excrement Specialist, Leon, was on this job. He'd leave the master a "gift" Kian would never forget.

Taking a path that hugged the base of the Citadel, Rube worked his way beneath the dining hall's balcony. Thick, tangled vines climbed toward the balustrade. Pulling himself up with ease, Rube landed on all fours and pushed open the window he'd unlatched earlier.

He found the room deserted. No sounds came from the hallway outside or from the kitchen. Sniffing the air experimentally, Rube followed his nose toward the supply cabinets at the back of the cooking area. It would be unprofessional to be this close and not "shop" a little.

When Giallo's voice came into his thoughts, the raccoon was

stuffing a half wheel of cheese into his waist pack. Startled, Rube jumped back and dropped the cheddar.

"For the love of the Trash Gods don't *do* that, Captain Iguana! You're gonna give me one of them cardiac inflections."

"You will be in the jungle for hours, Reuben, not days."

"Now you got like x-ray vision or something? How do you know what I'm doing?"

"You are in the proximity of food. I surmised you would avail yourself. Am I mistaken?"

"Everybody's a freaking diet doctor. I got an active meta-embolism, okay?"

"It is time."

Rube went to the door and squinted into the dining room. "But didn't the sun just go down?"

"The flow of time quickens this night. I feel it. Dawn will catch you shortly after you reach the jungle."

"Good deal," Rube said. "Gimme a sec."

He retrieved the cheese, grunting as he shoved it into the pack and closed the zipper.

"I am curious, Reuben. How much will your enchanted pack hold?"

"Beats me," Rube shrugged. "I ain't got it full yet. I'll let you know. So where am I going?"

At the dragon's direction, the raccoon threaded through a series of rooms until he reached the deserted ground floor corridor.

"Marta approaches. Remain out of sight."

Rube heard a tapping sound from the far end of the hall. He made out the outline of the old woman's form. She carried a basket covered with a cloth. When she passed where Rube was hiding, Giallo said, *"Follow her."*

Staying in the shadows, the raccoon started after the woman.

When she descended a stairway to the lower level, he quickly surveyed his options, scaled the wall, and used the exposed beams to make his descent.

"Who goes there?" the guard barked.

Marta laughed. "No one you need fear, Michael. You were not at supper."

The young man relaxed. "Hello, Marta. I didn't know it was you. Kian wouldn't let us take turns to get our food the way we normally would. He ordered us to stay at our posts. He's worried about the strangers from the ship."

"Kian worries about things that should not concern him and ignores others that should have his full attention."

Michael started to laugh at the accurate characterization of his superior, but stopped himself. "What's in the basket?"

"Plates for each of you," Marta smiled. "I assume you are hungry."

The guard's eyes lit up. "More like starving. Thank you!"

"Shall I take the others their plates in the artifact chamber?"

Indecision registered on Michael's face. "Please don't be offended, but Kian ordered me not to let anyone in no matter how much I trust them."

Marta nodded sympathetically. "I am not offended. You deliver the food, and I will stay here until you return."

The guard considered the suggestion. "I guess that would be okay," he said haltingly. "Couldn't you leave the basket?"

She shook her head. "I cannot. It is my favorite. I can carry it without hurting my back. Humor an old woman."

Michael's expression softened. "Sure, Marta. Wait here. I won't be long."

When the guard accepted the basket and went into the antechamber, Marta turned her back on the staircase and gazed contemplatively out the window.

She might not know all the details of the heist, Rube thought, but her timing is still perfect.

The raccoon swung down, darted through the door, and dove behind the tapestry Giallo told him would be there, pulling his tail under the fabric as Michael's returning footsteps echoed across the floor.

"Robert and John send their thanks, Marta," the guard said. "Do you need help climbing the stairs?"

"No, no," she said. "I am slow, but not ready to stop."

Peeking cautiously through the curtain, Rube saw two guards through the open doorway into the main room. They sat facing one another cross-legged on a bench tucking into their food. The Hourglass of the Horae rested on a pedestal in the center of the space.

As Rube watched, the grains in the glass emptied into the bottom bulb. The artifact, which was roughly the size of a quart jar, upended itself smoothly and began to empty again.

While one of the guards launched into a protracted lament about his inability to get a dragon rider named Megan to take notice of him, Rube slipped round the corner, hiding under yet another wall hanging.

Pausing to catch his breath, he slipped off the waist pack, flattened himself on the floor, and began inching toward the pedestal.

Completely wrapped up in their discussion, the two men didn't notice the raccoon until he lay mere inches from his target.

"*Hey!*" one of the guards yelled suddenly. "What is that thing doing in here?"

Shoving his plate aside, the guard jumped up and made a grab for Rube. The raccoon rolled out of the way, baring his teeth and growling when the man reached for him again.

"Don't you growl at me, you mongrel," the man snarled. "I'll mount your head on my wall."

"If you think you're big enough," Rube snarled back, "go for it."

The man's stunned reaction gave the raccoon the advantage he needed. Leaping for the pedestal, Rube wrapped his paws around the cylindrical base. Using his body weight for momentum, he whirled toward the guard kicking him solidly in the groin with both back feet.

Groaning, the man sank to his knees as Rube's paw closed around the hourglass. He turned the artifact on its side and felt the air in the room thicken and still.

The second guard, who was slow on the uptake, was caught in an awkward half-upright crouch, a long piece of roast beef dangling from his lips.

Careful to keep hold of the hourglass, Rube took out his iPhone, positioned himself and the object, and took a selfie with each of the men.

Snickering, he returned the phone to his pack. "Thanks guys. My Post-A-Pic peeps are gonna love you two."

Still chortling, the raccoon extracted a map, settled on his route through the Citadel, and waddled out of the room.

Minutes later, he found himself in Eingana's quarters. Blair and Giallo were there as well, all struck immobile by the cessation of time. Each of the dragons wore a set of saddlebags, and a heavy rucksack sat on the floor at Blair's feet.

A second pack bore the note, "Take this one, and be careful."

"People with kids," Rube said. "Always thinking the munchkins are gonna break. You ain't gonna break, are you egglet?"

To his surprise, the backpack vibrated slightly.

"Still awake in there, huh? Okay, don't worry. Uncle Rube's got this nailed."

Carefully shrugging into one strap and then the next, he settled the pack on his shoulders. "Okay, here we go. Hang on tight."

Retracing his steps, Rube returned to the dining room, went out the window and over the balcony, and headed into the jungle. He stopped when he spotted Jilly and Lucy frozen on a limb above his head.

Making sure he couldn't be seen from the Citadel, Rube upended the hourglass. As soon as the grains of sand began to fall again, the sounds of the jungle burst to life. Inside the fortress a man's voice shouted, "The Hourglass is gone! Awaken the riders!"

Blinking to clear her vision, Jilly looked down at Rube. "You got it?"

Rube shook his head. "You wound me, Jilly, you *wound* me. Of course I got it. The egg, too. Come on. We gotta get out of here."

Behind them a rumbling, wheezing growl echoed from somewhere deep inside the Citadel. The voice increased in volume as others joined in. Torches flared in the windows illuminating glowing sets of eyes.

"Oh, *crap*," Rube said. "Crap, crap, *crap!* I thought McGregor said them weretigers don't work in packs."

"Normally they don't," Jilly said. "Now what?"

A rustling in the bushes sent Rube halfway up the tree trunk before a man's voice whispered, "Please. Do not be alarmed. I am not affiliated with the people within those walls."

"Show yourself," Lucy demanded.

A figure stepped into a shaft of light. He stared at Lucy's black form silhouetted against the moon. "You are a raven," he said in an awed voice, "and you speak."

Jilly jumped down onto a lower branch and stared at the man. "Do I know you?" she asked.

"My name is Edgar Poe," he replied with a bow. "At your service."

No one spoke until Jilly asked, "Edgar *Allan* Poe?"

"Yes," the man replied. "I have, at times, used that variation of my moniker. Tell me, raven, do you perchance know one of your kind named Seneca?"

"We all know Seneca," Lucy said, "How do..."

"Geez, *Lou-eeze!*" Rube interrupted. "I don't care if he's Danielle Freaking Steele. This ain't no book club meeting. We got weretigers about to bust in on us any second. You dames can fly. Me? I'm gonna be cat chow if we don't get a move on."

Glancing toward the Citadel, Edgar said, "Tigers do not hunt by scent. Climb onto my back and I will carry you. They cannot track us. We will go to my abode. No one will think to look for you there."

"Not meaning to insult you, Eddie," Rube said, "but you better got a good reason for thinking that."

"I do," Edgar replied. "The dragon riders see me as a terrified, insane hermit. I have given them no reason to believe I possess the courage to participate in any action against them. Look, the sky lightens to the east. They will not remain in their feline form by daylight hours."

"He's right," Lucy said. "Weretigers won't stay shifted when the sun is up. If we can stay hidden until first light, we'll be in the clear. We can still make our rendezvous with the *Tempus Fugit* on time."

"Hold on," Jilly said, looking at Edgar. "Why are you helping us?"

His earnest eyes met hers. "I want to go home."

"Join the freaking club," Rube said. "Okay, give me a paw up. First we ditch the big pissed off puddy cats, then we'll work on the specificities."

As Rube settled on his shoulders, Edgar asked Jilly, "You will be able to follow?"

"Don't worry about us," she said. "Just go."

With that, Edgar plunged into the jungle, moving confidently through the undergrowth. He chose a zigzagging path that circled wide away from the Citadel and ultimately approached his dwelling from the river.

When he stepped into the clearing around his home, he stopped and waited for Jilly and Lucy. "There are snares and trip wires," he warned, "stay close."

He led them to a back entrance, going up one flight and into a cluttered central room. Papers littered the floor and covered most of the furniture.

Leaning down beside a chair, Edgar let Rube slide off his shoulders. The raccoon immediately shrugged out of the pack he wore and checked the egg. "We're good," he announced. "Baby Iguana is solid."

Looking around the room, Jilly said, "Edgar, what is this place?"

"It is the hospital in Baltimore where I was taken to die," he replied. "The raven Seneca came to me and told me I must come to this place or lose my life by order of Ruling Elder Isherwood. Please, do you know how long I have been here?"

"Forgive me," Jilly said, "but do you remember the date when you arrived?"

Edgar nodded. "It haunts me still. The month was October and the year 1849."

"Then you've been here roughly 167 years."

"Seneca told me Reynold Isherwood is dead," Edgar said, his voice breaking. "He implied that I might pick up the threads of my life. Will you take me with you when you leave this place."

Rube held up a paw. "Uh, Jilly, a word please?"

"Excuse me," the parrot said, hopping across a sagging couch to reach Rube. Dropping her voice she said, "What?"

"I feel behoven to point out that McGregor ain't gonna like this."

"Leave Festus to me."

The raccoon held up two black paws. "Lady, he is all yours, but I gotta admit, I am looking forward to hearing you explain this one."

Chapter Thirty-One

The Tempus Fugit, *Festus*

We didn't feel the moment when time stopped, but the uproar in the Citadel left no doubt about its resumption. I expected shouting, not roaring weretigers. Rube was good, but he couldn't outrun a pride of big cats ditching their solitary imperative and working together.

When Blair, Giallo, and Eingana landed on the deck, Miranda and I were halfway down the gangplank intent on a foolhardy rescue mission.

"Stop, McGregor!" Giallo ordered. *"Look! The night passes. The sun comes."*

A rosy glow suffused the eastern sky. Inside the fortress, the tigers grew quiet.

"They're still coming," Blair said, sliding off Giallo's back, "but on wings, not paws."

As the first rays of the sun struck the cliff face dragons spilled out of the alcoves diving straight for the pier and by extension us.

"You said they wouldn't fly," I growled at Giallo. "That looks like flying to me."

"Flying to watch and flying to fight are different things."

As the creatures neared the base of the mountain, a fierce crosswind caught them unawares. They struggled against its power, wheeling to the left and right, snorting fire. Only one force could toss dragons aside like rag dolls—the baobhan sith.

"Everybody stand back," I yelled. "Vampire coming in for a landing."

The sails strained against the gusting blast until I heard the masts groan in protest. "Come on, Greer," I muttered under my breath. "Tone it down. We need this tub."

Even over the screaming gale, Miranda heard the word "tub."

"What did you call my ship?" she yelled at me.

"You can deal with me later," I yelled back. "Shouldn't you be battening hatches or something?"

The pirate turned her head against the stinging wind whipping at her hair. "Too late," she shouted. "Hold on."

The *Tempus Fugit* rocked wildly to port, then careened back to starboard. A bone-jarring collision sent me flying off my feet and sliding across the deck toward the water. If Miranda hadn't grabbed my belt, I'd have gone into the drink.

Then, as quickly as it had come up, the storm settled. The rocking stopped, and I looked up into the amused eyes of the baobhan sith.

Jinx stood on her left with Addie cradled in her arms, Tori on the right running a hand through her wildly disheveled hair.

Since I'd seen Addie last, she had grown. I put her at about one year of age. Before anyone could say a word, the kid pumped her fists toward the sky and yelled, "Do it again, Aunt Gigi!"

My eyebrows shot up. "Gigi?" I asked Greer. "Did she call you *Gigi?*"

The vampire held out her hand and pulled me to my feet. "She cannot pronounce 'Greer' properly and so settled on an abbreviation of her own making. I find it oddly endearing."

A wise inner voice told me that teasing Greer about having a cute aunt name probably wouldn't be the best option at the moment—especially since Addie looked at me and burbled, "Hello Kitty Cat!"

I shot the kid a quick grin. "Morning, squirt," I said before directing my attention to Jinx and Tori. "You two okay?"

Both women nodded. Then I saw Jinx's eyes track over my shoulder. I knew what I would see before I even looked. Recovered from their collision with the flight of the baobhan sith, the dragons now sat in a regimented line on the shore, wings folded, watchful heads erect, drifts of smoke curling from their nostrils.

A lone figure moved down the stone steps that led to the pier —Master Kian.

Jinx handed Addie to Tori. "Take her below," she said. "Stay with her."

The child protested. "Wanna watch!"

"No," Jinx said firmly in that mother's voice that brooks no argument. "You go with Aunt Tori and you mind her. Mama has to help Uncle Kitty Cat with some business."

As Tori carried the toddler away, I said under my breath, "I will not, under any circumstances, be known as 'Uncle Kitty Cat.'"

"You want to be called 'Fess-fluff' because that's the best she's done so far with your name."

From the pier, Kian puffed out his chest and said in a clear, ringing voice, "Festus McGregor, I charge you and your people with the theft of the Hourglass of the Horae. You will hand over the artifact or face the justice of the Citadel."

Out of the corner of my mouth I said to Jinx, "We are not done with this discussion." Then, raising my voice, I greeted the Master. "Good morning, Kian."

My nonchalance instantly took his sour countenance from glower to apoplectic. "I am not in the mood to bandy words with you, werecat. Prepare to be boarded."

The sound of a saber clearing leather told me all I needed to know about Miranda's reaction to that suggestion.

"Captain Winter doesn't feel like entertaining guests at the moment," I said. "Besides, the Hourglass of the Horae isn't onboard."

"More *lies*," Kian spat. "If you will not hand over the Hourglass, we will take it. Riders, to the skies!"

The dragons sat placidly immobile. Two or three of the riders tried to urge their mounts forward, but to no avail.

Kian's big mic drop moment amounted to a massive, silent splat.

"I said *fly,* you fools!," Kian screamed. "I am *master* of this Citadel. You will obey me."

Giallo unfurled his neck and looked down at Kian. *"True leaders do not command obedience, they simply receive it."*

"*You!*" the master accused, jabbing his index finger toward the dragon's head. "You are behind this. You and that insurrectionist rider of yours."

Blair stepped to the rail and looked down at the irate figure on the pier. "This is beneath you and your position," she said sincerely. "We aren't trying to stage an insurrection. We only want to live our lives as we believe the Natural Order calls us to do. Let us go, Kian."

"There is more than one way to deal with a traitor," Kian said, his voice dropping to a throaty rumble. "If the riders won't deal with you, I will."

A rolling shimmer of magic enveloped him. When it reached his boots, a Bengal tiger crouched against the planks.

Without a moment's hesitation, I shifted, sprang onto the pier, and confronted Kian.

A male Bengal tips the scales at around 400 pounds—roughly twice my body weight. Nobody ever said I had good sense. Kian snarled and started forward only to stop, ears back and whiskers flat when a white tigress hit the pier beside me.

"You would raise your paw against your master?" Kian demanded.

"You are not my master," Blair answered, her own voice a low, menacing purr. "I stand with Chief McGregor."

Gathering his muscles to spring, Kian said, "Then die with Chief McGregor."

Man, I would like to tell you we dusted the pier with his orange butt, but I can't. Anybody who has ever been around felines knows the fastest way to break up a cat fight is to throw water on the situation, which is exactly what Jinx did.

With a sweep of her hand she scooped up gallons of river water and dumped them right on our heads. "Festus McGregor, you get back on this ship this instant," she said. "You too, Blair."

Dripping and furious at the affront to our dignity, we complied. Kian coughed water and glared at the Witch of the Oak. "It will take more than your cheap tricks to stop me."

"Will it now," Jinx said, turning her hand over and letting blue light fill her eyes.

Miranda's cannonballs rose from the river to hang suspended in a circle around the tiger. Kian's eyes cut nervously left and right.

"I am not a violent woman," Jinx said, "but I'm tired, and I've had enough of you, Kian Abercrombie. We have the authority to take the Hourglass and we are exercising that authority. Blair,

Giallo, and their whelp have sought the protection of the Witch of the Oak, which I have extended."

Kian's lips curled. "By what right do you kidnap a dragon egg?"

Jinx wiggled her fingers and brought the cannonballs closer. In spite of his bluster, the tiger cringed lower and let out a defensive hiss.

"You really are a pain in the backside, you know that?" she said. "We haven't kidnapped anyone. If you had a particle of human feeling you'd know that good parents do not leave their children. This ship is setting sail. Any of your riders who want to come with us to the Otherworld are welcome."

In response, two dragons lifted off the shore and hovered over the vessel. "We'll take you up on that invitation," a man's voice called out.

"Who are you?" Jinx asked.

"I'm Davin and this is Maeve. Blair will vouch for us."

The white tigress gazed at them with eyes the color of sapphires. "They are my friends," she said, "my family."

"Then you're especially welcome," Jinx said. "Miranda, push off."

As the *Tempus Fugit* moved away from the pier, Kian threw back his head and roared. "This is not over, Witch of the Oak."

"Blair," Jinx asked, "can tigers swim?"

"Superbly," the tigress replied. "Why?"

"Because," Jinx said, dropping her hand. "I think the Master needs to cool off a little."

The circle of cannonballs crashed into the wood, punching a neat circle through the pier and plunging Kian into the river.

As the ship negotiated the first bend in the tributary, I looked back and saw the master pull himself onto the shore, soaking wet, furious, and completely deflated.

"McGregor," Miranda called down from the quarterdeck,

"are you just going to stand there and drip? We have a date to pick up a coon."

Giving Blair a friendly feline shoulder bump, I said, "Let me get bipedal and then I'll take your clothes below and show you where you can shift."

"Thank you."

"I should be thanking you," I told her. "You went against your instinct to stand beside me and against Kian."

The tigress blinked slowly. "Instincts, like traditions, can be cages, can't they?"

"They can," I agreed. "Your father would be proud of you."

Looking back at the fortress, she said, "My father *is* proud of me. He dreamed of returning to the Otherworld. What I do now, I do for his honor and for that of my mother."

Giallo reached out with his forefoot and stroked the sleek, thick fur at her neck. *"You did well this day,* a sheòid."

Nuzzling against him she purred, "As did you."

Tears fell from her lovely blue eyes. I padded away softly, leaving Giallo to comfort his friend. All other considerations aside, Blair had to leave the only home she knew, to be her true self. In some part of her heart, that would always hurt, but never more than it did as she watched the Citadel fade in the distance.

∼

Abandoned Building, The Spica Jungle

"I lost everything when I was sent here," Edgar said. "You cannot ask me to leave my words behind."

Rube scanned the piece of paper in his hand. "Eddie, man, this stuff don't make no sense."

"But that is the point!" he cried, grabbing a handful of manuscript pages and shaking them in the raccoon's face.

"These ideas are as lost as I have been. I must rescue them from their oblivion as I am being rescued."

Rube looked at Jilly. "You try, 'cause he ain't listening to me."

"He does have suitcases," the wereparrot said.

"Yeah," Rube said, "and we'd need a truck to get them all to the river, which we ain't got."

Lucy stopped pecking at the mango Edgar had sliced for her and said, "What about your waist pack, Rube? You told me you won a capacity spell off a witch in Vegas. Can your pack hold Edgar's papers?"

"Honest to the Trash Gods, I don't know," Rube said, "but it's worth a try."

"I have begun sorting the best of the lot," Edgar said excitedly. "These stacks are the most crucial."

The raccoon shook his head. "Eddie, come on, have a heart. That's gotta be like six, maybe seven reams."

"Eight," Edgar said. "I have worked in publishing. This body of work comprises approximately 4,000 pages."

Rube unzipped his pack. "Okay, but I ain't giving up the emergency chow I got stashed in here. Hold on. Let me rearrange some stuff."

His arm disappeared into the pack as rattles and clunks emanated from its depths.

"What the heck do you have in there, anyway?" Lucy asked.

"Essentials," Rube replied. "Okay, give me the first stack."

The werebirds watched as Edgar handed pile after pile to the raccoon. Periodically Rube paused, cursed, made noise inside the pack, and then put his paw out for more paper. When the last sheet went in, he jumped up and down several times, wiggled his hips, and tugged at the zipper.

"Okay," he panted, "we got it all. *Now* can we blow this pop stand?"

"Assuming that means may we leave, yes," Edgar said,

looping the strap of his field glasses around his neck. "Thank you, Rube. I am deeply grateful."

"Be gratitudinal when we're back home," the raccoon said, pulling his pack on again. "We ain't there yet."

As they moved for the back stairs, Edgar paused and surveyed the room. Jilly landed on his shoulder. "Are you alright?"

"Yes," he said, "you would think a man in my position would not harbor sentiment for his prison, but these walls sheltered and protected me. Some aspect of my being will miss this solitary haven."

Jilly squeezed his shoulder comfortingly. "We carry with us all the places we've been and all the places we hope to be. Our truest home is within, Edgar."

"Indeed it is, madam," he said, "but there are other outward homes I wish to see again, so let us make a start."

Chapter Thirty-Two

The Tempus Fugit, *Festus*

"How in the name of Bastet's litter box did you manage to go into the jungle to guide Rube to the rendezvous and come out with Edgar Allan Poe?" I demanded.

Jilly clacked her beak. "Do *not* take that tone with me, Festus James McGregor."

All three names. Bad sign. I waited a beat and tried again. "Why exactly did you tell Poe we'd take him with us?"

"Why did *you* tell three dragons and their riders they could come with us *and* bring an unhatched egg?"

I couldn't escape that logic, but I tried anyway. "Some of that was Jinx."

"Sell that load of moldy bird seed to someone who's buying."

Across the deck, Poe sat under the canopy drinking tea with Greer and answering Tori's excited questions.

"So how did you come up with the idea for *The Cask of Amontillado*?" she asked, almost bouncing in her chair. "That one *totally* creeps me out. When he taps that last brick in? *Cold.* Stone cold awesome."

Although he seemed taken aback by the phrasing, the man obviously basked in the praise.

"What are we supposed to do with him?" I asked. "Edgar Allan Poe can't exactly pop back into the human realm. Their history records his death in 1849. If he tries to resume his life, he'll probably wind up in a looney bin sucking lithium lollipops."

Jilly knows how to play a good hand of poker. She promptly produced her ace in the hole. "He knows Seneca."

At first I thought she was joking. "Right. Of course he does. Next you're going to tell me Seneca inspired the poem."

She tilted her head and patiently waited for my brain to catch up with my mouth.

"Get *out!*" I said. "Seneca is *The Raven*?"

"He is," Jilly said, "and Reynold Isherwood ordered Edgar sent to the Spica Mountains."

That took the evolving plot from reed thin to thick as sorghum molasses. "How did Poe get hooked up with Isherwood?"

"I don't know," she said. "There wasn't time to find out and, well, Edgar seems fragile. He's been alone a long time. You should have seen the building where he lived. It was the shade of the hospital in Baltimore where history says Poe died. The poor man dragged everything into a second floor room and made himself a hermit's cave."

"It's a wonder he didn't lose his mind."

Jilly dropped her voice. "I'm not sure he didn't—at least for a time. There was broken glass on the floor by his desk, a hangman's noose, a knife, and a note addressed 'To Whom It May Concern.'"

"All that time in the jungle and he never reached out to the people in the Citadel?"

"He thought they were demons," Jilly said. "Then Seneca

came to him in a vision and told him to seek the aid of an odd 'collection of confederates.'"

I was going to have a feather to pick with that damn bird when we got home. "I suppose that means us?"

"Yes."

I scrubbed my face, absently registering how badly I needed a shave. "Okay, fine. As soon as we get back, we take him to Seneca. Let him and the Key Man sort this out."

She leaned forward and nipped my nose. "Thank you. You're a sweetheart."

"Don't be saying that where people can hear you," I grumbled.

We made excellent time once the *Tempus Fugit* reached the main river. Rube, who professed to be "fammy-shed," sat on the deck amidst a litter of empty MRE envelopes. Giallo and Eingana lay nearby in a sun puddle. The draikana held the padded pack containing her egg protectively in her slumbering embrace.

The two dragon riders, Maeve and Davin, were flying close on either side of the bow, talking with Blair, who was once again in human form. She seemed delighted and relieved by the presence of her friends.

We continued to benefit from the increased pace of time. By early afternoon, we spotted the rainbow hanging over the waterfall and prepared for our descent to the Sea of Ages.

Eingana and Giallo chose to fly through the opening into the Middle Realm. A vessel riding a temporal waterfall makes for a majestic sight, but with a four-dragon escort we came home in epic style.

Rube, who had resumed guardianship of the egg while Eingana was airborne, let out a yelp when the hull touched the surface of the sea.

"What's wrong with you?" I asked.

He hastily shrugged out of the pack and set it on the deck. "Egglet's moving," he said. "As in hatching."

With that, the raccoon looked up, put two fingers in his mouth, whistled, and yelled, "*Hey!* Mrs. Captain Iguana! I think you and the mister better get down here."

Eingana hit the deck first, her talons coming to rest inches from Rube. Giallo circled the *Tempus Fugit* once to allow the impact from his mate's landing to disperse before he jarred the ship all over again.

With the two of them hovering over the pack, Rube unzipped the top and pulled back the sides. The morning sun fell on the egg's surface as a jagged crack spread across the shell.

From behind us, Tori yelled, "Addie! *Stop!* Come back here, you little rascal!"

The sound of tiny feet hitting the deck made us all look. Addie trundled toward our group as fast as her chubby legs would carry her. At the last minute, she dropped into a perfect slide and came to rest against the pack.

The crack in the shell sprang open and a dragon head the color of new red wine poked out. The whelp's lavender eyes rested on Addie and filled with instant love. The child threw her arms around the whelp and sighed happily, "My draggy-on!"

Eingana shifted to let Jinx and Tori into our circle. "What just happened here?" Jinx asked, staring down at her daughter hugging the baby dragon.

"They have bonded," Giallo said. *"The life ahead will be shared by your child and mine."*

With exuberant energy, the whelp cast off the remaining shell and hopped out, landing upright on wobbly legs.

"Put out your wings, daughter," Eingana purred. *"Balance yourself."*

"Man," Rube said, "I wish we had a baby pool going, 'cause I woulda been two for two picking the chicklets. What you gonna name her, Lady Iguana?"

Eingana lowered her head to Addie's level. *"Do you know her name?"*

Suddenly serious, Addie nodded. "My draggy-on Nysa."

"Yes, Nysa," Eingana said. *"A perfect choice."*

Looking shell-shocked—pun intended—Jinx asked, "What does it mean?"

"It is Greek," Greer said. "It means 'new beginning.'"

Tori put an arm around Jinx to steady her. "And you thought bringing home stray cats was bad."

Jinx's shoulders started to shake. I honestly didn't think I could take one second more of a weeping female, but then she burst out laughing. Yawns and belly laughs have one thing in common; they're contagious.

Addie and the whelp looked up at the circle of cackling adults and scooted closer to one another.

"It's okay, baby," Jinx assured her, sitting down on the deck beside her daughter. "Hi Nysa, welcome to the family."

When she held out her hand, the dragon sniffed experimentally before waddling three steps and landing in her lap.

"I suppose we're going to have to work out a lot of playdates and sleepovers," Jinx said to Eingana.

The draikana bent and nuzzled her daughter. *"They will not want to be separated for long. It will grow more complicated when my child begins to speak. They will share every secret."*

Jinx looked up at Tori and reached for her hand. "I have some experience with that kind of relationship," she told Eingana. "We'll make it work."

From the distance of a few steps, Edgar cleared his throat. "May I see the young dragon?"

"Yes," Giallo said. *"We regret causing you fear this many years."*

"Many things from my tenure in the jungle cause me regret,"

Edgar said, "including my failure to know such remarkable creatures."

When he knelt beside Jinx, she said, "There are wonderful things waiting in the Otherworld for you to experience."

"I fear, madam, that I will not know how to find my way," he admitted.

Rube laid a paw on his knee. "You got friends now, Eddie. Don't worry. We ain't going nowhere."

From the vantage point of hindsight, I can tell you that Rube's offer of help turned out to be prophetic.

The dragons declined to come to Cibolita with us, asking instead to be taken to the ruins of Drake Abbey. We had some trouble prying Addie and Nysa apart. It took a promise of a reunion the next day to get them to let go of one another.

"Are you sure you want to stay here?" I asked Giallo. "You don't have any supplies."

"We have long awaited this return. I am sure."

Blair, Davin, and Maeve didn't look so certain, but relaxed when Miranda promised to be back by dawn with everything they would need to start rebuilding and to live with some degree of comfort in the interim.

"How can we repay you?" Blair asked.

The captain shook her head. "Consider it a donation to the restoration of the abbey. Besides, you helped us recover the second piece of the Temporal Arcana. We owe you."

When the *Tempus Fugit* docked in Cibolita, a man in a fedora stood waiting on the pier. "Lucas!" Jinx cried. "You're here!

He took off his hat and waved. "Hi! Lou gave me a mirror call when the ship came down the waterfall. I thought I'd surprise you and greet you in person."

Tori and Jinx exchanged a look and started to laugh.

"What's so funny?" Lucas asked.

"Trust me, buddy," Tori said. "Jinksy totally has you beat in the surprise department."

Miranda let down the gangplank and he bounded aboard. "How was your . . . " He stopped mid-sentence when he saw Jinx holding Addie. "Who's this?"

"This," Jinx said, "is your daughter, Adeline Kathleen Grayson. She grew faster than we expected in the Land of Virgo."

The child gave him no chance to process that news. She held out her arms and cried, *"Daddy!"*

Lucas didn't hesitate. He didn't ask questions. He recognized his child immediately and from that moment forward, she's had the man totally wrapped around her little finger. Any time they might have missed together in the beginning did nothing to harm their bond.

Taking the girl from her mother, he held her close as Addie encircled his neck tightly. Lucas held his hand out to Jinx and brought her into the embrace.

"Did you know when you left?" he asked, kissing her hair.

"No," she said, leaning into him. "It's a long story. Can we go home so I only have to tell it once?"

"Home, Daddy!" Addie said, leaning back and pounding her fist on his chest. "Draggy-on gonna come soon."

He laughed. "What on earth is she talking about?"

"Well," Jinx said, looping her arm in his. "You know how Dad adopts dogs and I bring home cats?"

"Yes," he said suspiciously.

"Brace yourself. It's a hereditary trait."

A black bird swooped past them and landed on the railing. He nodded at me and then spoke to Poe. "Hello, Edgar. Welcome to the Otherworld."

Poe smiled. "You were right, Seneca. I was aided by an unlikely gang of new associates."

"Are we really so unlikely?" Jilly asked.

Edgar turned at the sound of the female voice and stared at the two women coming toward us.

He studied Jilly intently and then his jaw dropped. "You were the parrot," he exclaimed.

"I *am* the parrot, or more precisely wereparrot," Jilly said, "and this is Lucy, the raven. You thought tigers were the only ones who could shift forms?"

Poe regarded Seneca questioningly. "If your kind has the capacity to so alter their physical being, why have you never come to me as a human?"

"Because," the bird said, "I am not like them. We have much to discuss, Edgar. Will you travel with me to my shop in Londinium? My brother and I will assist with your adjustment to this new world."

Before he left, Poe held his hand out to me. As we shook, he said, "I hope we will see one another again, sir. I am indebted to you for your kindness to me in my reduced state."

"My pleasure, Mr. Poe," I replied. "I, too, look forward to our next meeting. I have long been an admirer of your work."

The Lair, Briar Hollow

That night, back on four legs in the lair, I quietly padded off to my war room when I couldn't take one more second of disgusting baby talk. Not from the kid. From the adoring adults.

In addition to cooing over Addie, all the witches were combing their grimoires to put together a false memory spell powerful enough to blanket Briar Hollow. The humans needed to remember a pregnancy that never happened and the first year of Addie's life.

First, however, Jinx faced the daunting task of making Addie understand that she couldn't carry her wand all the time or use magic in front of humans.

The kid had already thoughtfully levitated Rodney from the floor to his shelf-top desk and choreographed Glory's pens in a darn good version of the *Jailhouse Rock* number from the movie—much to the Elvis-loving Pickle's delight.

After a few minutes, Rube came looking for me. "You being anti-sociable again, McGregor?" he asked, scaling the leg of my desk and plopping down next to the MonsterPad.

"Yes, and I had to file my mission report about the Hourglass of the Horae. We need to go to Londinium tomorrow and deliver it to Stank at BEAR headquarters for evaluation."

Unzipping his omnipresent waist pack, Rube pulled out a burrito and a can of orange pop. "Good deal. After that we need to swing by Seneca's joint so I can give Eddie all the papers from his crib back in the jungle. They're crowding out my snacks."

"How tragic for you," I murmured, reaching for the screen of the MonsterPad to check my InBox.

The first email was from Seneca.

Festus, it is imperative that we confer at your earliest convenience. We must discuss Edgar, Nevermore, and the Compass of Chronos. Time is of the essence.

Rube rolled over, read the message, and groaned. "We ain't even been home a day and the black bird has to go using words like im-perry-a-tive. No good comes of them kind of words, McGregor. Like, *never*. Besides that, I ain't so sure Eddie's got all his marbles."

Still staring at the screen, I said, "'*Men have called me mad; but the question is not yet settled, whether madness is or is not the loftiest intelligence.*'"

Taking a bite out of his burrito, Rube asked, "Where'd you get that from?"

"Edgar Allan Poe."

The raccoon sighed melodramatically. "Geez *Lou-eeze!* Here we go. I knew one way or the other that guy was gonna be trouble."

A Word from Juliette

Thank you for reading *Once Upon Nevermore*, the 13th book in The Jinx Hamilton Series.

I hope you'll want to continue the adventure with Jinx and the gang in Book 14, *To Raise a Witch*, coming in June 2020.

There are many things I love about being an author, but building a relationship with my readers is far and away the best.

Once a month I send out a newsletter with information on new releases, sneak peeks, and inside articles on Jinx Hamilton as well as other books and series I'm currently developing.

You can get all this and more by signing up at JulietteHarper.com.

About the Author

"It's kind of fun to do the impossible." Walt Disney said that, and the two halves of Juliette Harper believe it wholeheartedly. Together, Massachusetts-based Patricia Pauletti, and Texan Rana K. Williamson combine their writing talents as Juliette. "She" loves to create strong female characters and place them in interesting, challenging, painful, and often comical situations. Refusing to be bound by genre, Juliette's primary interest lies in telling good stories. Patti, who fell in love with writing when she won her first 8th grade poetry contest, has a background in music, with a love of art and design. Rana, a former journalist and university history instructor, is happiest with a camera in hand and a cat or two at home.

For more information...
www.JulietteHarper.com
admin@julietteharper.com

By Juliette Harper
Copyright 2019, Juliette Harper

Skye House Publishing, LLC

License Notes

eBooks are not transferable. All rights are reserved. No part of this book may be used or reproduced in any manner without written permission, except in the case of brief quotations embodied in critical articles and reviews. The unauthorized reproduction or distribution of this copyrighted work is illegal. No part of this book may be scanned, uploaded, or distributed via the Internet or any other means, electronic or print, without the author's permission.

This is a work of fiction. Names, characters, businesses, places, events, and incidents are either the products of the author's imagination or used in a fictitious manner. Any resemblance to actual persons, living or dead, or actual events is purely coincidental.

ISBN: 978-1-943516-00-1

❀ Created with Vellum

Made in the USA
Columbia, SC
11 October 2020